To Mom and Dad

FOLLOW HER HOME

A JUNIPER SONG NOVEL

STEPH CHA

faber

First published in the UK in 2020
by Faber & Faber Ltd
Bloomsbury House
74–77 Great Russell Street
London WC1B 3DA

First published in the US in 2013
by St Martin's Press
175 Fifth Avenue
New York NY 10010

This paperback edition first published in 2021

Printed and bound by CPI Group (UK) Ltd, Croydon CR0 4YY

A CIP record for this book
is available from the British Library

ISBN 978–0–571–36044–4

2 4 6 8 10 9 7 5 3 1

Acknowledgments

Thanks to Mom and Dad for your unquestioning love and support. This book could not have happened without you, and I will never stop being grateful.

Thanks to Michael Wittenberg and Nwamaka Ejebe for the first reads, and for letting me think my writing was not an embarrassment. If you were lying, I believed you.

Thanks to my agent, Ethan Bassoff, who saw something of worth in my flawed little germ of a manuscript. Thank you for investing in me, and for sweating with me through each new round of edits. We made this book together.

Thanks to Karyn Marcus, my first editor, for the good ideas, and for giving Song and me a home.

Thanks to my editor, Anne Brewer, who is tireless. I can only hope to be worthy of your hard work and enthusiasm. Thank you for making my problems your problems, and for holding my hand through every step of this process.

Thanks to Justin Velella and Cassandra Galante and all the

fine folks at St. Martin's who continue to work hard on my behalf. I am new to this all, and you have been indispensable.

Thanks to Jeremy Michaelson for the love of books, and to Joyce Moser for the love of noir.

Thanks to Andrew and Peter, the best brothers I could ever want, and to my son, Duke, who is a basset hound.

And finally, thanks to Duke's father, Matt Barbabella, who taught me how to drive stick, at least on paper.

One

It was about ten o' clock on a Friday in mid-July, the Los Angeles night warm and dry, the only wind rising from the whoosh and zoom of traffic on Rossmore. I was wearing a slinky black dress, black patent leather platform pumps, silver cascade earrings, and a black lambskin clutch. I was perfumed, manicured, and impeccably coiffed. I was everything a half-employed twentysomething should be on the sober end of a Friday night. I was calling on an open bar at Luke's new apartment, ready to spend a little time and respectability on a blurry and colorful evening.

Luke's place was in the Marlowe Apartments in Hancock Park, a complex towering pretty as a castle just north of the Wilshire Country Club. It stood less than two miles south of Hollywood and Ivar, where its namesake found his vocation. But the Marlowe was a luxury apartment more likely to house the rich degenerates of Chandler's novels than his wisecracking private eye with a heart of noir gold.

Luke's loft was on the third floor. I entered the building from

Rosewood through an iron gate propped open by yesterday's *Wall Street Journal*, then passed through a plush outdoor patio and a furnished lobby offering complimentary coffee. The Marlowe featured a fleur-de-lis floating in the valley of an M as its logo, and fleur-de-lis peppered every plausible surface of the place, from the spikes on the gate to the hallway walls and elevator doors. I rode up to the third floor and found Luke's apartment tucked in a corner behind a black door with three squares staggered in white geometric outlines from top to bottom.

A printout taped to the door commanded in bold black font: COME ON IN AND LOSE THE SHOES. I turned the knob and laughter and hip-hop spilled out at the first crack in the doorway, the pulse of the subwoofer smacking my ribs with a little less force than cardiac arrest.

A landfill of footwear clogged the entrance—flip-flops, Birkenstocks, loafers brown and black, Nikes and Converse, floral printed espadrilles, round-toed ballet flats in twelve colors. I looked down at my glossy pin-thin heels and scoured the floor for a friend. A wadded yellow sock peered at me from an unlaced sneaker, and as I started to surrender, I saw the pair that made mine look like Sunday shoes. They were tall, pointy, and painted in glitter, with bloodred soles and scarce worn in-soles reading CHRISTIAN LOUBOUTIN.

She was about as hard to spot as a clown in a prison cafeteria, wearing just a shade less makeup, tarred and sequined in steel gray from bust to midthigh, earlobes hoisting oversize Eiffel Tower chandeliers. She clocked in at about five foot one on a tall day, and except for some heavily jeweled wrists, she would have been easy enough to smuggle in carry-on luggage. Her left hand held the conic bowl of a martini glass in a loose circle between thumb and forefinger, and her right hand gripped the sleeve of Luke's button-down midbicep. Her long, dark eyes squinted as her wide red mouth gaped with silver laughter. Loose curls dyed a toasted honey brown fell past her shoulders, ends trembling on a modest bosom. She crinkled a nose that could hide behind a penny. One crooked incisor poked just a couple millimeters ahead of her front teeth—this would be her moneymaker, the Cheshire detail, the bite mark in your memory.

He looked like a giant next to the girl. He had always been tall—when I met him he was six foot two and 140 pounds. Sometime in college, he had filled out and grown into impressive good looks, with soft toffee-brown hair, an unearned surfer's tan, and kind eyes the mellow green of new sage. He wore dark jeans and a gray dress shirt with a thread count higher than most people's sheets. Luke, like many of his classmates at the USC School of Cinematic Arts, had an indulging father with deep pockets, and, though he didn't like to admit it, expensive taste.

Luke and I had been friends since high school, though back then we spent little time together off campus. We were both good students, and we developed a comfortable rapport over a series of shared classes, without getting to know each other particularly well. In December of our senior year, we were both admitted early to Yale, and we started to hang out and become friends. By a stroke of fate, we were placed in the same residential college our freshman year, and soon after that, I fell in love with his roommate. Except for a brief hiccup after Diego and I broke up, the three of us went through college like peas in a pod.

After my freshman year, my family left Los Angeles for Houston. No one expected me to settle down in Texas, and after graduation I moved back to my hometown. When I did, Luke was the reason I still felt at home. I did most of my moviegoing, grocery shopping, and eating out with him. He spent the year after graduation contemplating life goals, then ended up in film school with an aspiration to produce documentaries with deep, important social messages. He was a fitting companion for a private tutor without higher ambitions. Most weeks I worked twenty hours for an hourly rate high enough to keep me afloat. We both had plenty of free time and lacked the credentials to judge each other, and two consecutive days without contact was a strange and infrequent occurrence.

Luke cupped his hand and curled his fingers to call me over. I was his exact height in five-inch heels and enjoyed standing shoulder to shoulder, but I obeyed the sign before stepping over to Luke and the girl.

"Song! Thank God you're here."

I raised an eyebrow and looked at the girl enjoying his company. "Are you in need of rescue?"

He glanced at her and shook his head with a guilty smirk. "Just happy to see you."

"Likewise, then. The place is really coming together." When I had visited on Wednesday, there had been nowhere to sit.

"Like it?"

"Well, you did let me pick the couch. And you know how much I love Philip Marlowe."

He smiled. "So much that no flesh-and-blood man can compete."

"With witty brooding Philip Marlowe? Of course not." I gave him a light punch on the shoulder. Luke was also between relationships, but my perpetual singledom was still a favorite topic.

He remembered the girl on his arm and introduced us. "Sorry, Song, this is Lori Lim. Lori, Juniper Song. But everyone calls her Song. I guess you can understand why."

"Oh, shush, my parents were immigrants. Not all of us get to have names that wear sweater-vests, Lucas William Cook." I turned to Lori and put out a hand and a "good to meet you" with my best meeting smile.

She slid her tongue over the jutting corner of her jagged tooth and clamped it lightly in a lazy smile. Her dark eyes were sugar-glazed and sleepy, glitter lids fluttering and drooping. A lightweight. She took my hand in two dainty paws and planted a kiss, staining it with sparkling, plum-tinted lip gloss. Her glass pushed against her cheek and a few drops of clear liquid spilled onto the floor.

"You're tall, aren't you?" She looked at me, pupils hidden coyly behind a wall of mascaraed lashes.

"Can you tell she's a little drunk?" Luke yelled in whisper-tones. "Did you Korean girls get together and decide this was a cocktail party, by the way?"

After a four-second delay, Lori bent over dripping with laughter and socked Luke in the shoulder.

I watched her and smiled. "I guess I didn't realize we were still nineteen. When do we start taking body shots?"

"Aren't you hilarious."

"I'm kidding. Congrats on the new place. I did overdress, but in my defense it's been a while since I've been out among non-you people. So I decided to pull out the stops for this thing."

"Well, you look good. I'll buy you a drink from my fridge."

"Thanks. I'll take a beer."

"I'll be back in a second."

"Hold it." I pointed at the petite lush and mouthed, *What do I do with this?* She was humming now.

Luke turned and twisted his mouth. "Give her a boy to play with, she'll know what to do."

I turned to Lori. "I'll be right back. Want anything?"

She squinted her eyes and gave me a dreamy pouty smile and a belabored shake of the head. I followed Luke to the kitchen.

"Hostile, much? She's drunk, not insensate. Who is she anyway?"

He opened the refrigerator and looked thoughtfully at the beer supply. "She works for my dad's firm. Some kind of secretary or paralegal or who the fuck knows."

"I can tell you're a fan."

"I'm oozing with adoration. This is me oozing." He tilted his head down at me and gave me his best impression of a jaded student in a lecture on fractals.

"She is adorable. She's a my-size Barbie with an A-cup. I kind of want to take her home and have her look pretty on my couch. Can she even talk, or is that Joker mouth for show?"

He pulled two cold beers from the fridge and snapped off the caps. They hissed and smoked deliciously.

"Oh, definitely not for show." He chuckled and took a sip of his beer. "Actually, I have to talk to you about something."

I was about to take a swig but brought the bottle back down. "Yeah?"

He furrowed his brows and his eyes were long triangles as he pointed at Lori with his chin. "I need to find out if she's banging my dad." I started to laugh but inhaled it. Staring back at me were two pools of green sobriety. "Seriously, Song, I think she's sleeping with him."

❧

Luke didn't make a habit of second-guessing his father. He was an only child, and he grew up with an admiration of the elder

Cook that bordered on worship. Mr. Cook was about as warm and playful as an onion, but he doted on his son. He never threw a ball around with him, but he was as present as an ambitious lawyer could be. He worked seventy-hour weeks, and by the time his son was in middle school, he had founded Stokel, Levinson & Cook. Even at his busiest, he managed to drive Luke to play dates and doctors' appointments, and he never missed a school function.

He had hoped that Luke would become a lawyer, or better, a powerful client, but he was supportive when Luke told him he wanted to make documentaries. The decision cost Mr. Cook tuition money and living expenses for a few more years, but he never acted like he was doing his son a favor.

Though Luke never came out and said so, I gathered that his busy father's committed involvement in his everyday life stemmed from the relative absence of his mother. Erin Cook was a stay-at-home wife who didn't do much when she stayed at home. She didn't cook or clean, and she took only a nominal role in watching and raising Luke. Much of his childhood was spent with a series of Spanish-speaking nannies, but he never spent enough time with any one to develop a significant attachment— not a single one lasted a year before getting the slip from Erin.

What I knew about Luke's relationship with his mother, I learned from a few long, late-night conversations scattered over the span of our friendship. He didn't resent her, and when he spoke of her, it was with a fond, faraway tone you might use to talk about an old neighbor. She was never entirely present—she traveled often, spending dollars like pennies, and when she was home, she kept to the bedroom. In all the years I knew Luke, I had only met her a couple of times.

She had been clinically depressed for decades. When he was a toddler, Luke asked her for a baby brother and she broke down sobbing. That was one of his earliest memories. Like a Fitzgerald heroine, Erin was frail and neurotic with a penchant for woeful melodrama. But this was her disease—there was no play-acting element to it.

She tried to kill herself just days before Luke's tenth birthday. He heard the reason from his mother's mouth, hours after she recovered—his father had been unfaithful. Luke was young enough to pretend he didn't understand, and she didn't bring it up again. He never did find out if it was true, and he didn't dwell on the question.

If Mr. Cook had transgressed, he was a model husband and father in the years before and after. He was the central figure in Luke's family life, and I knew Luke's casual intimation of an affair came from a place of genuine agony. I grabbed him by the elbow and we peeled off from the party into his bedroom. I closed the door, and the music reached us more in throbs than in sounds.

Luke had been living at the Marlowe for all of one week. While he had managed to slap up enough house for a housewarming, he had yet to settle into his bedroom. A new queen bed sat kitty-corner from the door, his disheveled comforter spread across it end to end in an homage to a made bed. The only other furniture was a bare, L-shaped desk and a rolling desk chair, both new. The carpet was littered with poster tubes, a framed diploma, cardboard boxes in various sizes, taped and untaped, some open showing white plastic hangers, a baseball glove, books with worn covers. I could only imagine the state of his closet.

He sat on a corner of his bed, palms flat and pushing into the mattress. I took the chair and rolled it close. I crossed and un-crossed my legs four times in the silence that followed.

I clucked my tongue. "Talk to me."

"I went home for dinner today and mentioned to my dad that I was short on cash. He said he'd give me whatever was in his wallet, and I don't know if I should have, but I took that to mean I could help myself. When I did, I found a receipt. Chanel, three grand, dated last week." He leaned forward, fingers locked, and looked up at me, chewing on his lower lip.

I could read the distress clear as lettering on his face. Luke looked up to his father with a childlike devotion, and for the first time since I'd known him, it was being tested. I felt a flush of relief. He was waiting for me to speak, and I gathered from his silence that there had been no further discoveries. If this was his evidence, there were a hundred ways for his suspicions to be wrong. "And you think this means your dad is having an affair?"

He nodded, slowly, evaluating my response.

"Your dad makes millions a year. You don't think he was just shopping for himself?"

"I know my dad," he said. "He doesn't spend that kind of money on anything for himself unless it comes with wheels. And Chanel? Not the brand for an aging lawyer."

"So you think he was buying something for Lori. Not, say, your mom?"

"There's no occasion, and I mean, he isn't really spontaneous with the gifts. My mom hates surprises, even when they're expensive."

"He could've been picking something up for her. Or something. I guess it's weird, but I think you're being a little paranoid, no? It's a receipt. People buy things."

He scratched his nose with a fast knuckle. "I don't know. I just have this feeling that that's what's going on. Did you happen to notice what was on Lori's arm?"

"An arsenal of bangles, but other than that, no."

"You would've noticed. She must've put it down. Any guesses?"

"I'm going to guess there were some linking Cs involved."

"Could easily have been three grand worth. I mean, a pair of Chanel socks goes for what, a thousand dollars?"

"Give or take."

"I wouldn't have noticed, but it just makes so much sense. How else do you explain it? She can't make more than a few thousand a month."

"Maybe she has a rich boyfriend. One who isn't about to die." I paused and opened my mouth. "Sorry. It's just, she's a total knockout. She could be on Nickelodeon, dating a boy who wears bow ties."

"Please, Song. I can't kick this feeling that something's wrong. I'm just asking you to help me find out."

"Why," I started. "Has your dad been acting weird lately? I don't get where this is coming from."

"No, nothing like that. I mean, I don't see him enough to notice strange behavior." He stood up and started to pace. "But you know, it's an anxiety I've had since I was a kid. On the one hand, I tell myself he would never have an affair, not after my mom took those pills. On the other—it'd be so easy for him to fall into one. He has money, and status, and he's in good shape for his age. I'm sure women don't ignore him. And look." He stopped and ran a hand through his hair. When he spoke again his voice was lower. "My mom is a handful, and he would never say it but she must make him miserable sometimes. He might love her anyway, but I doubt they've had sex in the last several years."

"You mean you wouldn't blame him if he did have an affair?"

"No, of course I would. My mom is ill. Last time she thought he cheated, she tried to die. I know that wasn't a reasonable response, and I know my mom is a difficult person to live with. But my dad is who he is because for thirty years he's stood by her and taken care of her when most people would've quit. If he's sleeping with someone younger than I am, I'll never see him the same way again."

He was just short of breaking into a paranoid sweat. I leaned forward with my head in my hands, looking down at my elbows. "Do you remember when you thought Diego was cheating on me?"

He sighed. "I remember. Not my best moment."

"Well, at the time you had enough to go on that jumping to conclusions didn't seem crazy. Diego and I had kind of a big fight because I ended up getting suspicious and asked him about it."

"Yeah, that was my bad. Sorry."

"Ancient history. But my point is, people look weird and suspicious all the time, even people as virtuous as Diego. And when they do things that make you look sideways, logical explanations can be counterintuitive. Let's say your dad went and bought boxes of nail polish for charity. It'd be pretty bizarre, but it would still be an explanation. Honestly, it's at least as likely as what you're thinking. You have to admit, an affair requires something of a leap. Your dad and Lori just don't seem plausible."

He rubbed his nose with the back of a hand so that his voice had to tumble through his wrist. "I don't know, Song. If 'plausible' means 'capable of happening,' you of all people should know that it is."

I felt a sting of irritation in my sinuses. I stood up, smoothed out imaginary wrinkles in my skirt, and glared down at my best friend, whose eyes rested on blank wall. "I'm going to let that slide because you're obviously distressed, but if you're referring to what happened to Iris, then you can cry on someone else's fucking shoulder."

He touched my hand and threw me a pleading look. "Sorry, Song, that was out of line. I just want you to help me out here." I kept my eyes on his and felt their white films shudder with heat. He squeezed my fingers and didn't look away. "Song, forgive me. Please."

I blinked. "Is that why you asked me? Because you knew I couldn't say no?"

"Look, I—of course I thought about Iris. I would be lying, and you would know it if I said otherwise."

I nodded, and felt my anger subside with a degree of surprise— it was rare for me to lash out at Luke, and I was dismayed by the rawness of that eight-year-old wound.

"I know you don't like talking about what happened, and I promise you that this is not about Iris. I just know you might have a knack for figuring this sort of thing out. You did it before, and no matter what you think, it was the right thing to do." He waited for me to speak, but I let him continue. "But more than that, I'm asking because you're my best friend and I need your help."

He looked abandoned. I felt my shoulders relax and after a moment I clapped my hand on his. "Okay," I said. "Look, did you think Lori was trouble before she showed up tonight?"

He squeezed my hand and straightened his back. "Yes, yes I did. Diego told me she was all over his bones at a happy hour the other week."

"Diego did not say that. Does she know he's married?"

"Maybe he didn't use those words, but she made him uncomfortable. In any case, if she didn't know he was married then, she sure does now. One of the other associates practically pried her off of him with a spatula and told her. After which she went right back to humping his leg."

"I'll ask Diego about her if you don't want him privy to your theories. My hunch is that she's just a touchy girl, though." I showed him the plum-colored lip print on my hand. "Unless I made her fall for me already."

"Could you do that? I mean, you can tell him why, but he'll definitely think I'm nuts."

"At least you're a little bit self-aware." I rubbed my temples with the meat of my palms. "Sure, I'll ask him. But let's keep this realistic. I can't bug your dad's phone. I can pry around, but anything else is pretty out of my league."

"Of course. Maybe you could talk to Diego and chat up Lori? She seems to like you."

"I'll do what I can, okay? Lucky for you, I like the idea of posing as a dick."

I got up and rejoined the party, leaving Luke to untangle the tubes of his bothered brain.

Two

I was thirteen when I first read *The Big Sleep*. I was smitten. It was my introduction to Marlowe, to hard-boiled detective fiction, to the very notion of noir, and I could not get enough. As I grew my last three inches, I went from book to book, consuming everything that was Philip Marlowe. I savored his words, studied his manners and methods. I carried him with me like an idol. Marlowe, the honorable, lonely detective—he was my hero, and playing his part appealed to me, as Luke knew it would.

I had a job and a client. That meant something. When Marlowe took on a case, it was a matter of pride. He never gave up until he turned over answers, whether his client wanted them or not. I was no Marlowe, and Luke no violet-eyed knockout, but he was someone I wanted to help. There were only a few of those left.

I felt optimistic. When I set out to deal with what happened to Iris, I didn't mean to uncover a trail, had no intention of solving a mystery. It was only after I started that there was a mystery at all. And then, I was starting with a harsh truth. There were papers, rides to the doctor, my sister, drawn in the face and holding her flat belly, scarred on the inside. Luke had a receipt, a handbag, and a man's intuition. I had every reason to expect innocuous results.

I had no game plan, but Marlowe never did, either. By the time he took three steps, he would face a whole new path, an unforeseen story. The first step, though, was always straightforward. A lead, a person to question. I had two. I scoped the room, but there was no sign of Diego. That left Lori.

I found her sitting on Luke's couch, knees knocked together and feet apart, toes pointing in. My eyes went straight to her hands—she was holding the Chanel.

It was an evening purse, a domed clutch in gleaming black with metallic undertones, about the size and shape of the top half of a football, wide at the bottom and tapering up to a clean ridge with a shiny silver clasp of interlocking Cs. Luke was right about one thing—the purse matched her dress a sight more than it did her salary.

She held it open, and it took me a few seconds to notice that she was fishing out her car keys. I bolted over to the couch and plopped down next to her.

"I hope you're not planning to use those." I pushed out an open palm. "I need them, is all," I said. It was worth a try. "They're mine."

Her eyes widened slight and sudden like the bellies of two fish inhaling. "I'm—I'm so sorry!" The keys fell to the carpet with a jingle of tiny bells attached to a jeweled charm of a winking monkey in a sailor cap, holding a tiny green banana in its tiny humanoid fingers. Her head dropped heavily as she darted to pick them up, but her hand stopped short of the floor. I stooped down on my heels and swiped them.

"I got it. Thanks."

She went back to peering into the little Chanel, which now held only a bullet-shaped lipstick and a cell phone in a hard magenta shell. She looked up at no one in particular with knit brows and parted lips. "Have you seen my keys?"

"Are you leaving?"

"I have to be home by midnight." Textbook drunk driver, down to the slurred speech.

"You're tossed, babe."

"Like salad?" Her brows sat on her eyelids. "I'm not salad."

I almost smiled. "You're drunk."

"I have to go home," she whined.

Luke's request reflected itself in the dark gunmetal sheen of her clutch. "Where do you live? I'm leaving in a minute."

"But my car."

"You got a ride here, remember?"

"I did not."

"Don't worry about it." She was concentrating. I wasn't above enjoying it. "Where do you live? I'll take you."

She mumbled some half words in protest, but finally gave me an address: 432 South Citrus Avenue. Between Fourth and Sixth near Highland, an easy three-minute drive through Hancock Park.

"Don't forget your hat." I watched as her hands darted to the sides of her head in panic, feeling for a phantom brim. "I'm messing with you. Seriously, you were going to drive?"

"Have to be home." She extended a hand up toward me, her head drooping, her eyes doing their best to touch the ceiling. I took it and pulled her up, angelically light despite her rag-doll posture. I breathed relief that she was able to stand on her own. I was feeling gallant enough without having to carry the two of us back to my car.

"Get your shoes," I said. She walked to the pile of shoes at the entrance and found her pair. The thousand-dollar Louboutins. I gave myself a mental pat on the back and decided not to mention them to Luke. I strapped my platforms back on and put her keys in my clutch, switching out my own.

We left the Marlowe, and I turned back to look at its dark outline against the ink-blue sky. I smirked. I had entered with Marlowe on my mind and left with a case and a femme fatale wearing four months' rent in accessories.

The night was still pleasant, and muddled stars hung somewhere above us as we stumbled, collectively eight inches taller and several drinks deeper than base level, to my car on Lillian Way. I keyed open the front door of the Volvo 850 and the interior brightened with an air of surprise. "Where's your car?" I asked. She flicked vaguely at a tree. I started to get irritated but noticed the dark outline of a dirty black Jetta parked squarely under the branches. I fished in my purse for her keys, and bingo, a match. Not that the make of her car mattered in the least to solving Luke's mystery, but I thought it might pay to look thorough.

I opened the passenger door of my sedan and let her crawl in before I took the driver's seat and changed into my driving flip-flops. I threw the platforms into the passenger foot well, where they joined my minicloset of accumulated uncomfortable footwear without, apparently, bothering Lori. "Buckle up," I said. She strapped herself in and let her head roll to a painful eighty degrees against the taut seat belt above her shoulders. She didn't seem primed for conversation.

Now that Iris was on my mind, I saw the resemblance between the two girls. It wasn't a direct likeness as much as it was a common thread. Their features shared a slippery, nymphish quality and their bodies a young litheness, though Iris was several inches taller.

At the very least, Lori and Iris were more likely sisters than Iris and me. Since the beginning of my school days, I had been tall and bony. Until late in high school I wore unstylish glasses and a series of blunt haircuts. Austerity suited me, and it was only after I got into college that I spent time on my appearance at all. Iris was attractive from the minute she emerged from childhood. Before she was old enough to drive, she turned heads just by setting foot inside a grocery store. She had well-defined features that she learned to enhance with makeup, set in a face the size of a fist. She had the long almond eyes that ran in our family, but they carried a look of gentle innocence that differentiated them from mine. Her nose was angular and her small mouth fitted with full, shapely lips. She dressed well—she was proud of her figure.

We grew up in Northridge, hot, quiet, and suburban, with our strict Korean mother. Our father died of liver cancer when I was five and Iris three. We missed him in a way, but by the time we were thinking people, he was little more than a myth. Our mom was an accountant before we were born, and when she was widowed, she went back to her job. She would have stayed at home if it had been an option—she was meticulous about our upbringing and education and resented the job that kept her away.

She nurtured me with a watchful eye. I never touched a video game, and when I graduated from kindergarten, television was out of my life. I never thought to turn on cartoons when she was at work. I was an obedient child. I loved my mother. Though she was sometimes shrill and demanding, she showed love and affection even in her harshest words. I suppose my childhood didn't match the American television ideal, but I was neither bored nor unhappy. I did well in school and earned my mom's praise at every corner.

To fill the hours when I wasn't eating, sleeping, or studying, I read. My mom yelled at me for reading in the dark, and, true to her invectives, my eyes started to go before I turned ten. I was drawn to the stories. They existed outside what I knew, and as a girl from a family of women, I adopted Marlowe. He was quick-witted and masculine, fascinating and foreign, and I took to him right away. After what happened to Iris, the favorite character of my youth became a fixture in my life. I found more than fantasy in the world of noir, and I sank into the scorching bleakness with self-punishing relish.

Iris was just two years my junior, but by the time she was in high school, she had, in a calm way devoid of rebellion, fashioned herself a different upbringing. She didn't care for the piano lessons I had attacked with duty and gusto, and after a few years of lukewarm strokes of the ivory keys, she was allowed to quit. She wasn't a bad student, but she bristled with nerves when our mom mentioned my study habits or my grades. By the time Iris started middle school, our mom learned to respect the differences between her daughters. Where I could be pushed and scolded, Iris would shrivel and question her self-worth. She was a shy, delicate child who cried easily and melted under pressure.

But she wasn't stupid, and she had talents that I lacked, which the traditional bent of our mom's early parenting had neglected to nurture. She had always excelled in art class, but her gift for paint and pencil did not get the same attention as mine for letters

and numbers. By high school our mom had become more affirm-
ing, and without a finger in her back, Iris bloomed. She developed a fascination with fashion and design, and while an interest
in arts was not quite uncommon at our private high school, she
was serious. She dressed with maturity and a strange, elusive style
that ignored the norms of her classmates. As soon as I got my
driver's license, I ferried her to thrift shops and fabric stores. For
her fourteenth birthday, our mom gave her a sewing machine. She
started to wear makeup and perm and dye her hair, and while
she never stopped being quiet, sweet-tempered, self-effacing Iris,
she gained a little confidence to go with her burgeoning beauty.

Despite our differences, we were as close as sisters could be.
Growing up in a house with no father and a working mother, we
had little entertainment outside ourselves. From childhood, we
were best friends, and though we had the usual skirmishes,
we were, on the whole, inseparable. We shared a bedroom for
fifteen years, and we rarely spent less than an hour trading whispers between crawling under our covers and saying good night.
She called me *unni*, the Korean word for older sister, though she
spoke little Korean.

We both took it hard when I left for Connecticut, but I was
thrown into a dormitory and assailed with new situations and
eager new faces. It was an adjustment for me, and it took time
and effort that I couldn't often spare for missing home. I talked
to Iris several times a week, and in the beginning she cried during most of our phone calls. I felt guilty sometimes for the lack of
tears on my end, but she knew I missed her—I had never been
the expressive sister.

When I went home for Christmas, she was glowing with joy,
and as I was happy to be home, I credited our reunion. I wasn't
wrong, but I was less than half right.

Over the next few months, we talked once or twice a week. I was, for the first time, excited about a boy, and a lot of our time was devoted to discussing my blossoming relationship with Diego. In retrospect, I should have heard her silence on her love life. I must have presumed it was the result of her steady relationship with her recently acquired first boyfriend. She was a perpetual romantic, prone to crushes and analytical speculation, but she avoided the subject of her love life for months.

In April, my mom asked me if I knew why Iris was depressed. I had never before been blindsided by my sister, and that first conversation with our mom did nothing to change my certainty that everything was okay. I told her she was imagining things, and I didn't dwell on the possibility that Iris had been less than truthful with me.

The next couple weeks tested my capacity for denial. Iris refused to get out of bed or go to school, and in early May I got a phone call.

We had been talking about nothing, about food or school, when she said, in a voice calm as a frozen lake, "I think I'm pregnant."

I laughed. It was just past dinnertime in L.A. "How much did you eat?"

"I haven't been to the doctor yet, but I took three tests."

That my sister could be pregnant, and that I could have missed the loss of her virginity—these new facts unlocked a quadrant of the universe that I had never before encountered. I spent a lot of time reading about dramatic events and emotional turmoil, but I had avoided all the heartbreak that inspired the literature, and took a happy, peaceful life as my due.

Sex was not a closed topic between Iris and me. We had spent hours discussing the mechanics and implications, spinning out situations, the who and where and how. I had friends who had lost their virginity in high school, and the concept of sexual purity had never meant much to me. Our mom never talked to us about sex, one way or another, so we built our own understanding.

If Luke thought I would be interested in sniffing out foul play involving another half-grown girl, he wasn't too far off the mark.

I took Sixth past Rimpau, Mansfield, June, McCadden, and Highland and turned onto Citrus. The address belonged to a peach house on a residential strip. It had the feel of a parent's house. Two triplets of stairs led up to the front door, beside which hung the digits 4, 3, and 2 in pebbly iron calligraphy. The rounded butt of a Lexus SUV glinted from its perch on the sharply inclined driveway.

I stopped my car and saw fit to pry. Light filled the front seat, giving the tight quarters the air of an interrogation room. I couldn't be quite as aggressive as Marlowe, but I didn't think Lori would be tough to crack.

"We didn't really get to talk at the party too much. I hear you work for the Big Cook."

She puckered her lips and rubbed her head against the textured seat belt. "Uh-huh."

"Since when?"

"Mmm . . . last year?"

"Were you in school before that?"

She nodded, her cheek cuddling the seat belt.

"So, what, that makes you like twenty-three?"

She nodded again, then shook her head and lifted two fingers in a V. "Two." That made her four years younger than me. I thought again of Iris.

I was off track and decided to get straight to the point. Given her current state, I doubted that subtlety was necessary. "What do you think of Mr. Cook?"

She closed her eyes with an air of peace. "Funny."

"Funny?" I tried to picture Mr. Cook cracking a joke and had to laugh. He might have strained a cheek from the effort. I had known the man since the end of high school, when Luke and I started hanging out off campus. When we got around to planning our summers in the spring of freshman year, Mr. Cook offered us easy employment at his firm. He was nice enough, but with all the edge of a Mormon on a Sunday.

"He's awkward. And adorable."

"Adorable?" I felt something icy spread through me at the word. Maybe Luke was onto something. When Mr. Cook was in the room, I would remember to straighten my back and pull down the hem of my skirt. Not because he was looking, either.

"I think he likes me."

I tilted back my head and looked down my nose at her. "Really."

"Don't tell anyone, okay?"

"Who would I tell?" There was at least one obvious answer here, but she didn't quite grasp it. "What makes you think that anyway? The man's married."

She giggled. "He doesn't want to, you know, *do* me, he just *likes* me."

"Then how does he like you?"

She mused with a whimpering hum. "I dunno." She undid her seat belt. It was a messy operation that needed several attempts.

"Are you friends with Diego too?"

"Not really."

"You know I went to college with him and Luke. He's a good guy."

She nodded in angles, apparently too drunk to feign interest.

"Thanks for the ride," she said. She struggled with the door for a couple seconds without looking at her hand before letting herself out.

I got out of the car to walk her to the front door.

"I'm fine," she said. "Thanks so much though." She circled her arms around my neck in a high-school-dance hug, her head resting on my shoulder, pelvis a comfortable couple inches removed from my thigh. "Night, Junie. Drive safe." I grimaced. The only person who called me Junie after the fourth grade was Diego, and the nickname faded out after we broke up. She disengaged herself and I took her palm in mine, pressed her keys into it, and folded her fingers like I was wrapping a gift. I smiled and shrugged, and after reopening her hand to stare at what I'd given her, she did the same. She turned around and tripped up the steps to her front door. She waved, with her head tilted and fingers splayed every which way, and then she let herself in.

I got into my car and brought it back to life. I started to turn into an opposing driveway to go the other way on Citrus, but stopped. Something bothered me about the BMW parked at the curb, sitting quietly in the path of my headlights. The yellow-white beams fell onto the car like a spotlight, and I knew instinctively that something was off. The image before me was like one of those subliminal ads in magazines that makes you look a little bit longer. I steadied my foot on the brake and studied the car under the scrutiny of my headlights. It was a 5 Series, license plate 5PXK766, antenna like a shark fin sticking out of the rear windshield, paint job a hard, glinting Goth-manicure black.

There was the problem. The car was black inside and out. I switched on my high beams. Buckets of white light spilled on the BMW, but its insides remained tarry and inscrutable. I dropped my car into Neutral, rolled down the window, propped my left foot on my right knee, and lit a Lucky Strike. When I'd smoked about half of it, I let it hang from my lips as I texted Luke: "On the job. 5pxk766?" I looked back at the BMW. Nothing new.

I backed my car close to the curb in front of 432, then cut the headlights and killed the engine. The space around me turned milky bright again. I stared at the BMW and wondered if it was any of my business. Luke hadn't mentioned it, and I couldn't think how it would answer any of his questions. I knew Luke would be missing me, and it was time to head back to his party and get properly drunk on this nice Friday night.

When I got out of the car, I told myself it was just to finish my cigarette. I smoked without hurry, standing next to the driver's side door. I stared and stared at the BMW, waiting for my night vision to kick in. My cigarette waned, and I felt the creep of a thrill as I realized I wasn't leaving without a closer look. Luke had called on me to be his detective, and now the dark windows seemed to emit a tempting, dangerous gleam, tickling my curiosity until it became an undeniable itch.

I approached the beemer and went around to the passenger side to try the door. Locked, of course. I knew a couple of tricks that could, in theory, on television, fix that, but my audacity ended before breaking into strange vehicles through untried means. Marlowe might've opened a suspicious car and checked the glove compartment for the name on the registration, but he didn't seem to face many locks in his day, let alone alarm systems. I brought my face as close as I could to the window, even opening my cell phone to shine some light on it, but the glass must have been tinted with obsidian.

I felt it before I heard it. I heard it before I registered it. A dull cotton explosion and the copper taste of blood behind my nose, the memory of a whoosh in the air, footsteps receding in a dream. The chronology of sensation blurred, but it ended in thick, oily, all-consuming black.

Three

When I came to, it was in a cloud of disbelief mixed with the stale taste of morning breath. I gritted my teeth in a stiffened grin, constricting my throat and swallowing with a hard sound that echoed between my ears. I had a headache. I groaned and lay still with my eyes shut tight. As far as I could tell, I had been sapped.

It took me a seventy-second minute to remember the BMW, Lori's house, Luke's party, Iris, and I spent the next minute drawing the line that led to my stint as an unconscious detective. It made me want to laugh and cry. Half an hour of being my own noir hero and I ran into something as real and unrealistic as I could have hoped for.

It was different for Marlowe. Chandler wrote seven Marlowe novels and the hero got knocked out in almost every one. When it happened, he would wake up, shake it off, and calculate to the minute how long he'd been out. He was a private detective, after all, paid to stick his nose in places where it was liable to get punched into his skull. He was never surprised by it, never even mentioned being offended. For all my fascination with the violence of noir, I had never fantasized its intrusion into my own life. I stayed still for several minutes, blinking often.

I sat up where I lay on a hard bench, letting my feet fall wooden on the ground, and looked around. The timid light and the pale blue sky said it was early, maybe six or seven. I was no longer on Citrus. The geometric head of a Koo Koo Roo chicken winked down at me from behind. Someone had seen fit to cart me unconscious to Larchmont, on the Beverly end. At a red light at the empty intersection, one car waited patiently to continue down Beverly.

My clutch lay miraculously at my side, where it must have been tucked behind my back as I slept off the sapping. I snapped open the clasp and looked inside. Cash, credit card, driver's license, car keys, cigarettes, matches—check, check, check, check, check, check, and check again. Cell phone—no such luck. I still had my shoes. Even better—my clothes.

I lit a Lucky Strike and tried to think. I considered that I might have been violated and re-dressed, and I felt the mist of a cold sweat forming on my forehead. This was a detail Marlowe never seemed to deal with when he woke up from forced slumber. I checked my clothes and all seemed to be in order, and I didn't feel like I'd been touched beyond my injury in the last few hours. I liked that I still had all my cash—I figured passing up petty thievery would be like stinting on the after-dinner mint after a double cheeseburger with fries. I decided I had greater causes for panic.

I stood up with the feeling that my brain was swelling out of my skull. I put a hand to the back of my head and stroked the welted, tender bulge right below my hairline's end with the tip of my middle finger. It stung but I couldn't leave it alone, and I marveled at it with all fingers and both hands in turn as I walked down Beverly. I was at the entrance to the Marlowe Apartments within minutes.

I buzzed for Luke. One buzz didn't do it, and neither did two. I jammed my thumb into the smooth concave buzzer and held it, the quack from the intercom vying with my headache for the use of my ears.

A boy in ratty, fraying sneakers and oversize gym clothes came huffing to the door, keys in hand. He gave me a wry grin as he opened it and held it for me. I nodded and gave him the sweetest smile I could muster, which might have been one notch above a frothing snarl. I walked to the elevator and hit the Up button. The boy stood next to me, feeling free to stare. I heard a series of words and snickers dribble out the side of his mouth over the ringing in my head. I looked back at him, unable to make sense of his mumbles. "Are you talking to me?"

He shuffled for a second, then tried to look cool, standing tall in his sneakers with elbows straight, hands folded in front of him. "I said, looks like someone had a fun night."

I opened my mouth with my lower jaw locked wide and tight, tongue pressing up against my back teeth. I furrowed my brows and blinked twice, slow, deliberate, annoyed. "You have no idea."

"You look cute, though. Do you live here?"

I smiled a real one. "Are you hitting on me?"

He stuttered a string of apologetic words.

"How old are you? And Jesus, what time is it?"

"I'm seventeen, and it's—"

I shook my head. "That's called a rhetorical question. You'll learn all about it in English."

We rode up to the third floor in unpleasant silence thick as jam. I got out and noticed that he did not, though he'd also failed to press the button for another floor. I felt a little sorry for him. Seventeen. He was only a boy.

✦

The week after Iris missed her junior prom, I tracked down her intended escort, a clean-cut kid named Paul. It was the beginning of my summer vacation, but Greenwood High was still in full swing. It was a Monday. I had been home for four days.

It was a gorgeous campus in Studio City with old, distinguished buildings and state-of-the-art furnishings. The tuition was more than our mom could afford, but Iris and I got just enough aid that she decided our private education in the hands of L.A.'s most reputable school was worth the remaining figures. Our classmates were a mix of rich kids and smart kids who were, for the most part, as easy to tell apart as goats and sheep. The ones with Rolexes and famous parents tended to be rich. The ones in AP Calculus, smart. There was some overlap. Luke was a notable example.

Paul Kim was a smart kid, or so I'd always thought. I found him eating lunch with two friends, their table strewn with napkins and homework. I saw him smiling from a hundred feet away. Someone was telling a story, and the mood was light. It made me stop walking, for a moment. My steps were hard-heeled and heavy, and it felt incongruous to stomp to a table of boys shooting the breeze on a school day.

He was a good-looking kid, tall and tan with a perpetual cowlick and a disarming set of large teeth. He was the year between Iris and me, and when I was a senior, the three of us had been on the same campus. I saw his face around school before they started dating, but I had never known more than his name.

She started calling him her boyfriend in the middle of my senior year. Iris was fifteen, and our mom grumbled but gave her acquiescence. After all, Paul spoke beautiful Korean, and he had done admirably on his SAT. He and Iris spent a lot of weekends on the family couch, watching television, and he was good about getting up and greeting our mom when she walked into or out of the room. They were never caught with the door closed.

Based on what Iris had told me, I liked him well enough. He was from Glendale. He played the cello. He had an older sister and a beagle named Bob. He and Iris met in the Asian-American Club, and he pursued her in various nonthreatening ways. Toward the beginning of his courtship, I saw him walking with her to class, holding her books. I smiled at Iris, and she turned bright red.

She had never had a boyfriend, and she flourished under the attention. I watched her affection for Paul grow night by night. She told me about their dates, and about sweet things he had said to her, and kisses they'd shared. I realized later that after I left for college, she stopped talking about him unless I asked.

"Hi Paul," I said. My arms were crossed and my tone shaped to inspire fear.

He looked up with his mouth open, his soggy sandwich gripped in one hand. It took him a second to register me standing there. His eyes jumped wide.

"Juniper, hey. What're you doing here?"

His friends had stopped talking, and they were staring at me. I recognized them as faces from old scenery, but they probably knew me as Iris's big sister.

"We need to talk," I said.

He looked to his friends, and one of them shrugged.

"Sure." He turned to the shrugger. "Can you guys watch my stuff?"

"Bring it," I said.

He gave me a look that was less scared than confused. I felt a ripple of anger spread through my chest.

"Okay." He followed me toward the visitor parking lot with an eager gait.

As soon as we were out of earshot, he asked, "Is Iris okay?"

I threw him a glare that kept him silent until we reached my car.

Once we were inside, I locked the door. "I find it hard to believe that you're just hanging out at school, eating a sandwich."

He backed into the far corner of the passenger seat. "What?"

"Do you have any idea what your girlfriend is going through?" I heard my tone go harsh at "your girlfriend."

He leaned forward and looked at me until I gave him eye contact. When I did, he lowered his eyebrows and raised his cheekbones in an unhappy smile. "Am I crazy? What girlfriend?"

The next words nearly stopped in my throat, but I pressed on. "My sister. Iris Song. Your girlfriend."

He sighed, slow and quiet. We sat without talking while my mind raced. I had come to yell at Paul, to blame him for taking advantage of my sister, for being cruel and insensitive and unforgivably dumb. It was an impulse visit born of my own sense of failure, the anger and disappointment I could turn nowhere else.

"I think you have something wrong here. Iris broke up with me in October." He managed a smile when I didn't respond. "Is she okay? I haven't seen her around school."

I could picture my stunned expression. I pinched my sinuses and closed my eyes. I didn't know what to say, so I repeated what he had told me. "You broke up more than six months ago?"

He nodded.

"I don't know if I believe you."

"Believe me. It was tough."

"How did it happen?"

I hadn't decided whether I was embarrassed or convinced he was lying to my face. Either way, Paul must have felt it best to say what he knew.

"She was kind of depressed when you left, but I thought things were fine between us. We were talking about where I might apply to school, and what we would do if I left the state. She broke up with me a week after my birthday. She made sure I got my present first."

"Did she say why?"

"She was vague about it. She said I was a great guy, and she actually thanked me for treating her well. And of course, she asked if we could still be friends." He paused, shaking his head, savoring the sour taste of the words. "I think when it comes down to it, she never liked me the same way I liked her. There's no good way to tell someone that."

I was finding it hard to suspect him of lying. The Paul Iris painted was guileless and gentle, and while I had to admit my sister was capable of deception, I could not accept that she had masterminded his entire portrait.

I had come to chastise the source of Iris's misery, but now I had a new set of questions. Of course, "What happened to my sister?" was qualitatively different from the mysteries of a Chandler yarn. I had no client but my own thirst for knowledge and a contrite explanation. But there was the whodunit aspect—my sister was pregnant and I needed a name. The culprit had no identifiable marks, but I found myself in closed quarters with a potential lead.

I chose my words with care. "Do you think Iris might have been interested in someone else?"

He winced and gave me a sad smile. He was full of them, and they made me sorry. "I thought about it. It was so sudden it seemed kind of passionate. I thought there must be someone else. But I think I was just being jealous. I never found anyone likely."

I wanted to pat Paul on the head, and I realized I had lost all doubt that he was telling the truth. He didn't seem to know anything, and I was thankful I hadn't mentioned Iris's pregnancy in my accusations.

"So are you guys still friends?"

"I think so, but I don't know. She seems to have disappeared lately. I was happy to see you, to be honest. Is she doing okay?"

I shook my head. There was no use saying there was nothing wrong. "She's been really depressed these last few months. I guess she hasn't been going to school. She missed prom, didn't she?" I caught myself. "Though I guess you weren't her date."

"No, I did ask her to prom. She let me know she wasn't coming. I went with a group." I must have looked at him with something like pity, because he added, "It was fine." He scratched his head and looked down at his shoes.

As I walked out of the elevator, I felt a glimmer of guilt toward the teenage boy, but my headache took over by the time I was halfway to Luke's apartment.

I stomped to his door, saw the sign from the night before torn off and lying in the hallway, and knocked. I tried my best to be obnoxious about it, with loud, stiff-knuckled raps and nonsensical rhythms. I was at it a solid minute before Luke came to the door in an undershirt and yellow athletic shorts, his hair a nest wrought by blind birds.

"Song?" He blinked squinted eyes. I could almost hear the dry wrinkle of his slept-in contact lenses. "You look a mess. What the hell happened?"

He opened the door wide and I barged in, kicking off my shoes. A man I didn't recognize slept like a heap of laundry on Luke's couch. There were four pairs of shoes left in the entrance, including a tiny pair of jeweled flat sandals whose owner was either out a pair of shoes or behind closed doors. Bottles, cans, loose playing cards, and crushed tortilla chips littered Luke's floor. The place looked like hours of work for whatever poor soul was cleaning up.

I plopped down on a chair at his dining table, across the room from the couch.

"What time is it?" he asked.

"I don't know. Seven?"

"Good grief." He sat across from me, dragging wooden chair feet in a fibrous rustle through the carpet. "You must've had a fun night."

"So I've heard. Do I really look like I just did a walk of shame?" My head throbbed.

"Well, those are last night's clothes, and you don't look like you spent much time sleeping." He propped his wrists on the table and held his hands together. "I got your text around midnight after you went and disappeared. What the hell happened?"

"To be honest, I can't say for sure, but nothing good." I drummed the table with my fingers. "Luke, is there anything I should know about this little mission you've sent me on?"

"What do you mean?"

"I don't know, any reason to think it's dangerous?"

"I don't think so."

"Let's say your dad was having an affair with this girl. Would he take drastic measures to keep it quiet?" I bit my lip and looked up to see his face tighten with apprehension.

"Jesus, what are you getting at?"

I stood up, walked over to his side, and leaned on the table next to him, half seated. "Feel this." I indicated the swollen bump on the back of my head with a few light taps.

He reached up and ran his fingertips across my hair. "Holy shit. What happened?"

I outlined the events of the night before, from the Chanel to the ride, to the BMW. "Anyway, I was trying to look in the window to see if I could make anything out, and that's it. When I woke up, I was on Larchmont, so I came here."

He wore a look of puzzled horror and rubbed his knuckles against the tabletop. "What do you mean, that's it? What happened?"

"Well, I'm pretty sure I got sapped."

"You mean like by a cop?"

"More likely a bad guy." I sighed. "You know, Marlowe gets cold cocked in like every Chandler novel."

"I didn't know that. Whatever I know about Chandler I've gotten from you."

"Okay, well, did you know *The Big Lebowski* is based on *The Big Sleep*? I think that's why Lebowski gets knocked out twice."

"Occupational hazard?"

"Yeah. Occupational. It's always because someone doesn't want him snooping around, or because someone wants to know what he knows—because he's doing his job. Do you see what I'm getting at?"

He started to give a tentative nod.

"I'm not a detective, Luke. This shouldn't have happened to me."

He brought both hands to his cheeks and dropped his elbows onto the table. "I'm sorry. I'm still processing this, but I swear, I didn't think anything like this was even possible. Do you believe me?"

I nodded. "Yeah, I believe you."

"Good. I'd be really sad if you didn't. Are you okay?"

"My head feels pretty abused, and truthfully, I'm a little shaken. But I guess I'm as okay as I can be." I rubbed my eyes with the heels of my hands. "I'm glad they left me near your house."

We sat for a few minutes, absorbing the changes in the air.

Luke spoke first. "Do you think we should call the police?"

It took me a few seconds to register the question. "I hadn't thought of it, to be honest."

"Really?"

"Yeah. I think I've been thinking a lot more about private eyes than police since I woke up. Strange how fast you can disconnect from the real world."

"Well, what do you think?"

"About the cops? I don't know. Should I? What do I tell them?"

"That you were attacked, I guess. And . . ." He lowered his voice. "Do you think this happened because of my dad?"

"I don't know, Luke."

"It would kill me if he was part of this."

"Honestly, I have no idea. I will say something untoward could be up with Lori. You were probably right about that. Whether your dad is what's untoward, I can't say."

He found a pen on the table and twirled it between two fingers. "This wasn't supposed to happen. I want to know whether my dad's cheating, not whether he can be put in jail."

"Look, I don't feel like talking to cops right now anyway. They'd brush me off. I really don't have much to give them."

He nodded. "So what now then?"

"I guess first thing, I need my car. Can you drive me?"

"Yeah, of course." He hesitated but he didn't say anything. I assumed it had to do with the passed-out drunk on his sofa and the nameless Cinderella in his bedroom. I took a split second to consider being considerate, and pretended not to notice.

"Great. Can I borrow your bathroom first? And some tooth-paste? And some Advil?"

"Go for it. Toothpaste is on the sink. Advil's in the medicine cabinet."

I shuffled across the room and through a short hallway to the bathroom, noting the closed bedroom door before shutting my-self in and switching on the light. I locked my elbows, gripped the hard, white sides of the sink, and stared at my reflection.

I did look a mess. My teen admirer must have been missing his glasses. Wisps of hair stood in waves and lumps on top of my head where my ponytail had come loose. My bangs were no longer swept to the side but hung sadly in a greasy black curtain over the rightmost two-thirds of my forehead, leaving the last third bare. My eyes were rimmed in smudged charcoal a full cen-timeter around, giving me more the look of a gaunt, overworked hooker than of a panda bear. Blackened gobs of sleep gathered in the inner corners of my eyes. I was missing an earring.

I washed my hands with a pump of soap, pushed a finger into each eye in turn, and coaxed my contacts out from where they stuck to my irises, shifting them slowly up and down and side to side. I blinked hard and my eyes watered. I found Luke's tooth-paste and squeezed a tricolored dollop onto my right index finger. I loosed a thin stream from the faucet and wet the paste, then shoved it this way and that into my mouth, across my teeth, over my gums, down my tongue. It failed to foam, but the mint tasted clean. I gargled and spit, gargled and spit. I rinsed my hands and splashed my face, then helped myself to the cleanser by the faucet and washed up, scrubbing well around my eyes. It took me a good twenty seconds to get rid of all the black. I dried my face and hands on a feather soft towel hanging on the wall, then retied my hair. A mirror check showed a tired but socially acceptable face. I wet my bangs and combed them out of my eyes. I opened the medicine cabinet and zeroed in on the Advil. I pressed open the cap and shook out two burgundy pills. I shoved them in my mouth and gulped them down with a palmful of sink water. I wiped my lips dry on my wrist and hobbled out to the living room.

"Thanks. I feel human again," I said. I took up my purse and dropped in my widowed earring. "Shall we?"

We trudged, dazed and dog-tired, to the elevator, down to Luke's dirt-speckled black Porsche in a Porsche-heavy garage. It was a Cayenne hybrid, pretty and fast, a car designed for the Saks Fifth Avenue liberal. Luke was still in his pajamas, a pair of dirty sandals on his feet. I asked, "Dude, did you brush your teeth?"

He pulled out a pack of Orbit. "Want one?"

We chewed as we got in the car.

"So where are we going?"

"Fourth and Citrus. Take a right on Sixth and another right after Highland." I patted down his disaster cloud of cappuccino hair. "I take it you had a better night than I did."

He took a second to contemplate whether he had to address my innuendo and realized that he did. "You could say that."

Luke had a couple girlfriends in high school and a couple more in college, and when he did, his eyes never wandered. But as he shed his smooth layer of boyish dough in his first years at Yale, girls started to notice him. He was never one to spew testosterone, but he learned the rhythms of flirtation with relative ease. When he was single, he had his pick.

"After all your judging last night, you get to sleep with whoever you want. Some feminist you are. Who's the girl?"

"We have a couple classes together. Took me by surprise, though. She isn't anyone you've heard about."

Luke and I kept each other up-to-date on our personal lives, but given the circumstances, that was the extent of my curiosity. We drove without talking through smooth curves on Sixth.

After a minute, Luke exhaled. "I still can't believe someone knocked you out."

"It's unreal. Pretty scary, and I'm pissed off, too. The back of my head feels like a placenta. Or what I think a placenta would feel like, anyway." I palmed the gooey bump. "Do you know anything about a black BMW with the license plate I texted you?"

"Doesn't ring any bells." He paused. "But whoever knocked you out last night obviously wasn't in the car, right?"

"Right." I thought for a second. "Right. But I can't—they have to be related, right?"

"I guess so. I mean, unless someone just didn't like that you were curious in general."

"Maybe. I kind of doubt it, though, because it would've been pretty easy for another car to just kind of chill while I sniffed out the beemer, you know? Though we can't rule out that whoever did this to me is a total idiot. My guess would be that the sapper was looking out for the shady bastard in the beemer. What do you think?"

"I mean, I have no idea. It doesn't really make sense to me."

We pulled up to 432 South Citrus. I caught myself breathing easier at the sight of my darling car parked safe and demure where I'd left it. I fished out my keys and unbuckled my seat belt. Luke parked his car behind mine and killed the engine, and we lumbered out into the gauzy warmth of a Los Angeles summer morning unbothered by wind and damp, unbothered by the crimes and follies of the night before.

"Uh, Song? Isn't that your mystery car?"

It hadn't occurred to me that the BMW might still be there, so I hadn't even thought to check across the street until Luke pointed directly at the spot where I'd ended my waking night. Sure enough, it sat parked where I'd seen it last, in mannered concert with my Volvo.

I power walked across the street and stood right in front of the windshield, arms akimbo, leaning forward at the hips, staring inside. Luke came up next to me and mirrored my pose. The black tint was solid and unapologetic, even in daylight.

He sucked in air noisily through his teeth. "This confuses me. Does it confuse you?"

"Well." I kept staring. "Well, fuck."

"It's a shady vehicle, I'll give you that."

"Don't tell me this is just a neighbor's car. Who tints their windows like that?"

"So where does this leave you?"

"Where does it leave me? Nowhere, apparently. My big lead was this license plate."

"Lead to what?"

"Who knocked me out, why, and what Lori Lim's got to do with it all."

He was quiet for a second. "You know, maybe you don't want to keep investigating her. I had no idea it could be dangerous."

"I guess I should be more careful, but I can still talk to Diego. And I can try and talk to Lori again. In daylight."

He shuffled his feet and made an arc on the concrete with one toe. "I'm scared of what you'll find out."

"Do you not want to know anymore?"

He thought about it. "No. I think I need to know, especially now. I'm rooting for you to clear my dad."

"I am too."

"And you know, if you think it's better that you call the police, don't hold back for my sake. I didn't mean to discourage you."

"Thanks, Luke. We'll talk later. I haven't really had a chance to think this through, and I'm not a hundred percent right now." I walked toward my car. "I'm going home to shower, and then I have to do a thousand things. Don't worry, though. I'm not going to tell the police to arrest your dad. That would be absurd."

"I guess so, huh?" He gave me a weak smile. "Can we catch up later? Get lunch or something?"

"I can do dinner. I just have a lot to take care of today. I should probably take a nap, too."

"Okay, dinner works."

"I don't have my cell, remember, but I'll try to get a new one today. Otherwise try me at home."

"Okay, that sounds good." He gave me one of his mild, brotherly hugs, a loose circle draped over my head, clasped with wrists resting above the small of my back. "I'm sorry this happened to you."

"Me too." I gave his torso a good squeeze and got into my car. He stepped back and waved. I started the car, eased my foot onto the accelerator, and left South Citrus to swallow my dust.

Four

The single-mile drive from Lori's to Park La Brea took two smooth, uneventful minutes. I didn't hit one red light.

I pulled into the garage and slammed the brakes on the slope to my spot as a jogger with a death wish bunny-hopped across the ramp. A thud sounded from the trunk and I felt my stomach drop as if my intestines had been yanked out from underneath it like a magician's tablecloth.

It could have been a bag of bowling balls, maybe a floor lamp. It was definitely not the shopping bag of dry cleaning that I had put into my empty trunk the morning before.

I slid my car into its space crooked and hasty like I was stealing home. I slipped the stick to Neutral, yanked on the emergency brake, and stepped out of my seat without turning off the engine. I let myself hesitate for just a few seconds, then reached in for the latch. I closed my eyes and pulled until it popped, and the trunk was open   I gave the door enough force to rise, and I stood back as it rose, with the measured theatrical pace of an elevator unsealing, revealing.

Bile bloomed harsh and thorny at the back of my throat. I suppose I already knew what was in there. In the dark of a Los Angeles night, I had been clubbed down and left out cold—this was a new reality with new rules, and it was about time to toll the body count.

Marlowe always managed to describe every detail of a room before coolly settling his writer's eye on the petrified body with bound ankles and a knife in its face, sprawled out in a pool of gore on the middle of the musty oriental carpet that looked, forty years ago, like it had seen better days. My trunk offered little to work with, but I wouldn't have noticed the gardens of Versailles jammed into that spare space for the fact of death staring at me from within.

I grabbed my knees, turned my head to the right, and threw up. A spotted confection of brown, orange, and pink hit the pavement like spilled chunky soup. By the time it settled into a couple of motionless pools, I was vomiting again. I huffed deeply, one, two, one, two, then heaved until there was nothing left.

I spit and lifted a hand from where it gripped my kneecap to wipe the slime from my mouth on the flat of my wrist. I forced myself to look at the body.

It was a he—a strange he, thank heavens. His long, string-bean frame lay crumpled at the hips, knees collapsed and pointing to the back of my trunk. His candy-bright red hair was well kept, even after what had to have been a bumpier night than mine, spiffy with gel in a perfectly executed interpretation of bed head. He wore a close-fitting button-down shirt in white and lilac pinstripes, unbuttoned a button or two too low. The lean expanse of tan skin peeking out from underneath was unnaturally hairless. Brown Ferragamo loafers and thin, distressed blue jeans finished the outfit. His torso was contorted so that he lay on his back with his face looking up at me.

It was an unlovable face, with twisted eyebrows, meager chapped lips, and a nose so narrow it barely had a bulb. When it mattered, maybe hours, maybe days ago, he might have been somewhere in the neighborhood of twenty-nine, thirty-one—it didn't matter anymore. His muddy brown eyes were open, fixed in panic and disbelief.

There was no blood that I could see, no holes, but a crude ribbon of bruises and narrow scratches spread across his neck. Strangled, if I had to guess. The fingernail marks might have been his own.

I lowered the back of my hand into the trunk space and touched it, just barely, to the dead man's cheek. I don't know what I expected to gain from this gesture, but it proved pointless. The temperature—neither notably hot nor cold—was unrevealing, and the skin felt like regular old cheek skin, only I knew it was dead, and I couldn't untouch it. I scraped the back of my hand against the skirt of my dress, but I couldn't unfeel the touch I absorbed with my skin even as the fact of sensation fled from my mind. I rubbed and rubbed, trying not to keep staring at the corpse. I stopped when it started to smart, and I shook out my hand, then popped the wrist. The sound was crisp and satisfying, and I popped the other and cracked every knuckle I knew I had. The garage echoed.

I pulled down on the lid of my trunk and squatted on the floor of the garage, my heels hovering in their flip-flops. I held it like that, not quite closed, and I buried one eye in the stretched skin of an extended arm. I whimpered like a stupid pup, and I was aware of how pathetic I looked, squatting and shivering among the splashes of my vomit.

A minute later, I closed the trunk and forced myself to my feet. I needed a phone like I'd never needed a phone. I rounded the side of my car, got in, and killed the engine. I smiled a little at my brain's use of that stock phrase—a killed engine up front, a murdered body in back. The garage held a tight silence, the type that comes between the drips of a leaky faucet. My shoes scratched the pavement like rude critters scurrying, cluttering. I left the garage and plodded to my apartment tower, one heavy shuffle at a time, trying to keep my balance while the world swirled around me.

I walked into the entryway of my building and hit the button for the elevator. A doorman seated on a metal stool watched me from a corner, wedged between a courtesy phone and a wall of mailboxes. I crossed my arms and shifted my weight from foot to foot. The elevators in my building were in dire need of remodeling. A pressed button gave no light, and there was no telling when a car would arrive. The doorman stared at me for a full two minutes before letting me know that the elevators were down.

"Thanks. I've only been standing here since Tuesday." I spun on a used-up heel and rounded my way through a very heavy door into the echoing concrete cave of a stairwell. The iron steps wobbled and clanged in lazy noisy baritones under my tired, plodding gait. I gripped the railing as I wound my way up.

I heard the old telephone ringing from the hallway as I approached 4J. I was the last twenty-something in the Los Angeles area who still had a landline. Even the cable guy gave me a look when I requested it, all high eyebrows and crooked smile. The phone itself was an antique—rotary dial, earpiece like a fancy black barbell, fat trapezoid body, and, of course, a ring like the angry clatter of the entire cookware section of Bed Bath & Beyond falling into the aisles at once. I loved that ring as much as everyone else hated it, and as I shimmied my keys into the lock, I was aware that I had never dreaded hearing it until now. I gave the door a shove with my upper arm and stumbled into my studio bursting with that furious tin sound.

I stood still in the doorway and let it ring, and ring, and ring, the receiver nearly jumping in its seat. The clock in the TV stand said 7:42 A.M. in rude red dots and dashes. The ringing stopped, and I slipped out of my shoes and approached the old phone where it sat, dressing up a vanilla-wooden Ikea coffee table with screw-in peg legs. I dropped onto the couch and forgot to relax, forgot to appreciate the way the old leather cushion sank in just enough to welcome a worn-out behind. I leaned forward, propped my elbows on my knees, rested nose and chin in a two-handed finger gun, and waited for the next call.

The only person who might call me on my landline, especially at this hour, was Luke, who knew there was no other way to reach me. Even so, I sat stone still as terror churned in my stomach.

The wait was short. This time I picked up after one ring. I took a deep, quiet breath, careful not to make a sound. "Hello?" The greeting did not come out as bright and clear and cool as it had in the split-second preview that played in my head, but neither did my booming heartbeat leak into the cadence.

"Welcome home, Miss Song." The voice was gentle, teasing. I pictured a man of medium height and unknowable age with Talented Mr. Ripley hair, smiling wryly over a cup of coffee. My murderer had good PR.

I swallowed, running my tongue across the roof of my mouth. "Can you tell me what you're driving so I can hang up and call my building manager?"

There was just the tiniest window of silence on the line, and I might have imagined that. "I'm afraid that wouldn't be in your best interest."

"Please, tell me what is."

"Stay out of trouble, and you might be left alone. You're just a girl, Miss Song. I don't know what possessed you to stick your nose where it doesn't belong. Bad things happen when you do that." His tone was sweet, but cold and stiff.

I could hear him waiting, unmoved but impatient, for a response. Marlowe always had thugs warning him to keep his nose clean—it was a requisite conversation in every book. Marlowe never listened. If I had learned one thing in the last ten hours, it was that I was no Marlowe. I couldn't take violence and death with his even, evaluative stance, and danger did what danger does—it scared me.

"I will stay out of trouble," I said, then put down the receiver with a passive click. I couldn't have delayed more than a few seconds before going for the phone again to call the cops, but the bad guy had my number.

The sugar was gone from his voice, and he enunciated like he was cutting steel. "I assume that you won't be involving the police. I will be listening." I heard three dry taps, fingernails hitting the speaker on the other end of the line.

I hesitated, and before I could respond, he started to speak again. "My employer"—he said it just like in the movies, with utter certainty and awed loyalty—"is a busy person, but my employer is willing to take the time to meet with your family, all the way out in Texas. I've heard all about your beautiful little sister. Your poor mother. Two daughters who just can't stay out of trouble."

I could tell from the lilt in his voice that he smiled with just the corners of his mouth as he spoke. He knew he was dealing in clichés, and he knew that the clichés would do just fine. Worse, he knew about Iris, and he was taunting me, knowing it wouldn't matter. The strongest poker hands never change, never lose. There was no need for cleverness. The bald, pulp threats glued my tongue to the roof of my mouth, and when the dial tone sounded a minute later, I realized I had no conception of when, cat-footed, he had disappeared from the other end of the line.

I waited a full day to approach Iris after I talked to Paul. She had been avoiding me since I came home, though not in the physical sense. We shared a room, after all, and she accepted my gentle attentions, my shy, open-ended inquiries as to her general state of mind. It felt strange to be home, knowing that for the first time, I was not in tune with my sister. She'd had experiences, important life moments, without reporting them in whispers before we fell asleep. I had moved away, left our room, and lost her confidence. Now that I was home for the next three months, I needed to win her back. I decided to let her get used to me, let her recall my smell and the sound of my voice without the filter of telephone wire. I spent those first days blending back into the space that we had shared for years.

On my fifth night home, I turned our light back on twenty minutes after we went to bed. I didn't need to ask if she was still awake.

I cleared my throat. "Iris, do you trust me?" My words hung in the air, cold and without echo. "You trust me, don't you?" I could hear her holding her breath, lying still, hoping I'd let her pretend to sleep. "I know you're awake. We have to talk about this sometime." I sat up and leaned on one elbow, facing her. Our twin beds were separated by less than three feet of carpet. Iris lay in fetal position, her head down, knees pointed toward me. "This is important. If you won't talk to me I'm going to have to tell Mom."

The threat tasted dirty leaving my mouth, but I knew as it did that I meant it, and that I was in the right. Iris and I had buried each other's secrets since we were children. As much as we loved each other, we were siblings born two years apart—until at least middle school, our fights were routine and sometimes furious. Still, we never stooped to tattling. Our stern mother wasn't a last resort so much as a nonoption.

She opened her eyes but kept them averted. "You can't tell Mom. I will die if you do."

"I have to do something, Iris."

"No, you don't."

I collected my words. I avoided landmines like *keep* and *baby*. "What's your plan?"

She melted into herself on the other bed, shivering with tears. I got out from under my covers and sat beside her, stroking her unwashed hair. Comforting Iris came naturally, like it was something I was born to do. I waited for her sobs to subside.

Minutes later, she whispered, "I can't keep it."

"Do you want to?"

"I don't know. I want it to come back in ten years."

She was finally talking to me, and I figured out fast that she would stop talking about her health, her pregnancy, and her state of mind if I said a word about the father. I stroked her back until she fell asleep, and I drifted off as I held her.

A few days later, she rested her hand on mine as I drove her home from the clinic. Iris, who had never had a job or a large allowance, paid for the procedure with a small number of clean bills. I waited another few nights to ask more questions.

❖

Iris's teenage face spread across my mind like a picture coming into focus. I lowered the receiver into its cradle, letting it drop gently with a slow uncurling of my fingers from around its waist.

Marlowe would've picked it back up and called the police. Even he didn't mess around too much when a corpse was involved. But Marlowe never spoke of a family, or close relationships. There were few threats that could stop him cold.

I let myself linger on the edge of the couch for a few seconds before bolting upright and marching to the bathroom. I peeled myself out of my dress, unhooked my bra, and stepped out of my underwear. I picked up each article of clothing in turn and passed it inch by inch over the flat edge of my sink, scanning the cloth with two fingers. I didn't know how high-tech criminals were these days, and I didn't really know what I was doing, but it made me feel better to do something, so I settled on checking for bugs. I satisfied myself that I was clean, at least as far as I could tell, and grabbed a coarse milk-and-coffee towel and set it on top of the closed toilet.

I turned on the hot water in my bathtub and lifted the pull for a shower. I cupped a hand in the path of the spray, which this morning seemed much too limp to scour me clean. I waited for it to get warm, then I stepped in, facing away from the shower-head. My scalp stung, but I shampooed twice, conditioned twice, soaped twice, and stood soaking in the hot pour for minutes after, breathing in the antiseptic, lemon vapor before it washed down the drain with the emulsified sweat and fatigue of my body. I pondered my next move, and whether I even had a turn coming.

One important question became clear amid the steam—was my tormentor bluffing? He implied that my phone had been bugged, but he would have done that whether or not it was true. My apartment looked undisturbed, and, for all I knew, he was a bumbling one-man team with a smooth voice, a cell phone, and a rudimentary knowledge of the conventions of crime movies. If I knew he was bluffing, I could call the police right now. If I was wrong, and called the police anyway, he might be powerless even then. He was outside my building and would have to flee.

But then what? I knew nothing of his identity or where-abouts—I knew only that he was unfazed by murder, that he was a man who had ditched the norms that controlled the animal im-pulses of human society. I might run the risk that he would track down my family whether or not he had anything to gain.

The entire situation felt unreal, and I considered how the body in my trunk had come to be. I ran scenarios through the fuzzy projector of my mind's eye and, squinting as water ran down my stinging head, watched them unfold on the sweaty white plaster wall in front of me.

I watched as a man in a black trench and matching fedora ap-proached the malnourished redhead on Citrus. He held a nonde-script belt in two downturned fists like bicycle handlebars, giving and taking up slack as he tiptoed toward his victim. He caught up to the tall redhead and, with a sudden fast-forward flourish, looped him from behind, kicked out the backs of his knees to get him to bend down to where he could pull up on the belt, and yanked hard and steady while the soon-to-be corpse kicked the concrete beneath him. Midstrangle, the killer saw my car pull up in front of Lori's house, watched as I watched her to her door, watched as I almost left, watched as I watched the BMW, watched as I lurked solo in the dark street, poking into other people's business. Maybe his eyes, gleaming and bloodshot in the velvet warmth of the night, were fixed on me as he felt the body in his arms fill with death as with so much cement. Maybe he was watching, worrying, and missed the moment when his victim made the binary leap from 1 to 0. I closed my eyes and watched him watch me as he dropped the body and crept, sliding as if he had no feet, across the street. His hand disappeared into a deep pocket and came out holding a heavy flashlight. Maybe when he caught up to me and brought the weapon down on the back of my head, he wielded it with a wrist stiffened by resentment that my interference had deprived him of his victim's crossover moment.

Then what? He must have gone through my purse at some point, gotten my keys, and lugged the body to my trunk. Why? So it wasn't his problem anymore? No—a corpse in my trunk wouldn't make me the murderer, not in a competent policeman's eye. It had to be a message, a drastic way of saying, *This is what I can do.*

I pulled back the shower curtain, grabbed the towel, and gave myself a rough, quick pat-dry before stepping out of the misted warmth and onto the sterile linoleum floor. I swept to my closet to swap the towel for a navy thong and a loose gray V-neck, dressing with Olympic speed. By the time I grabbed my Mac-Book and plopped back onto the couch, the drenched ends of my hair had left dark wet splotches on the front of my T-shirt. I opened up the laptop and woke it up by hitting the space bar. It gave a brief whirring groan and was at my service. I entered my password and opened a Web browser.

I would have to count on my computer being secure. It was one thing to put a wire on a phone, and quite another to monitor e-mail on a password-protected laptop. I clamped my teeth together and hoped I was right.

I opened a new message and addressed it to lucaswcook@ gmail.com. It was just past eight thirty in the morning, and I estimated the chances of Luke being awake as fifty-fifty, solely because of what had happened during the night. I added diego. diaz@stokel.com to the recipient list. I needed to reach Luke, and I wanted Diego's advice.

I typed: "Hi guys, I'm in a pretty urgent situation right now, and I want to talk to you in person. Diego—I know you're up. Could you call Luke for me and make sure he's getting this? Can we meet up as soon as possible? I'm ready to leave my apartment whenever. I don't have a phone."

I thought about e-mailing my mom and found I couldn't re- member the last time I'd spoken to her. We were never officially out of touch, but I could go about my days and realize I hadn't heard from my family in months. For now, I would do what I could to keep my mess out of their lives.

I decided to start getting ready. I had to leave the building, and I didn't want Luke and Diego to be seen coming in. I found a black padded bra in the folds of my unmade bed and put it on under my T-shirt, feeding the straps through the armholes and hooking it in the back. I pulled open the bottom drawer of my dresser and found a pair of denim shorts and threw those on. When I sat back on the couch, there was a message from Diego in my in-box. "Come over whenever you want. I'm not getting through to Luke right now but I'll try again in a few minutes. Is everything okay?"

I closed my laptop and got up again. I unclasped my clutch and emptied its contents into a roomy black leather shoulder bag. I glanced at the block of sharpened knives on my counter, but I knew I couldn't wield a blade outside the kitchen. Instead, I scanned the room for something heavy and breakable, and settled on a thick, black ceramic ashtray. I put that in my bag. Its weight was reassuring. I put on my flip-flops, left my studio, and locked the door behind me.

I could have asked Diego to call the police. They may not have gotten my villain without a description, but they would have kept him away from me and taken a body off my hands. Still, I ruled out involving the law just yet. The likelihood that this man would commit violence against my family before I could get the police to protect them and track him down was very small, but greater than zero. If I had Diego call the police, he would know, and if he was a murderer, he was also part madman.

He would know because after he hung up the phone, there was nothing for him to do but watch for my next move. He would see the police pull into my garage because he would be lying in wait nearby. If I was right, I could see how crazy he was for my-self, just by setting foot outside.

Five

A man in a smart blue suit and polished brown oxfords leaned on the corner of the 850's closed trunk, his feet crossed jauntily at the ankles, relaxed as a lizard on a rock. He held one of his elbows in a cupped hand and examined his fingernails, a sculpted interpretation of nonchalance. It might have passed but for the subject's middling height, which forced him to keep his heels tense on the ground to maintain his noncommittal perch on the car. His glazed gold-and-chestnut hair parted right at the 30/70 line of a short forehead, falling into a tall, swept-back shell around his head, the gel-crusted crest of which you could bounce a ball on. His cool eyes, black or green or both, like the chitinous shell of a housefly, were downcast as he continued looking for grime and snagged cuticles. They held a devilish gleam that wasn't uncharming, and he had a nose that could cut glass. He looked up with a slow, exaggerated raise of the chin, a lopsided smile, and an affected widening of the eyes that spread across his face as he heard my stomping footsteps. If he'd had a hat, he would've tipped it, no doubt.

I stopped when his eyes met mine, and the slap of my rubber-soled foot on concrete boomed brassily around us. "You look exactly like you sound."

"Thank you." He pushed off the car with a backward thrust of his tailbone and his feet touched the ground with a soft pat.

My throat felt dusty and my voice was on the verge of cracking. "Are you going to kill me?"

"I would like to avoid it if possible."

"You could have killed me last night."

He shrugged and tilted his head to look at his fingernails.

"Who are you?"

"You can call me Humphrey."

"Do you have a last name?"

He smiled. "Bogart."

I scanned the parking lot but Bogart and I were alone. It worried me that he showed himself, what it would mean for it not to matter that I could identify him. With my assailant before me, the ashtray in my purse felt stupid, pointless, a minute's reach away. "What do you want me to do?"

"I want you to come with me."

"Where?"

He shook his head.

I tried to stall. "Who is that in my trunk?"

"That's none of your concern, Miss Song."

"Did you kill him?"

"Tsk-tsk."

I looked at the ground and perked up at the sound of a door opening. A girl around my age came through it, a neighbor going to her car. It was a brief window, but it was there and it had a witness.

"I won't go with you," I said with volume, and I took my car key out of my purse. I stepped quickly to my Volvo's door and unlocked it.

Suddenly there was a navy-clad forearm in my field of vision and pressure on my shoulder and at the side of my neck. I felt the warmth of a live human body all along my back. It was the negative of an embrace, the same gesture in a world of black teeth and white eyes.

His mouth at my ear let out hot breath and as he whispered I saw like a bat the quivering damp of his inner cheeks, red and uneven. "I can kill you, you know. You and your pathetic scrap of a family."

My hands, at my sides, sprung open and stiff, and I had to fumble to recover my key. I nodded slowly and my voicebox managed to puff up under the hold of his arm, "I know."

He laughed. It was an airy laugh that was almost nervous, like that of a child who had lost his temper on the playground and wanted back in the games. His hold relaxed and he withdrew his arm, the fabric of his jacket rustling as it slid over my shoulder. He patted me on the back, jocularity in his very fingertips.

"We will see each other again." He emphasized the second word, certainty buoyant in his voice.

He was still behind me and I said without turning, "Yes."

I stood for a long moment, waiting, then opened the door and climbed into the driver's seat. I jammed my foot on the clutch and started the engine with teleport speed. I backed out and sped out of the lot.

I listened to the hum of my engine as I switched gears, and I left him to figure out whether to follow me, satisfied that no amount of scrambling would allow him to tail me directly. The wait for the garage door to sense my presence and crawl open was strange and strained, but he was too far away to share my darting eye contact. He didn't move, even as I drove away and he became a vague, suited Waldo in the rearview mirror. When he was out of sight, I noticed I was breathing normally, and that this was a change.

It was eight twenty now. Diego lived on Kings Road and First Street, a five-minute drive from my apartment. I rolled down the windows and tried to relax, breathing with the sound of the passing air as the Volvo knifed through it.

I still depended on Diego, but when I was eighteen, I could forget how to breathe without him. My first weeks home that summer were lonely and difficult, and not only because of Iris. After months of virtual cohabitation with Diego—and, in turn, Luke—I was getting my first taste of a long-distance relationship.

When Iris told me she was pregnant, she asked me not to tell anybody. I told her I wouldn't breathe a word to our mom, but I asked for permission to talk to Diego. I told her he had a cousin who'd had a baby in high school and that he might have some good insight. She was reluctant, but she said she couldn't stop me.

It was true that he had that cousin, but I needed Diego's ear more than his experience. We talked every day, and Diego listened to me gripe over the phone. He said that Iris would come around, that she would open up if I gave her time. But my newly secretive sister was driving me mad.

I avoided trapping her in a lie. I didn't ask, *What does Paul think?* or *How have things been with him?* If there was any consideration in this open strategy, it was incidental. I was protecting myself.

Hearing a new-spun lie out of Iris's mouth would have hurt me, mind, heart, and stomach.

"I heard you broke up with Paul," I said.

We were getting ready for bed, and she caught my eye in the mirror, with her toothbrush in her mouth. She finished brushing, took her time rinsing, splashed water onto her face, and dried off on a towel.

"Where did you hear that?" Her tone was sharper than I'd heard it in a while. She had her hands pressed down on the bathroom counter in the posture of a push-up. Her head was down and sought neither my eyes behind her nor their reflection in the glass.

"Doesn't matter."

"Of course it matters. I didn't tell you that. You went behind my back."

I smirked. "Well, gee, Iris. Why the hell would I go behind your back when you've been so up front with me?"

She turned on the faucet to splash more water onto her face and let the water run as she squinted at my reflection. We were only minutes into the fight and I already felt the wear of battle. "Don't be bitchy, *unni*. You have no idea what I'm going through."

"You're right. You haven't told me fucking anything. Every time we talked in the last—I don't even know how long—you've been lying to me."

Her eyes glassed over with malice and she turned off the faucet with a hard twist. "You never asked. You stopped listening to me. You left me here, and ever since, you've been in your own little world and it's all you ever want to talk about."

There was violence in her tempo—she whetted her words so they could break skin. I gasped, but before I could protest, she continued.

"You went to college and stopped caring about your sad little sister all the way across the country. I could tell. I know I annoyed you, crying on the phone, saying how miserable I was. You acted patient, but I could hear you zoning out. So, obviously, I made an effort. To stop being such a drag. I let you have my ear, and I listened to every detail of your new life, wishing you were here instead." Her voice dissolved, shaking with tears.

I remembered those long phone calls. Hours and hours of comforting Iris, knowing that she was, consciously or not, spinning her resentment into veiled guilt trips because I had left her for college. I couldn't deny that on occasion, I found her tiresome. I never admitted it to her, but sometimes I dreaded her calls, a few times even ignored them. After some of the more frustrating conversations, I complained to Luke and Diego. About my downer of a sister.

"Do you ever listen to yourself when you talk about Diego? You go on for days. I know all about his family, I know how hard he works and how sweet he is—I know what he eats. When did I have time to talk about Paul or anyone else? After we've been on the phone for half an hour and you remember to ask, 'How's Mom?' and, 'How's Paul?' all in one breath? I didn't tell you about Paul because I wasn't sure you gave a shit anymore. You were relieved that I stopped talking about my problems."

Tears stung my eyes, and for several seconds I was too stunned to defend myself. Iris waited, watching me struggle in the mirror.

When I slumped over to embrace her back, she didn't protest. "Of course I gave a shit. You're my sister. I'm sorry if I was distant, or self-absorbed. I didn't realize you felt like that. You should've said something."

"I couldn't say anything. I couldn't force you to care about me, and I didn't want to make you pretend." Her weight was still resting on her palms, and she trembled like the struck string of a violin.

"But we should be able to talk to each other about everything. I can't believe you felt this way for months. And now, you can't tell me what's going on in your life? How can you have been pregnant without me even knowing who the father was? It wasn't Paul, was it?"

She shook her head. "Paul and I never slept together."

"Would you have told me if you had?"

She nodded. "But I'm not saying anything else."

She wriggled out of my arms and hurried out of the bathroom, her fingertips dripping water.

I arrived in less than five minutes and parked on the street. I walked up a flight of white wooden steps to the front door of Diego and Jackie's one-bedroom. They lived in a complex with four or five units between two stories, all of which looked out onto a shared lawn that shone green and dewy all year round. The letterbox outside their door read D DIAZ & J BLUMENTHAL. I rapped on the door one two three.

Diego opened it at two and a half, before the knuckle of my index finger could kiss the wood. He wore boot-cut jeans and a black polo that hung too square on his frame.

"Hey." I gave him a clinging hug and he put his arms around me in return. They had a tranquilizing effect, imparting the warmth of relief. Dependable Diego.

"Come in. Sorry, it's kind of a mess. I haven't vacuumed in days."

I surveyed the broad living room. One dirty plate and an open DVD case sat on the polished wood coffee table. Diego's

Toshiba sat on his couch. One pair of mahogany leather loafers made twin islands near the door in a sea of café-au-lait carpet. I guess you could say it was a notch more cluttered than a monastery, if that was worth apologizing for.

Diego was a skinny Puerto Rican man born in the Bronx and raised in Plymouth, Minnesota. He had a young face with a small, uncertain mouth, thick, expressive brows, and saucerous eyes that were ever wet with a maple-syrup gleam. Their dark irises were the dark brown of black coffee, their whites the white of White-Out. His hair was blacker than mine, and the short curls stuck tight about his head gave the impression of a swim cap. He was one inch taller than me with a one-inch slouch.

It was not love at first sight, but we built a fast friendship. I spent a lot of time in Luke and Diego's room, and the three of us had frequent late-night discussions about life and family and religion and politics, often accompanied by alcohol, clumsily obtained. Freshman year was the time for introspection and discovery, and Luke and Diego were my shipmates. My own roommate was a spoiled, prissy archetype, delivered straight from the loins of a banker and a Manhattan socialite to the front steps of Yale. There was a building named for her grandfather, and she barely took the time to learn my name.

Luke was the most outgoing of our little pod, while Diego and I found that we were content to spend our social time together. We talked and watched movies, and within a few months we were cuddling on his Ikea futon and taking shy walks in the cold. It was the first relationship for us both, and it lasted just over a year and a half. Most of the affection between us melted back into friendship soon after our breakup.

While Luke and I moved back to L.A. after graduation, Diego stayed in New Haven, for law school. He put in three honest years of diligent study and came out with a shiny degree and a pretty wife. He landed a competitive job at Stokel without so much as a thumb's weight of help from Luke or Mr. Cook. None of this changed him in the least.

I took off my shoes and settled onto one end of his couch, slouching diagonally in the corner with my bag in my lap. He transferred his computer onto the coffee table and sat on the other side. He leaned toward me, forearms resting on his quads.

"Did you get in touch with Luke?" I asked.

"I tried him a couple times but he wasn't picking up. He's probably sleeping in."

"On a day like this." I palmed my forehead and rubbed my eyes. "Can I get some coffee?"

"Of course." He got up and brewed me a cup while I contemplated what and how to tell him. A few minutes later, he set a hot cup of black coffee on the table.

"So, what's going on? Is everything alright?"

"I've had a long day, and it's not even nine. Where's Jackie?"

"At the gym."

I took a long sip of coffee and organized my thoughts. "I met a co-worker of yours at the party last night, Lori Lim."

He opened his mouth a little and looked ready to smile on one side. "Oh."

"What can you tell me about her?"

"Not much. She works at the firm, hasn't been there too long. She's young, twenty-two, twenty-three. Very friendly."

"Is that your way of saying she's loose?"

He played with the ring on his finger, rotating it with his thumb. "I wouldn't know. But she is very friendly in a touchy way."

I almost smiled. Diego would never call a woman's virtue into question. "I hear she tried to jump you the other week."

"You should know better than to take Luke's gossip at face value."

"What happened?"

"She got a little tipsy at a happy hour and she just started talking to me, but she was handsier about it than necessary. I guess it was kind of inappropriate, but I don't think she meant anything by it."

"Inappropriate?"

"Enough to make me uncomfortable. Anyway, one of the other first-years told her I was married and she hasn't done anything like that since. Why? What's this all about?"

I took a deep breath and let it out with puffed cheeks. "Before I say anything, I need you to sign onto a couple things."

"Such as?"

"This stays between you and me. No Jackie, no one. You, me, and Luke. That's the loop."

"Okay, sure."

"And you have to promise that you won't tell me what to do."

He nodded, hesitant, and gave me a worried look. "I'll try."

I pounded a knuckle on my forehead. "Don't freak out, Diego, but there's a dead body in my car and I need your advice."

He stood up like the seat of his pants had caught fire. "What?"

I explained what had happened, from my jaunt on Citrus to my run-in with the villain. He listened with balled fists and wide eyes.

"Oh my God. You're not joking." His mocha complexion soured into lemon-curd yellow. "You must be scared to death."

"I am."

"Do you need a hug?"

"I do."

We sat quietly for a minute on the couch, side by side, my

back resting on his arm. I almost started to cry, then remembered I didn't have the time. I rotated out of his arm and faced him. "Should I go to the cops?"

He thought for a second. "I know it would make me feel better. Why haven't you called them already?"

"I didn't want to call them from home because he'd know. He threatened my family."

"I know, but what makes you think he could hurt them? You can't just walk around committing crimes. You get caught. Your family's in Texas. We could notify police there."

"I know. It's just, I don't know anything about the guy. My guess is that he's a little unhinged but not necessarily a criminal mastermind. Putting the body in my trunk was a scare tactic and a really dumb move. Then he showed himself when I had no way of identifying him before. I don't think he's in control."

"Is that a good thing?"

"I don't think so. At least if I knew he was some kind of professional criminal, I could credit him with logic and strategy. I could take for granted that he wouldn't do anything suicidal. Can't do that with a pure lunatic."

"But if he's just some crazy guy, he probably couldn't reach your family without getting caught."

"There's something more to it, though. One, he alluded to an employer, which might be bullshit. But if it's true, he could have someone else track down my family." I hesitated.

"And two?"

"He knew about Iris. He mocked pity for our poor mom, with two daughters getting into trouble."

His mouth fell open. It had been a long time since I'd referred to my sister in a meaningful way. "Oh no."

"I think he was trying to piss me off, but he was also trying to scare me. I can't shake the feeling that he knows about every-thing that happened to her, and a lot of that is not public infor-mation. If he knows about that, he knows everything about my family. That makes me think that if he is a psycho, he's a psycho with means."

Diego shook his head. "I still think you should call the police."

"I'm thinking about it. The chance that he'd track down my family is probably minimal. The thing is that the one time in a hundred that it actually happens, my family gets hurt because of me. And I know firsthand that he's dangerous in a very real way."

"So what do you do? Pretend nothing happened?"

"I can't do that either. But the more I think about it, I really can't go to the police right away. I need information on what's hap-pening, who the guy is, and what power he has over me and my family. When I'm satisfied, then I call the cops."

After fifteen seconds of silence, Diego spoke up in a slow, clear whisper. "Are you saying you're going to keep playing detective? Are you out of your mind?"

"What choice do I have?"

"Song, you've been assaulted and threatened by someone you don't know anything about, not to mention there's a corpse in your trunk."

"I think I know what I'm doing." As soon as I said the words, I knew they were ridiculous.

"You have no idea what you're doing. You can't keep going with this."

"I told you not to tell me what to do." I felt my ears go hot. He placed a hand on my shoulder. It was warm and heavy through the white cotton of my shirt.

"I know you're tough, and in ninety-nine out of a hundred

situations I would trust you with my life, but this is an incredibly unusual situation, and your life could actually be in danger. You've had a traumatic day. My God, getting assaulted on a dark street was just the beginning. You found a dead body. I know you can't be okay right now, no matter how—"

"Stop stop stop!" I shook my head on the third *stop* like an insect had flown into my ear. The violence of the motion made my swollen crown smart. He flinched and jerked his hand away. I sat up, leaned forward, and focused on a spot on his shoulder. "God, Diego, I hate when you do this. Do you have any idea how annoying it is to hear you go on about what I'm feeling? I'm fine. You need to stop thinking I'm some fragile fucking snowflake just because you've seen me cry once or twice."

My face was hot and I was startled at my own anger. I forced myself to look him in the eye. He didn't return my gaze. His eyes were lowered and glued loosely somewhere on his coffee table. I waited for him to say something. It was a long wait.

He swiped twice at the bulb of his nose with the flat of his thumb. His voice came out bruised and soft. "You're asking me to let you put yourself in harm's way. You're right, I shouldn't assume I know how you're feeling, and if you say you're fine, I believe you and that's wonderful. But please, please take care of yourself."

"Look, I know I'm new to this sort of thing, but I know what I'm doing. I like living, you know, probably more than you like having me live."

"Clear your head, Song. Going after Iris's boyfriend didn't make you a detective, and reading all the books will never make you Marlowe. How on earth could you possibly know what you're doing?" He fixed those gleaming binoculars on me with the earnestness of a child.

The door opened like magic as I struggled for a plausible answer. Jackie Blumenthal Diaz walked in shoulder first in a plain white tank and gym shorts. Her forehead and bare arms glistened with the sweat of good health.

"I'm home." Her eyes took a second to find mine and she looked at me with surprise approaching panic. "Juniper, I didn't know you were coming."

Jackie was Diego's classmate in law school, a Columbia graduate who had taken a few years off after college to work in D.C. She was a few years older than Diego, having just turned thirty-one in February. They started dating toward the end of their second year of law school. It was Diego's first relationship after our breakup, but he and Jackie got hitched the week after their graduation last June. Luke and I used to tease Diego about their hasty marriage, attributing it to her insistent biological clock. We stopped once we noticed the shivering timbre of his laughter as he bore our immaturities.

Not that she looked old enough to worry. Five foot five, 110 pounds of lean muscle, she went to the gym as often as most people brushed their teeth. Short, dark hair fell jaunty and jagged about her ears, framing a milk-white, unmade face that didn't tan, didn't wrinkle. Her quiet eyes stayed squinted most of the time, but when they didn't, their cool auburn agate was captivating.

"Hey, Jackie." I tried to dissipate the solemn, intimate air that hung over the sofa. "I was in the area and thought I'd drop by."

"You're always in the area."

Jackie pretended to like me with the thespian flair of a nervous house cat. I didn't blame her for being wary of me, but I always thought it was silly. Diego and I hadn't shared so much as one strand of saliva since before we could drink legally. I suspected that the fact of my perpetual singledom since our breakup let her imagine I still carried a torch for him.

In her defense, she wasn't the only person who found my seven years of solitude a little bit curious. When Luke needled me about my lack of male companionship, I knew his jokes came bound with concern. It was a constant theme with my mother, who wanted to see her twenty-six-year-old daughter married before all the good men vanished from the dating field. Co-workers and acquaintances knew me as a staunch bachelorette and occasionally expressed interest in ending my misery. I went on dates now and then, attached men for brief romantic experiments, but I fell in love for the last time when I was eighteen. Diego was the only one who was judicious enough to withhold comment.

Jackie was an enthusiastic meddler in my love life, and I usually obliged her when she set me up with various men she guaranteed were perfect fits. I was often tempted to tell her that I did not have plans to seduce her husband, and that she should know he would kill himself before cheating on his wife. Diego couldn't be more loyal if he were in a coma. He was devoted and single-minded, and dating him was not unlike a full-time job with unpaid double overtime.

But now was not the time to make a point for Jackie. I stood up and motioned vaguely toward the door. "I was just about to head out. I'm going to track down Luke. I think I'll be hanging out with him today, so if you guys are free, let me know. Though I guess I don't have a phone right now."

Diego looked up at me, distress still evident in every inch of his face. "I'll walk out with you." He started to get up.

I still had no answer for what was probably a rhetorical question anyway. "No, it's cool. I parked pretty close." I twisted the doorknob with a pinch too much haste and opened the door halfway. "Later, guys."

I heard them say goodbye and closed the door soft and slow, the better to make my getaway.

Six

I had just turned on my engine when I saw Diego bound down
the stairs leading out of his apartment. I kept the car idling as I
watched him run up and knock on the passenger-side door.

I unlocked the car and Diego climbed in.

"You're coming with me, then?"

He nodded, looking at the windshield. "I guess so."

"What'd you tell Jackie?"

"I just said I'd be back."

I would have bet my car that Jackie was fuming behind the
front door and Diego didn't know it. I decided against awaken-
ing his conscience—despite his questions, I was grateful that he
came and I wanted his guidance. Marlowe may have worked
alone, but I had something he didn't—I had friends I could trust.

"You're going to help me, then?"

"Something like that. I'm going to make sure you don't get
yourself killed."

I tightened my fist around the shifter. "Thanks. And sorry I blew up at you."

"It's okay." He looked at his lap.

"You know, I did come to you for advice. Can you answer a legal question?"

"I'll do my best."

"Does finding the body and staying away from the police make me a criminal?"

He shook his head with some vigor. "No. You didn't do the killing, and California's pretty lax on Good Samaritan laws. Do you remember the Sherrice Iverson case a while back?"

I shook my head.

"Awful murder. Grown man molested and killed a seven-year-old girl in a casino bathroom. His friend walked in and saw him fondling her, and after he did the killing, the murderer confessed to the friend, who shrugged and walked away. There was a lot of outcry that nothing happened to the friend, but nothing ever did. You didn't try to hide the body or anything, so I think you're good."

"Good. I have enough on my plate."

"Yeah, as to that other stuff on your plate—legal or not, I still don't love that you're not en route to a police station right now."

"I—"

"But I get it. I do get it. That's why I'm here and not calling it in myself."

"Thank you."

After a while, he said, "So we're sitting in your car with a dead body in the backseat."

"Yep."

He blinked hard and scratched his ear. "Do you know who it is?"

"No one I know."

"Did you check for ID?"

"I—no." I started to wonder how I had failed to do so, and then I remembered the feeling of death against the back of my hand. Further handling had been far from my mind. "Should I? He's fully dressed."

"And we're not assuming that the murderer was careful, are we?"

I turned off my engine and sat, limp.

"Will you come with me?"

"Of course."

We got out of the car and stood behind the trunk. The street was clear for the time being. Wheat-colored insects, silent and faceless, made patterns in the warm summer air.

"We have to be quick," I said. I breathed in and out. "Just warning you again, there is a dead body in there."

"I know."

"You're not freaking out?"

"I am, but it's okay."

I stood with my keys in hand, staring at the trunk.

"Are you okay, Song?"

"I'm okay."

"Do you want to wait in the car? I can check for the wallet."

I dug my heels into the ground. "Thanks, Diego, but it's okay. I can do it."

I checked the street once more for people, then popped the trunk, keeping one hand on the door in case someone came by. I made a quick wish that the body wouldn't be there.

And it wasn't. My trunk was as it had been before last night, free of rotting flesh and fiery red hair. Marlowe had seen a corpse or two disappear in his day—in *The Big Sleep* he left a dead smut dealer on the floor for a few hours, and came back to a clean scene. Of course, he'd broken into someone else's house to find the body, so it hadn't been his floor.

"There was a body in here. A tall, skinny one, with bright red hair." I looked up at Diego, willing him to give me credit. "I wouldn't make this up. You know that."

He nodded slowly. "I don't need you to produce the body. But it was there when you came here?"

I reasoned through the events of the morning. It was an unpleasant process. "The only thing I can think of is that this Humphrey Bogart must have broken into my trunk and moved the body while I was in my apartment." I smirked. "I can't even be sure that I locked it when I left."

"But why would he do that?"

"Well." I sighed. "He put it there to scare me, and he accomplished that. Maybe he didn't want me to have the body on hand."

"Okay, but—" His jaw dropped and his dark eyes widened.

"But what?" I asked. I felt the ghostly approach of rejection, the idea that one of the people who knew me best could entertain the thought that I was now deranged, or a pathological liar. The possibility was scary and irritating.

"Tall and skinny with red hair, and he died outside of Lori Lim's house." His tone was breathy, like he was vocalizing while he did sums in his head. I realized with a thrill that he believed me, and that he might know something I didn't. "I think I know who he is. Was."

My mouth felt dry, and I swallowed. "Who?"

Diego took his phone from his pocket, and in a minute I was

looking at the Facebook page of the murdered man. His name was Greg Miller.

We clambered back into the car and sat in stunned silence. I put a hand on Diego's shoulder and gave it a squeeze. There was a bulbous tear forming in one of his eyes. "Are you okay?"

He leaned back against the headrest and exhaled. "I don't know."

"Who's Greg Miller?"

His voice hit the air brittle and coarse as old wire. "He's a Stokel associate. I work with him. He's in my class."

"Were you guys friends?"

He shook his head. "No. I didn't know him that well. He was kind of moody and quiet around the office, and you know how I am, so we never reached out to each other." He brought the heel of his hand up to his forehead, pushing some stray curls above his hairline. "He's the associate who told Lori I was married at that happy hour."

"And he was murdered on her block."

"He had a pretty big crush on her. It's one of those things everyone in the office knew about. Do you think that has something to do with—with this?"

"My inclination is to say yes, but it's hard to unravel the logic behind something so unreal."

"Is that what we're trying to do now?"

"Greg Miller was no one to me, and I would have no problem letting the police figure out what happened to him. But I do need to know more about who killed him and what their agenda is. If the whole mystery is embedded in those questions, then I guess we'll figure that out, too."

"So what now, then?"

"We need to talk to Luke."

✦

The drive from Diego's to Luke's took less than ten minutes. The three of us lived in a tight triangle in our sprawling city.

If I had to guess, Luke would not like that his father's suspected paramour was now linked to a murder victim who worked at his father's firm. I didn't like it either.

"Can you try calling Luke again so we don't have to knock down his door?"

Diego took out his cell phone. I heard the dribble of a ringtone followed by a voice mail message. "Still sleeping, I guess."

"Then we'll knock."

We were turning onto Lillian to park when Diego grabbed my shoulder. "Wait," he said. A short block away I recognized Lori Lim, standing at the window of a pewter Lexus SUV parked directly across from her Jetta, which I saw in the daylight was marvelously filthy.

She was extra doll-like today in a sweet, white cap-sleeve sundress and a round gold pendant I could see catching the sun from where I watched forty feet away. She was talking to the driver of the Lexus. We watched, idling, as she fumbled around in a butterscotch shoulder bag for her keys and crossed the street to her car.

The Lexus took off in our direction and I caught a glimpse of the driver as she passed us to turn on Rossmore. She was an Asian woman with short black hair, middle-aged but attractive. She had on dark sunglasses and her lips were pursed and stern. I guessed I was right about 432 South Citrus being a parent's house. She didn't notice us watching.

"Change of plans, Diego."

"Are you going to follow Lori?"

I nodded slowly as we crept up the block and watched the Jetta come to life. "It's called a tail. It's what Marlowe would do."

"Song, you're not Marlowe."

"I know I'm not. But I can follow his tactics. They probably work better than what I can spin out of air, right?"

Diego sighed. "What about Luke?"

"His lazy ass can wait. She's moving."

She pulled far away from the curb and made a sudden U-turn and started to drive right toward us.

"Look back," I said, and Diego and I turned our heads to look out my rear window. "I don't think she'd recognize my car, but she should know both our faces."

When the Jetta came into view, I let it ride for a few seconds, rolling down Lillian under low-hanging trees and the velvet gray of their leafy shadows. Then I made a similar U-turn farther down the block. If she didn't see us, it was only because she wasn't looking. Marlowe would never have been so sloppy. She turned left onto Rossmore and I followed, leaving a few car lengths between us.

"Look at her go," said Diego.

She drove like a drunk missing one eye and a thumb, and I patted myself on the back for saving the streets from a boozed-up version of this maniac the night before. I hoped she was concentrating on not getting herself killed rather than on the stealthy Volvo trying to stay small in her rearview mirror. There were no cars between us as we drove north on Rossmore. I maintained a safe distance, and let a nice bulky 4Runner cut behind her at the light on Melrose, where Lori shuffled over to the right-turn lane. No turn signal flickered from the Jetta's rear, but its front nosed halfway onto Melrose, so I prepared for a turn. I was right, and I followed her from the other side of the Toyota, and when that turned off a few blocks later, I stayed a few car lengths behind her. We were almost at Western when she made an illegal, mid-block three-point U-turn to head back west. I let her pull off the maneuver and followed suit at the next intersection. We coasted down Melrose, around three cars between us at any given time. Steady traffic kept her recklessness in check. We passed the flurry of glittery boutiques and kept driving west, the traffic thinner and the shopping more precious with every block. At Kings Road she yanked her Jetta ready for a U-turn in the middle of the intersection, let one car pass on the other side, and gunned it to the curb, wheels kissing sidewalk. I passed her, cutting just under the speed limit, and saw her park at a meter in my rearview. Diego and I watched her, forgetting to breathe.

I took my time and rolled up behind her after the brief delay caused by following the law. Her destination was Buttercream, a little bakery-café with wide windows ivied and latticed for easy spying. I kept the car running with a foot glued to the brake as I peered through the white-gridded window.

Lori sat with her back to the wall, facing the baked goods, and I had a decent view of her rear profile, one small ear, and the tip of her nose saying hi from beyond her mess of chestnut-tinted curls. She rested her upper back against her chair, lower back floating in a slight slouch. Her shoulders pointed up, pinched toward her neck, as she gripped the sides of her seat, twiddling her thumbs on the wicker. She had her legs crossed, the hem of her dress hiking up to show off warm, sunny thighs, and she tapped the heel of the burdened foot on the tile under the table. She was the damnedest fidgeter I'd ever seen.

I turned to Diego. "I'm seeing this right, aren't I?"

Across the glass-topped table behind an oversize coffee mug, staid as stone in a crisp, ironed shirt buttoned to the gills, sat William Cook. I eased tense toes off the brake and let the car melt back onto Melrose.

Iris was the first subject of my surveillance. In the weeks following our confrontation, I spied on her in an attempt to solve the mystery that had torpedoed into our lives. It was a loose surveillance—Iris only left the house a few times, and when she did, I was not so bold as to follow her. The thought occurred to me, of course, and if I could have gotten away with it, I have no doubt I would have attempted a tail.

Instead, I took every chance I had to pick up any clues she left in our home. I rifled through her desk, her backpack, and all her drawers. I hoped to find a diary, or love letters, something solid and incriminating that would give me the answers I needed. Once, she forgot her cell phone at home, and I spent over an hour culling through her texts and contacts.

I found nothing suspicious, and this lack of romantic remnants struck me as strange, even tragic. Love leaves mementos, I knew, and Iris was the type to hold on to them. While I found nothing mysterious in her belongings, I did find a birthday card and some sweet notes from Paul, and an origami crane a boy had made for her in the fifth grade. She was a hoarder of keepsakes—the top drawer of her desk was littered with movie-ticket stubs.

When a few thorough sweeps yielded zero evidence of a relationship I knew to exist, I realized that the lack of a trail was in itself a clue. As was, it occurred to me, Iris's demeanor. She had never been secretive with me, but now, all at once, she was hiding the very identity of someone who had hijacked her life.

Because it had been hidden from our mom and, it seemed, the world outside our bedroom, I had treated Iris's pregnancy as if it were her big secret. In one sense, it was. But Iris had been open with me about the pregnancy, and had asked me to go with her to the clinic. Her secret was her relationship with the father, of which the pregnancy was both a side effect and a solid proof.

Iris had never been shy about discussing Paul or her other numerous crushes and admirers. But since she started dating Paul I hadn't heard a breath about another boy. Her new paramour wasn't just someone our mom wouldn't approve of—he was someone whose very existence had to be hidden from me.

Iris was sixteen. If she was dating a truant or a drug dealer, she would have mentioned him with the assumption that I would not tell our mom. This wasn't a bad boy—whoever it was had no business seeing a sixteen-year-old girl. If I was right, I was looking at a new category—not boys, but men. I didn't know who he was, but I, my sister's angry keeper, vowed to find out. I was eighteen years old, and I guess I thought I was pretty smart.

I turned onto the next side street and stopped the car. I was breathing heavily.

"That looked a lot like a wealthy white law partner getting weekend breakfast with a hot little Asian employee under half his age."

He nodded and cringed. "Poor Luke."

I was in a mood to spit and seethe, but I remembered I wasn't the one this discovery would really hurt. "Poor Luke," I echoed.

Paranoia aside, it looked like there was some substance to Luke's hunch. There it was, skank and scandal all. William C. Cook, midfifties, founding partner of Stokel, Levinson & Cook, employer of two hundred attorneys at the downtown office and hundreds more in Newport, San Francisco, Chicago, New York, London, and Tokyo, father of one son with his first and only wife, gallivanting about town with Lori Lim, early twenties, potential drunk, alleged promiscuous scamp.

As far as fathers of friends went, Mr. Cook scaled to attractive. My summer at Stokel, I noticed that female employees dropped into his office with improbable frequency. Mr. Cook gave Luke his height and his poetic green eyes. His hair grayed handsomely, thick and regal. But wrinkles besieged his forehead and crows had stamped the skin around his eyes. Age eroded what had been a chiseled jawline, and slackened what had been a tighter waistline. I thought it was gross that girls wanted him seven years ago, and he hadn't become any more desirable in the interim. Lori, on the other hand, wore youth and beauty like others wore skin.

I wanted to punch something, but I settled for gripping the steering wheel until my knuckles turned white. "God, Mr. Cook and Lori? That's so disgusting. So, so disgusting. How can he do that to his wife, his family? And to a young girl like that? I don't care if she's consenting. She can't know what she's consenting to. She can't." I heard my voice crack.

Diego gave me a searching look and opened his mouth but closed it again. He knew without being told who was on my mind.

"I know she isn't Iris, Diego. She isn't a child, and for all we know she is loving the presents and the attention." I hesitated long enough for him to interject.

"But?"

"But obviously, I can't help but make the association. Lori and Mr. Cook getting coffee in that cute little bakery—that only ends in disaster. I know she isn't my sister, but I get this feeling like I want to save her. Like you'd want to save anyone, from a tornado, or from a monster."

Diego gave my shoulder a warm squeeze, and I noticed then that it was tense to the point of twitching. He talked to me in a soothing voice that was almost patronizing, like he was coaxing someone to come down from a ledge. "But we don't know that anything's going on. We don't know."

I exhaled. "No, we don't know. But I think it's safe to assume that we know better than Mrs. Cook where her husband is right now."

"You're probably right about that."

"And it's not just the affair. If he is seeing Lori, and the man in my trunk was an employee who had feelings for his mistress, Luke's dad could very well be a felon."

"That would be a hasty conclusion, don't you think?"

"True, but the fact that he's in there with her right now increases the odds he's in something deep."

He bit his lip and leaned back in his seat. "So what do we do?"

"I want to swing by Buttercream when they're not there anymore. Other than us, the people in there are the only ones we know have seen the two of them together."

"And Luke?"

"There's no reason to run to him if we're going to find out she's asking for tax advice." I wanted corroboration before reporting news that would ruin Luke's family. "How long would it take for you to have breakfast with your mistress?"

"If I had to guess, at most two hours?"

"That sounds reasonable. And it gives us time to get me a new phone. I need a cigarette pretty badly, too. What time is it now?"

He looked at his watch. "Just after ten."

We headed out to the Verizon store at the Beverly Connection on La Cienega. I struck a Lucky and smoked it in the parking lot until it almost singed my fingertips. When that was done, I reported my phone lost and treated myself to an iPhone with a brand new number. It was black and sleek, and it had Internet. It took me a few minutes to get used to the keyboard, but I managed to get a notice up on Facebook: "New phone number. Let me know if you heard from my old one after midnight last night." I decided to keep my new number close to my chest. I knew the numbers I needed by heart. I could do without announcing my direct line to the world.

It was a little after eleven, so we drove through the In-N-Out on Sunset and ate cheeseburgers in the parking lot. At 11:45, we headed back to the bakery. When we arrived, the clock read 11:52 A.M., and there was no sign of either person of interest in the bakery. "So what's the game plan?" asked Diego.

"We're just going to probe one of the workers about Lori and Mr. Cook. She stands out, and maybe even more so with an older man of a different race."

"Probe?"

I tried to remember Marlowe's approach, which often involved small bribes of unsavory characters. I thought I could be more subtle in a cake shop. "Yeah, nonchalant, sort of."

Diego shrugged. "Okay. Should I come in?"

"Maybe you should stay in the car. I'm just going to pretend I'm buying a piece of cake, and I don't want you looking all serious over my shoulder."

He frowned. "Fine. I'll wait in the car."

I parked at a meter, fed it a quarter, and sauntered in. The place was small and busy, but the counter was empty. I walked right up to it, and a skinny black cashier with implausibly wide eyes and an even wider grin stood ready to take my order.

"Hi! Welcome to Buttercream! How can I help you today?" From the sound of his voice, I guessed he'd been in back wolfing frosting all day.

"Yeah, uh." I realized with a short panic that my plan was ill defined. "This is my first time here and I just want like a piece of cake. Do you have a favorite?"

"Ohh." He sparkled. "Well, we're famous for our triple berry, so if it's your first time, you might want to get that. It's bitching good. And oh, the espresso cheesecake is fan-freaking-tastic, maybe the best thing she makes."

"I guess I'll try a slice of the triple berry. Can you box it?"

"Sure thing." He gave me a wink and a megawatt smile. His face muscles must have been as toned as a runner's thighs.

I amped up my energy level and quit stalling. "Hey, so, was there like, a petite little Asian girl in here earlier? With curly light brown hair?"

"Is she really cute with kind of a squeaky voice?"

"Yes!" I mirrored his wide eyes and clasped my hands together. "She's like, a pop singer in Korea and I have a huge girl crush on her. My sister was in here and saw her and texted me to come, but I guess I missed her. Sad." I mugged sad. If there was an advantage I had over Marlowe, it was that no one would peg me for a shamus—not with an alto voice and no hat. I was an Asian girl, and though not an actress, I knew a little pep and emoting would go a long way.

As I'd hoped, the cashier gave me credit. He leaned forward

with a show of fascination. "Whoa, seriously? I thought she was cute."

"What was she wearing?" I tried to sound starstruck.

"I think like a white dress with short sleeves and eyelets. Super cute. And she had a great bag too. It was this dreamy tan Prada."

"My sister said she was with some old guy. Was it her dad, you think?"

"Is she adopted? Because she was with a white guy."

"No, her parents are Korean." I was getting into it. "But I wonder who that was, then. God, this is going to bother me. You don't think . . . did it seem like a date? Were they like, touchy?" I shuddered with big shoulder shakes and a wince, hammier than Porky Pig.

"Maybe. I don't think they were touching at all, though. I would've noticed, cause gross! He was old enough to be her dad."

"Did you hear what they were talking about?"

"Nothing interesting. Trust me, I would've noticed." He laughed.

I giggled, one hand covering my mouth. "Duly noted." I paid for the cake and he handed me the box, a white cube sealed with a pastel pink sticker. "Thanks a bunch."

"Anytime! What's her name?"

"Huh?"

"The singer. I'm totally googling her when I get off work."

"Oh, duh." I giggled again while I came up with a moniker. "Her name is Lorelei."

Seven

I walked back to my car, opened the door, and entered cake-first. Before I was fully seated, Diego said, "I got in touch with Luke. He called me back."

"Great. I guess."

"I told him we had some news and he sounded very confused. Anyway, he's expecting us soon. What did you find out?"

"Well, nothing corroborative. In fact, if the guy who sold me the cake is to be believed, there was nothing about them that seemed sexual."

"That's good. But it might be weak testimony when you consider what we have to tell Luke."

"Yeah." I started the car and drove toward the Marlowe.

The streetlights were forgiving darlings, reds flickering to green the moment I touched on my brakes, greens stalling their blinking ascent into yellow until I could only spot them from the corner of my right eye as I jetted through intersections.

"Hey, Song? I think someone's following us."

"What?" My neck strained as I fought the instinct to jerk my head back with a stiff flinch. "Where?"

"See that black Mazda behind the blue Lexus, behind you in the right lane?" Pointing with his chin, he indicated the rearview mirror, where I saw a black Mazda with tinted windows.

"Shit. Are you sure?"

"It's blocked now, but the letters on the plate spell *cat*. It's a black cat. I happened to notice it while we were eating. You didn't see that guy's car this morning, did you?"

"No. Can you see a face?"

"No."

I smirked. In a way, all this had started with a black car with tinted windows. "I'll start driving. Let's see what he does."

I drove slowly, switching lanes now and then, and brought us to the parking lot of a Bank of America on Beverly. I stopped the car and watched as the Mazda found a spot on the curb right outside the lot. "Nice catch, Diego."

"Should we go over there?"

"Not yet. I'll have a cigarette. You go inside and look like we're here for an errand."

We got out of the car and Diego went into the bank with his hands stuck into his pockets. I took note of the black cat's license plate while I fiddled with a match. I committed the numbers to memory as I pulled on a Lucky Strike. I leaned against the hood of my car and tried to look relaxed, approachable. If it were Humphrey Bogart, he might come right over and sling his arm around my neck, friendly and lethal.

A minute later, someone else came out instead. The driver was a stocky man in his mid- to late forties, wearing dark sunglasses and a threadbare blue polo shirt over khaki shorts. The legs spilling onto the ground from the frayed hems were thick and hairy, and they ended abruptly in a wrap of white socks stuffed into cheap white tennis shoes. He had his head shaved in a matter-of-fact way that admitted oncoming baldness, and the flesh at the back of his neck folded along two deep lines. He shuffled casually past me and headed into the bank. No eye contact. I counted to ten and snuffed out the rest of my cigarette before following him inside.

I found our shadow sitting in an armchair with his face buried in an outdated issue of *Time* magazine. Diego was standing in line, waiting for a teller. He saw me come in and I pointed at the man with my eyes before taking an empty armchair.

There were at least a dozen people in the bank, and I felt comfortable addressing the man in the white tennis shoes who eyed me nervously as I sat down. "Hi," I said. "Do I know you from somewhere?"

He made a show of lowering his magazine. "Don't think so." His voice was low and breathy, and his face uneasy. From up close I saw that he was a few years younger than I'd thought. He had a wide nose and thin lips and I couldn't see his eyes behind the black lenses of his cheap, gold-rimmed glasses.

I held out my hand. "I'm the driver of that handsome Volvo, and you drive the black Mazda that's been on its ass."

"Don't think so," he said again.

I recited the license plate. "Look, I have a cousin at the DMV who can give me your name in a second. You can't just follow a stranger around town like that. I'll go to the police." I had no such cousin, but the bluff seemed to work. The man sat up and searched for words, with his mouth hanging open.

He cleared his throat. "Don't do that."

"Why are you following me?"

He took a second to think, and when he was finished, I could feel his straight gaze through his glasses. He spoke with a snap. "Why are you following the girl?"

"The girl? Who do you mean by the girl?"

"Lori, from Stokel Levinson. Why were you following her?"

My pulse jumped at the name. "You know what? You go first. I'm not in the hot seat here." I leaned forward and jabbed at the coffee table as I stressed each word. "Why are you following me?"

He leaned forward and extracted something from the back pocket of his shorts. With practiced indifference he tossed it onto the table, where it landed on a stack of magazines. It was a red nylon rectangle, thinner than a wallet, fastened with Velcro. As I stared, he reached for it and flipped it over. A photo identification card now peered out through smudged, clear plastic. It read "Private Investigator License" across the top and identified the man as Charles Oliver Lindley of Van Nuys, California.

I went over every letter of the license before giving Charles Lindley another thorough look. "Charles?"

"Chaz."

"Chaz. You're a private eye."

I'd suspected the modern shamus was no longer the tall, brooding Marlowe in a suit and fedora, but I had never seen one before and the difference amazed me.

"That's right."

"But you still haven't answered my question. Why follow me?"

He folded his arms and leaned back. "I'm looking for a man named Hector Lopez. Do you know him?"

"No."

"He's the asshole my sister decided to marry, and now he's gone missing." I felt his eyes fix in on mine. "She thinks he ran off with some Korean girl."

"Lori."

"Yeah, that girl."

"Mrs. Lopez—"

"Her name's Candy."

"So Candy is having you look for him? She didn't report him missing?"

"What do you think a private eye is for? Some matters need a more subtle touch." He scratched plaque from his bottom teeth with a thick fingernail.

"Again, then: why are you following me?"

"I said already. I was following her and then you started following her and I thought maybe you were in cahoots or something."

"You mean we both ran away with your brother-in-law."

"Well, you got that Mexican with you, too."

I laughed out loud and called to Diego. "Come here for a second." He sauntered over, with his face turning red. "This is Chaz. He's a private eye."

"Hi. I heard."

I stood up and put my arm around his shoulder. "This here is one of my best friends, and he's Puerto Rican, Chaz. I'm not part of a Mexican man-smuggling ring if that's what you're onto."

He put his hands up like he meant to show they were empty. "Hey, I didn't mean nothing like that. I just thought, you know, people got their affinities and—look, I was just following my gut, okay? You sure as hell looked suspicious." As his voice lost its tone of apology, I conceded, to myself, that he was right. "What's your angle on the girl?"

"I met her yesterday. I have my own case going."

"You a private investigator too?"

"I don't have a license."

"Who you working for?"

This was a question Marlowe never answered, no matter who asked. "That's not for you to know."

"Hey, girlie, I'm just asking, because maybe we can swap info or something, you know?"

I smiled. "You can start by telling me why you think your brother-in-law ran off with Lori."

"My sister—" He cleared his throat and I saw his eyes narrow despite the opacity of his shades. "If you can't even say who your client is, I don't have to tell you shit."

"Hold on a second." I pulled Diego a few feet away and whispered, "Do you think we should talk to him?"

"We have no reason to trust him."

"I mean, I think he's telling the truth. He had enough wits and dumb luck to figure out we were involved. He might have something that could help us."

"Do you want to tell this stranger about Luke and his dad? About Greg and the killer on your tail?"

I sucked air through my teeth. "I guess not."

"Get his number."

I sat back down and pulled out my new phone. "Let me have your number and maybe I'll get in touch later so we can help each other out."

He stayed motionless for a second before reciting his number. 818 area code, like mine. "But I ain't saying nothing unless we go tit for tat."

"Fine." I stood back up. "Don't follow me out or I will call the police, Chazzie."

✤

We made it back to Luke's apartment in less than ten minutes.

I was back at the Marlowe for the third time in less than

twenty-four hours. I parked again on Lillian and thought how much had happened since my car had left this street the night before. Again I passed through the iron gate, the warm patio, the opulent hallways, and again I was knocking on that black door.

He was in the same stupid T-shirt and athletic shorts I'd left him in and he hadn't combed his hair, but I could tell even from the snap with which he opened the door that he was feeling anything but lazy.

"Is everything okay?" He gave me a hug. "You guys look like hell."

"Hey, Luke, thanks for having us." Diego and Luke embraced.

I surveyed the entryway, and though the place was still a mess, there were no shoes but Luke's. Diego and I added our pairs to keep his company.

I slung my purse onto his couch and Diego and I sat down at the table. "Can I borrow your laptop?"

"Yeah, let me get it." He disappeared into his bedroom and reemerged with a closed PowerBook in one hand, extending it to me like a piece of mail.

I handed it to Diego. "Can you pull up a picture of Greg?" He took it and had it open before it hit the tabletop. I turned to Luke. "Do you know someone named Greg Miller?"

He scratched at the light scruff sprouting on his jaw while Diego pulled up Greg's Facebook page.

"Oh, that guy? I think he works at Stokel. I've seen him a couple times. What about him?"

"He's dead, Luke. Someone found it funny to strangle him and put him in my trunk."

He wheezed. "Get the fuck out of here."

"She's serious," Diego said.

Luke crumpled to the floor, falling first on his knees, then catching his weight on a hard wrist to one side. He sat there like a girl on a lawn and stared at me, inky pupils bleeding outward, threatening to tar out the green.

I recounted what had happened in the last few hours, up to when I went over to Diego's. I kept it short, and he stared at me with pupils moving, trying to make sense of my words.

He twisted a fist into his thigh, rotating the knuckles with a twitching slowness. "Wait, someone's threatening you? Who is this guy?"

"Around five foot eight, medium build, green eyes, blond hair. He dresses like a con man from another decade. Sound familiar?"

His knuckles stopped their turning and the muscles of his face tightened like he was courting long division and it was showing nothing but annoyance at his advances. "Don't think so. Do you have an idea why this dead guy ended up in your car?"

"I have an idea, yeah. I'm thinking Greg Miller had just been killed when he was stuffed in my trunk, and I think my untimely presence at the scene is the reason I was knocked out in the first place."

"Why your car, though? What was the point?"

"Well, I think someone must've seen me as a witness, and I might've been if I hadn't had my lights put out before I could see anything. The body was probably an attempt to scare me quiet." I huffed air from my nostrils in lieu of a chuckle. "Talk about irony. Now I know Greg Miller was killed and I can ID a suspect. Before the body showed up, I didn't know a thing."

He took a deep breath and let it out with a slump of his shoulders. "So what now?"

"Here, do you want some cake?" I produced the cardboard box stickered shut by a cursive label. "There's a fork in there."

He pulled the white flaps to undo the tape and placed the deconstructed box on the carpet by his knees. He took a few bites of the towering cake in silence. "It's good. Thanks." He stared at the slice.

I watched him sink the side of the plastic fork deep into the sponge. I watched him watch his hand, motionless after the fork hit the cardboard.

"You're buttering me up."

I looked at Diego and we both nodded. "You tell the rest," I said.

Diego sighed and narrated, and when he got to Buttercream, Luke turned his eyes on Diego, then me, with a heartbreaking sparkle. "She was with my dad, wasn't she?"

I nodded like a turtle with a weak neck. "Sorry, Luke."

He blinked his eyes wide and ran a hand through his hair. He seemed to forget we were there for a few seconds. "Right," he said. His voice was weak with the sound of choked tears. "Well, at least I wasn't crazy."

"We don't know that they're sleeping together," Diego offered.

"My dad doesn't have hot jailbait friends."

"But the cashier didn't peg them as a couple, if that helps any." Diego was desperate to help, and I felt the same way.

"It doesn't really."

We sat in grim silence for a few minutes before Luke voiced his fears. "Does this make my dad a murder suspect?"

I wanted to give him a happy answer, but I couldn't. "I don't know."

He turned to Diego. "What do you think?"

"I hope not, for your sake, Luke."

"So you think it's possible."

The air was heavy with commiseration when Diego's phone rang a few moments later.

Luke and I stayed where we were and pretended not to listen as Jackie's voice came pouring out in a loud, rapid stream, straight into Diego's ear. He spoke to her in bewildered tones that turned slowly contrite and hung up a couple minutes later.

"That was Jackie," he said, sounding uncomfortable. "I guess you heard."

We nodded.

"Sleeping on the couch tonight?" Luke asked.

"I hope not, but maybe. I kind of ran out of the house this morning and didn't tell her why."

"Well, she won't stay mad if you tell her about the extreme circumstances," I said.

"Sure, but you asked me not to tell."

"That's true. But can't you just tell her I was in big, big trouble?"

"Song," Luke cut in. "How would that be helpful?"

I put my hand over my mouth. "Right."

"No, it's not just that," Diego said. "Her parents are in town and we're supposed to take them to lunch. I completely forgot, and it's already two o'clock. She says she's coming to pick me up."

"I'm sorry, Diego," I said.

"No, obviously, it's not your problem. Anyway, I don't have to go."

"Of course you do. I'll be fine. We'll reconnect later."

He nodded. "Thanks. I guess she is on her way."

"How's she doing, by the way?" Luke asked. "Haven't seen her in a while."

Diego shrugged. "She's fine. Great, really. I'm surprised she's so mad at me."

Luke shook his head. "Oh, Diego, you have much to learn."

"Right," I said. "And you have much to teach the guy in the stable marriage."

Diego smiled. "Actually, I have something to tell you guys, but I'll save it for a better time."

Luke gave his shoulder a light shove. "Why so enigmatic?"

"Just context. This is not a good day for it." He sighed. "I really miss hanging out with you guys. I wish it didn't take something like this to get us in the same room."

Before this weekend, the three of us had not been together for weeks. "That's what you get when you're a married lawyer with two bums for best friends," I said.

"I wish you were around all the time," Luke said. "You would never call me a bum." We all laughed, tired, anemic chuckles.

Five minutes later, Jackie called back and Diego got up to leave. "I'll call you as soon as I can get away."

"Don't worry about me," I said with half a smile. "I told you I know what I'm doing."

He shook his head. "I know you sort of believe that."

"It's okay, I'll follow her around from here," Luke said. "Appease the wife and we'll catch up later."

Diego answered Luke's fist pound, then gave me a hug so tight it made me gasp. "Don't be stupid, Song."

"Never."

"Okay," he said, letting go. "Later."

We listened to his running footsteps fade. "You know," said Luke, "he seems to find his way into the doghouse when he hangs out with us."

"Yeah, that kind of sucks."

"And by that I mean, he seems to find his way into the dog-house when he hangs out with you."

"I know that's what you meant." I said. "But we have other things to worry about. I need to put on my detective hat again."

❖

With the help of that hat, I'd come up with a theory to explain Iris's behavior, but no likely suspects. That, as it turned out, was not hard to fix.

Iris chose not to tell me a lot of things in the months I was away. She omitted details and schedules and whole people from our conversations. She was able to do that because I was no longer living with her. I didn't know when she left the house or when she came home. I didn't know who she was seeing or who she even claimed to be seeing. I meant to keep tabs on her, but I'd failed. Her words stung. I had allowed myself to become so self-absorbed that I'd skimmed over her silence and missed the small sounds of her tracks rerouting.

One day in mid-June, I followed my mom to the Galleria Market, the Korean shopping center in Northridge. After shopping for groceries, we stopped for lunch at the food court.

My mom and I communicated in a mix of Korean and English that I found natural. Our conversations dipped in and out of each language sometimes two or three times in one sentence. Of course, my sentences were weighted toward English and hers toward Korean, but we jumbled and blabbered without much awareness of who was speaking what—it was a two-way street that we'd long forgotten to notice.

She was slurping down soup when I brought up Iris.

"Umma," I said.

"Yoon-Kyung," she said. My mom was the only person in the

world to address me by my Korean name. The sound of it was always soothing.

"What was Iris doing every day while I was gone?"

She lowered her spoon and gave me a blank stare. "What do you mean?"

"Just . . ." I hesitated. "I wasn't here, and I don't know how she got so depressed. Do you?"

She shook her head. "I don't know what to do."

"But you know what her life has been like, right? I don't know anything. Who was she seeing? Where was she going? Was she away from home a lot?"

Our mom never let us leave the house without knowing where we were going and when we'd be back. She was fastidious about schedules and quick to anger if we walked in any later than we promised to be home. Iris had gotten her license not long before I left for college, and I knew I could count on our mom to have a catalog of her excursions.

I questioned her gently and found that Iris went to church on Sundays and two or three nights per week she went over to Paul's. My mom still didn't know that Iris and Paul had broken up in October. This meant that for months, Iris had been lying to her two or three nights per week. I wondered if Iris really went to church, either.

I asked how Iris had been doing in school. It was a generic question, but it was the one that unlocked the door to my sister's dark room.

"Her semester grades were bad. Worse than usual. Straight Bs. B-minus in precalculus. Only As were in art and history."

"Really, history?" Facts and dates had never come easily to Iris, and history had been her most detested subject in years past.

But I didn't find a sudden improvement in school relevant or suspicious, so I heard my heart thump as the next words rolled off my mother's tongue: "She was doing so poorly that her teacher suggested she get tutoring."

"So she started seeing a tutor?"

"Her teacher offered to tutor her himself, actually."

I was starting to feel queasy, and I knew I was done with my lunch. I strained to keep my voice nonchalant. "Who's her teacher?"

"Mr. Quinn," she said. "He's a nice man."

Something emerged from the murk of memory—Iris had mentioned Mr. Quinn back in September. It was in passing, and I had never even spoken to Quinn, so the fact that he was her teacher didn't stick. I now remembered, curse words running through my brain, that Iris had commented that he was "cute."

Quinn was a new teacher when I was a junior, and he had a small following among the girls in my class. He wasn't the most popular choice—most preferred Mr. Lacey, in the English department, who doubled as our school's swim coach, and the two were rarely compared. But there was something about his face that was hard to forget, and though I had not thought of the man in over a year, his features floated into place. He was in his early to midthirties, with dark brown hair and a light complexion. His small, serious eyes seemed to be his main physical asset, though most considered them beady.

I saw him walking around campus from time to time, but I knew little about him. He was well liked by his students, but I had no idea how he ran a classroom, or why a sixteen-year-old would find him attractive.

I kept my face calm, but my forehead grew damp from the effort. "How long did he tutor her for?"

"Just the first semester."

"He came to our house?"

"No. He tutored her after school."

My hunch grew inside me until it was something hard and certain. I would corroborate it on my own, without giving Iris an opportunity to deny and warn her seducer.

❖

Luke sat across from me, eating Chinese delivery in silence. He never had food in his apartment. It didn't matter if he was moved in for a week or eight months. His pantries were always bare, and he never used a stove.

There was plenty to talk about, and none of it was easy. I was staring out the window when Luke swallowed audibly and started to speak.

"Do you think—" He lowered his voice and prefaced his query anew with a breathless pause. "Do you think my dad did it?"

"It?"

He wiped his mouth on a thin napkin. "You know. Do you think he knocked you out and killed Greg?"

"I honestly can't say. I hope not. He is in the pool of shady happenings, but I wouldn't go confronting him and losing your allowance just yet."

He lowered his head in a tentative nod and finished his lunch.

"I'm sorry I got you into this, Song. If I had known there was more to it than asking a few questions, I would never have considered it."

"I know. And at this point, God knows I'm not playing the gumshoe for you."

There was a brief pause as we both stared into air. "Not turning back?"

"I can't just yet. I need to find out a few things, then it's to the LAPD and back to my boring life."

"What if you get yourself killed?"

"Well, that'll just about serve me right for being a goddamn curious cat, don't you think?"

"Don't joke, Song."

"I won't get myself killed. I've lived twenty-six years now and haven't even done that once." I flicked his forearm.

"So no cops just yet?"

"Not yet."

"I guess I should be grateful, really. I don't love how my dad looks here." He shook his head. "I want to find out with you. What are you planning to do? Are you sure you don't want to follow up with this PI?"

"I have his number, but I don't think he can help us. Let's start with Miller. He's the most time-sensitive piece of this puzzle."

"Right." His voice was tight. "What do you propose?"

"Let's hit up Stokel and search his office."

He hesitated. "Are you going to be okay doing that? You did just find the man's body."

I managed a weak smile. "I think I'll be fine. It was a shock, but I didn't know the guy. Can I just steal some more Advil before we go? My head still feels like tiny people are playing freeze tag in my brain."

He pushed himself up and dashed into the bathroom, coming back with at least a dozen of the brick-hued pills in his outstretched palm.

"Am I an elephant?"

"You don't have to take them all now." He went to the kitchen and returned with a bottle of water. "Keep the rest in case."

"Thanks." I swallowed two smooth pills and dropped the rest into my purse. "Hey, what time is it?"

He looked at his phone. "Three thirty. Why?"

I sifted through my bag and groaned. "We have to stop by my place on the way."

"Sure. I just have to change first." He bent his chin to his chest. "I don't think the building people will recognize you, but if they see me strolling in in my pajamas, they might just mention it to my dad."

He took a few minutes in his bedroom and came out wearing clean, dark blue jeans and a gray button-down shirt. He shoved his bare feet into silk socks and black leather shoes as I slipped back into my flip-flops. We made our way to his car and left the Marlowe once again.

The July sunshine beat down on the windshield with the ruthlessness of a storm. Luke put on a pair of black sunglasses as we drove into the eye of the summer day.

"What's at your apartment?"

I sighed. "My pill. It's not in my bag."

"Wait. We're making a detour from investigating a matter of life and death for your birth control?"

"Like a ten-minute detour. And look, as I don't plan on dying today, I'd really rather take care of it."

"Who's even trying to knock you up these days?"

"Oh, everyone." I rooted through my purse again. It wasn't hiding anywhere I could see. "It's not just about pregnancy, anyway."

"Yeah, what then?"

"Do you really want to talk about my period? I mean we can talk about my period if that is what you want."

"Okay, okay, forget it. We're almost there anyway."

A few minutes later we were back at my apartment, and I invited Luke to take the spot I had deserted a few hours earlier. We stayed seated in the car well after he turned off the engine and I felt the pressure of silence wad up my ears as I looked around the parking lot. I opened my mouth and let out the hot, dry breath that had built up inside.

"Are you okay?" Luke asked.

I nodded and opened the door. "Yeah, he's not here."

"Hey, I'll go with you."

The door to 4J looked wrong. Luke noticed first, and I followed him with my eyes as he darted down the hall to my apartment. The alignment was off—the door stuck out from the wall like a puzzle piece nudged out of place.

I made my way to Luke. He stood between me and the door, holding the knob, and I felt his eyes on my head. I kept mine fixed on the doorknob and the crack of plaster doorjamb beside it.

"I'm going in first," Luke said, and before I could stop him he stepped into my apartment ahead of me.

I followed him in and he rushed forward, covering the space of the room, putting his body between me and whatever I might find. He opened my closets and I heard him draw back the shower curtain in my bathroom with a clatter of rings.

I nodded to myself and surveyed my apartment, head bobbing, until I fixed on my bed. It sat in the corner of the room, stone still, like a picture in a home catalog, the blue spread draped neatly over its edges. My bed had been made since I had last seen it.

Luke came out of the bathroom. "There's nothing here."

I threw the covers to the floor and tore the sheets apart, savagely.

✤

I leaned against Luke's car and smoked two without talking. Luke watched me with his hands in his pockets.

"Did you take your pill?"

I nodded.

He fell silent again and I lit up a third. "What're you going to do?"

I blew smoke out of a corner of my mouth. "I don't know. Nothing, I guess."

"Nothing?"

"What, I'm going to call 911 and say, 'Hey, someone broke into my apartment and made my bed, and by the way his name is Humphrey Bogart'?"

"You have more than that."

"Sure, I know. But this doesn't change anything. He knew that."

"Well, prove him wrong, then."

"Luke—I wasn't ready to go to the cops when he left a body in my car. I just can't do it yet."

He nodded. "Then what do we do?"

"We keep going, I guess." I pushed myself off the car and snuffed the cigarette on the cold asphalt. "I believe we were headed for the office."

✤

I squinted and turned my head away from the sun as we approached downtown. Marlowe never talked about the unpredictable stalls on Beverly, the inexplicable Saturday-afternoon traffic. His L.A. never felt quite so crowded and anonymous. Phone numbers were shorter in his day, easy to remember.

The buildings were shorter, too. Marlowe didn't live in a city of skyscrapers. The City Hall was the lone exception, the tallest building he knew by at least a hundred feet. It was still around, a designated landmark from another era, but its tower was quietly outgrown by a number of nameless office buildings. As downtown came into view, I took in the cold, industrial beauty of our skyline. There were a few more stray survivors of Marlowe's downtown—the Barclay Hotel, the Los Angeles Athletic Club— but they blended into a landscape dominated by younger giants of glass and steel.

Stokel, Levinson & Cook occupied six floors of the Gas Company Tower at 555 West Fifth. The soaring building came into view from miles away, its mercury windows reflecting blue skies. The tower was shaped like a lighter by design. Even in the shadow of the US Bank building it stood massive and alluring, gleaming with promise. *Find a big enough thumb, and I'll light the world on fire.*

Luke drove with one hand on the wheel, the other lying useless in his lap. "Are you okay?"

I scratched my head. "I'm rattled. But I've been rattled. I want to get to the bottom of this and nail that bastard. It won't help if I let him cow me even more."

"Sometimes, Song, you cow me."

We slipped into the underground parking structure on Olive and circled the garage to the reserved spaces. Mr. Cook's spot was beautifully empty, and Luke pulled into it with liquid grace.

"So what're we doing?"

"Well." I pounded my fists in a light drumroll on my thighs. "Okay, we're going to Miller's office."

"I don't know where that is."

"That's okay. We know where Diego's office is, yeah? He should have a roster. They print one every month. Don't you remember?"

"I forget that you worked there sometimes."

"We were cubicle neighbors for three months."

"Right. So what's the plan?"

When Marlowe was stumped, he followed leads—the stray address, the stranger to question—and the leads would generate more leads until he had answers he could hold in his fist.

"We hit up Miller's office. Search his desk. Search his computer."

"What are we looking for exactly?"

Even Marlowe didn't always know what he was looking for, so I hoped for the best. I shrugged. "You know, clues."

"Will they have bright blue paw prints on them?"

"Well, we don't know what they'll look like, so anything that might help. E-mail access would be nice."

"Too bad we have all the hacker knowledge of a couple of cheese rolls."

"Doesn't your crowned-prince status get us anything?"

He shrugged. "It'll get us in the office."

We made our way to the elevators and rode up to the lobby. It was as gratuitously grand as I remembered it, three stories of sparkling aluminum, glass, and stone, with a water garden on display, stout fountains gurgling onto marbled tile. The wall clock read 4:18.

A middle-aged security guard noticed our entry. She was small and unimposing, not much more than a head and shoulders above the check-in desk. She wore burgundy lipstick and a tired smile that peeled at the edges. I nudged Luke with the boniest part of my shoulder. "Do your thing, crowned prince."

He nodded and I loitered near the elevators. Luke talked to the guard in large gestures. His moving figure blocked her from view, but within a minute, he was walking back to me with two visitor badges. Both of them were printed with his face.

"I am not this ugly."

"It's just to get us through the sensors. You don't even have to wear it."

I slipped the sticker into my bag and we passed through to the elevators. I pushed the button for the forty-fourth floor, and it lit up in a ring of vermillion. Our journey was short and noiseless. The doors rolled open and we stepped onto close-mown taupe carpet. Luke led the way through frosted-glass doors to a row of numbered offices. Under the numbers hung name plaques in engraved silver. We tried not to look suspicious, and had the good luck to avoid any weekend litigators. Diego's office was at the western end of the row. We let ourselves in, relieved that the heavy wood doors lacked locks.

I plopped down into Diego's chair, which was less welcoming than it looked. His dark wood desk held nothing but a fat computer and two framed photographs. One showed him and Jackie on their wedding day, faces near goofy with happiness. The other was of us at our graduation—Luke with one arm around me and the other around Diego, the three of us linked in one long smile.

I picked it up and turned it for Luke to see. "Remember when we were twenty-one?"

"Ha, yeah." He took the frame and peered into it. "Not that anything's changed, really." His tone was weary, and I took in the serious expression on his face. Luke often joked about his financial dependence on his father, how it made him a child and kept him from acting his age. I decided it was best not to explore this mood.

"Well, not for us. And not until a couple days ago." I opened the top drawer of Diego's desk. "Holy shit."

"What?"

I picked up a waxy square of paper, holding it gently. On it was a black-ink fan interrupted with splotches of white.

Luke walked behind me and looked down over my shoulder. "That's not," he stuttered, "that's an ultrasound, isn't it?"

"Motherfucker." My voice came out in a whisper. "Did you know?"

"No. I guess you didn't either."

I bent my neck to see if I could make out anything human. "I can't believe he didn't call us when it happened."

"He's probably waiting to tell us in person."

I laughed. "Oh, of course. That was his important news. I can see why he didn't want to announce it today, bad luck and all. I have to say, though, that if I were thinking clearly, I would've guessed that. He's pretty transparent."

"I wonder how long it's been."

"Probably not long. Do you see so much as a bean's worth of human in here?"

Luke brought his face to the ultrasound and shook his head. "I'm sure it's cute, anyway."

"Should we call him?" asked Luke.

"No. Diego already dislikes what I'm doing. I don't think he'll be happy to know that I went searching around in his business. And anyway, we're not here to snoop through Diego's life."

I rifled through the drawer and found a pink stapled pamphlet with STOKEL, LEVINSON & COOK—JULY printed in block lettering on the cover. I flipped through the pages and found Gregory Miller listed under "Los Angeles Attorneys."

"He's on the forty-sixth floor." I extended a hand and Luke grabbed it and pulled me up.

"Let's do it."

We left Diego's office and took the elevator up two stories to an identical floor. We went through another set of frosted-glass doors and rounded the office, looking for Gregory Miller's nameplate. All the doors were closed, and halfway around the floor we found it. I touched the engraved name. The etched letters were cold. "R.I.P., Greg."

Luke opened the door. "Spooky." He turned on the light.

The office faced Fifth Street through a wide window that let in the thickening blue of the evening sky. I followed Luke inside. Miller's desk faced the door, which shared a wall with a large Matisse print hung in a simple black frame. His desk was cluttered silly with papers, pens, paperweights.

"Well." I gave my knuckles a good crack. They burst in sequence like bubble wrap. "Let's rummage."

I settled into Miller's chair, a leather recliner with a healthy spring to its back, and turned on the computer. "It would appear that we need a password."

Luke came around and stood behind me. "Shucks. Try 'password.'" I tried it, along with a couple iterations of Greg's name with Lori's.

"Couldn't he have left it on a Post-it on his monitor?" I pouted. "We'll need a hacker friend if we plan on doing this again. In any case, plan B." I pulled out every drawer of his desk in succession with exaggerated force and let them bounce back loudly on their rollers.

I tugged with a little less force at the top drawer so that it gaped open, revealing its contents with easy candor. It held an assortment of odds and ends, office supplies, a few folders, some loose paper. I removed everything but pens and paper clips and laid it on the desk. I then closed the top drawer and did the same with the middle drawer. More folders, more documents. The bottom drawer was the deepest, and it held folders in shades of manila, swamp green, and clay, hanging on to its sides by plastic tabs. Some were empty, some fat and sagging. I loosed the tabs and stacked the folders on the desk in sloppy piles.

Luke whistled.

Marlowe never seemed to wade through piles of paper, but that was a different day, before paper trails were long enough to trap every kind of sin. When he found a clue, it was clear and isolated—a name or phone number would stick out like a palm tree in an ocean—and all he would have to do was snatch it and move on. This was a law office in the twenty-first century, a place where records were kept with artisanal precision. We were looking at one office in one building, but it was filled with thousands and thousands of words, numbers, and objects. "We're looking for anything."

"Clues."

"Right. This should be mostly legal documents and whatever." I grabbed a stack of folders and pulled it onto my lap. "I guess just take some of this and cull through it for anything that could help."

Luke sat in one of the chairs on the opposite side of the desk, a plush affair in aged, oaky reddish leather with a resilient rounded seat. He reached for a stack near the edge of the desk and picked it up in a noisy flutter. "Yes, ma'am."

I sifted through the first pile, discarding what I'd viewed into the bottom drawer as I went along. I heard riffles and thuds coming from Luke's side as he thumbed through pages and dropped the occasional stack onto the carpet.

"I think this is roughly what Diego calls 'doc review.'"

"Yeah." I sighed. "It kind of sucks. Have you found anything?"

"Couple phone numbers. Take-out menus."

"Better than me. I got zip."

"I think I got the top drawer. You're stuck with all that legal jazz."

"Yeah." I stretched out my arms and got back to doc review.

My fourth pile of nondescript folders waned in my lap. The bottom folder was the fattest yet, and I groaned and gave it a violent glissando flip.

The bottom half of the papers refused to rise with the top, falling back to the folder after a brief start upward. I felt my heart rate pick up speed like a runner hitting his stride. I ran my fingers through the pages and found where the stack had stuck. Wedged between two stapled packets was a thin gray flash drive on a silver key ring. I picked it up with care and looked for a label. Nothing printed outside of a factory. I dangled the key ring by the tweezers of my thumb and middle finger.

"Luke. I think this is what a clue looks like."

Eight

Marlowe was no armchair detective, but he knew a clue when he saw one. He picked up the dirty books, the discarded scraps of paper, anything and everything he might find hidden in the band of a hat. There was never any question of a found object's significance. Marlowe was smart, but even he needed some hints to end up with answers.

We took our time and finished combing through Miller's office. It was almost seven when we were done.

"I think that's everything." Luke wiped his palms together, twice, with the dry-chalk sound of a mission complete.

"Give me your stuff. Let's keep it all together."

He handed me a thin stack of papers and I added it to my own. I folded them down the middle and stuffed them into my purse.

"Nothing else? No scented handkerchiefs or mysterious keys?"

I smirked. "No. I think we can get out of here now. We found what we needed in that USB drive."

What I didn't tell him was that I was certain, that the question was not whether the jump drive was important, but what was on it. There was an eerie sense of logic to the last couple days, the clean lines that construct the plots of noir. The tinted BMW was from another mode of life—I was done with red herrings the second a murderer bludgeoned the back of my head.

Luke led the way out the door. I scanned the office with that feeling you get when you leave a hotel room, the knowledge that you'd better check under the sofa because there's no coming back.

We padded softly to the elevator lobby, and I thought of Mr. Cook's empty office on the forty-eighth floor. "Luke," I said, "we have to check out your dad's office."

He paled.

"Look, I'm hoping almost as much as you are that we find nothing in there. But if there is, I have to know."

He nodded weakly and gave a grunt that had been a word at its conception. I summoned the elevator and it came, quick and obedient. I stepped in first and pressed the smooth dimple of the button for the forty-eighth floor.

The elevator deposited us into a lobby plush with dark wood and frosted glass. I led the way through the door on our left and padded across the freshly vacuumed carpet to the corner office. I'd been in Mr. Cook's office before for a few informal chats that always included Luke, but as we approached I was aware of how different it felt. It grew dark and imposing as it took over my field of vision—cavernous, ominous, pregnant with secrets. The massive door felt heavier, and, after everything I had seen in the last twenty-four hours, I was surprised to find it unlocked.

The office looked, in fact, exactly as I remembered it. A long couch took up one wall, and on the other end was a large mahogany desk with a dark leather office chair. The wall held Mr.

Cook's Harvard Law diploma, along with a few framed photographs. Luke and his mother were the subjects of most of these.

Erin Cook was once a striking woman, tall and slender and blond as the sun. She was five years younger than Mr. Cook, and they had met when he was in law school and she was a junior at Wellesley. Luke once confessed that he might have divorced his mother if he were in his father's shoes. Her depression often made her hard to deal with, but Mr. Cook met her again and again with patience. I felt for Luke—the villain of the hour was the person he admired most.

"Are you going to tell your mom about your dad and Lori?"

"I don't know. She's out of town till Tuesday, anyway."

Mrs. Cook was prone to sudden vacations, but this one, at least, seemed to suit Luke.

"Could you reach her if you had to?"

"I guess." He held his head in his hands. "I don't think I want her to know. I don't know what she'd do. I want to hold off on it, especially if it could be a misunderstanding."

"Okay, that's fair. That's why we're here. To find out what we can."

I rounded the room and took a seat behind Mr. Cook's desk. I hesitated and looked at Luke before settling in the chair. Luke had found his way to the couch, where he sat with a sulking look on his face.

"You don't have to help me, Luke. I'm sorry I even brought you here. Do you want to wait in the car?"

He shook his head with an air of misery. "It's okay. I'll just lie down." He slumped into a pile of Luke on the couch.

I tried the computer first, but it was locked down smart enough. I spent the next couple of hours going through every inch of the office, opening every drawer and examining each folder for something out of the ordinary. I checked behind photographs and between books as the sun set in a tangerine glow. Luke pretended to sleep on the couch and I let him. When I was finished, downtown L.A. twinkled like a switchboard outside the window.

"Luke," I said. "There's nothing here. Not a scrap of paper looks interesting."

He opened his eyes and sat upright. He looked up at me and nodded with relief. "I don't blame you for looking. Honest, I don't."

"Thanks."

"What time is it?"

I took my phone out of my purse. I had a missed call from Diego at 8:55 P.M. "It's nine thirty-six. I guess Diego called. Did he call you?"

He checked his phone. "No love."

"I'll try him now, I guess." I called him, but found myself facing his voice mail message. It was infuriating, a startled "Hello?" that always tricked me into thinking he'd picked up. It was a common prank, but in Diego's case, unintentional. "Not picking up. I guess we'll try again later."

I put everything back in order and we left the office spotless. Then, on the long path to the elevators, I saw a familiar bald head.

❧

Chaz Lindley was crouched in a cubicle, his back to me and Luke. The loose, folding skin of his neck looked damp with slow-gathered sweat, and he was fiddling with the keyboard to an unresponsive desktop on a disorganized desk. I could see that he was engaged in the same activity Luke and I had been attending to for the last several hours. I grabbed Luke by the wrist and pointed. "That's Chaz," I whispered. "That's the PI."

We padded softly to the elevator bank before Luke spoke. "What is he doing here?"

"I don't know. I think I have to talk to him."

"Who did you say he was looking for?"

"His brother-in-law. Who his sister thinks ran off with Lori." I groaned. "Of course he's a Stokel employee. How did I not just assume that?"

I left Luke alone by the elevators and found my way over to the cubicle and knocked on the desk. Chaz Lindley leaped in his seat.

"What the hell. Are you following me now?"

I shook my head. "Wouldn't dare tail a seasoned detective."

"I'm not following you, if that's what you're thinking."

"I didn't think you were." I felt my tongue grow thick in my mouth as I considered what his presence here meant. "I think we should swap stories."

He raised an eyebrow. Without the dark glasses, his eyes were almost friendly, but he didn't seem to like me much. "First thing. What the hell's your name?"

"It's Song. Juniper Song."

"What's your story?"

"Did you happen to pay any attention to Lori in that bakery or were you too busy keeping your eyes on me?"

"I saw her with an older man."

"That older man's son happens to be my best friend. He was wondering if his dad was fooling around with Lori Lim. Similar project, really."

He shook a wireless mouse back and forth in one hand. "So what do you know?"

"I know that she lives at home in Hancock Park, and that she didn't run off with your brother-in-law. I know exactly nothing about any Hector who isn't a Trojan prince. I'm guessing this is his desk?"

He nodded. "He works IT here. Been doing it a couple years."

"Do the names Greg Miller or William Cook mean anything to you?"

He frowned and scrubbed the inside of his ear, his index finger submerged to the second knuckle. "I don't know no Miller, but isn't Cook one of the bosses here?"

"Of Stokel, Levinson, and Cook. That's the one. Did Hector ever talk about him?"

"Not that I remember."

"Why does your sister think her husband is cheating on her with Lori of all people?"

He took a long time to answer, eyeing me with unmasked suspicion and chewing on his words. "She found some dirty pictures on his computer. When she confronted him about them, he said they were part of a photography project. That this Lori was a friend from work." He leaned forward. I smelled onions on his breath. "Between you and me, Hector's a greasy little gash hound—at least Candy thinks so. She had me put a tracker on his car a while back, cute little thing that tells me where he goes. Never led to much until he went and disappeared on her. Wanna know where his car is now?"

I nodded, with genuine interest.

"It's at a body shop in Koreatown. I did a little homework. Shop belongs to a guy named Taejin Chung. Taejin Chung has a cute little niece called Lori Lim. Now tell me what you know."

His broad face was without guile, and though he was sharper than I'd allowed, I hoped he was dumb enough. If Chaz was nothing like Marlowe, he wasn't unlike the occasional secondary investigator who crossed paths with him. That type tended to end up dead. I wished him health and safety, and I knew there was nothing wholesome about the web I'd wandered into.

I shrugged. "Sorry, Chaz. I've told you just about everything."

❧

Luke and I were back in his car, riding Wilshire past MacArthur Park.

"What do you think is on that drive?" Luke asked.

I plucked it out of my bag and rotated it slowly. "We'll find out soon enough. I'm very hopeful, though. I mean, this thing was tucked away in the back folder of the bottom drawer of a dead man's desk. Since my life is now an RPG, it has to be important."

He nodded and settled his eyes on the road as he merged onto Third. I turned on the air conditioning and reclined in my seat, hands folded on stomach as in a lazy prayer. Luke drove fast, and each bump was this princess's pea. Still, I relaxed and watched the ink-dipped, starless sky. The city sliding past our windows like painted screens was not quite Paris, but it was what we had.

I woke to the sound of Luke retrieving his key from the ignition. I must have nodded off for a while. It took a full half minute of rapid blinks to make my contacts feel at home again. The drowsiness faded as we made our way back to his apartment, and anticipation swam in the air, strong as bad cologne. He keyed us in and we dashed for his laptop on the coffee table without even shucking our shoes.

"Let me," I said. "I owe him something, you know?"

I plugged the USB key into the side of the PowerBook. A second later, a Finder window popped open on the desktop.

Multicolored thumbnails appeared in a column next to files labeled IMG_1351.JPG to IMG_1366.JPG. Next to the file names were the dates modified, all February 11, earlier this year. I selected the lot and double-clicked.

The window popped open with silent indifference. There was Lori, standing against a white background, hands held together in a honey-toned heart peeking out from the drooping sleeves of a heavy silk kimono.

❧

I thought about finding Quinn at school, but discarded the idea for the sake of Iris's privacy. In my head, our meeting was destined to be explosive. I planned to rain threats and accusations on Quinn's head in loud, clear tones. I decided the history office, where each teacher had a desk in arm's reach of the next, was not an ideal venue.

It took some maneuvering to find his home address. I got his phone number from the school by calling Iris's dean. In my best Korean accent, I told him I wanted to speak to Mr. Quinn about my daughter Iris. I mentioned that she had been missing a lot of school, and that she might require private tutoring. I noted that Iris's dean did not seem to think this an irregular request.

I took my time preparing to call him. I wrote out a short script and took many deep breaths before dialing his number. When he picked up, I didn't recognize his voice. It was, after all, our first interaction.

I borrowed the persona of Mrs. Winter, one of the women from the administrative office at my high school. I had met her a handful of times, and she had a quiet, muffled voice I thought I could imitate on the phone. I told Quinn that a system error had wiped his address, which I would need to process his paycheck. I

kept the conversation short and devoid of any strands of insinu-
ation, and within minutes, I knew where he lived.

His voice did not strike me as I feared it would. I must have
expected some sinister force to finger its way through the telephone, to slip into my core through the tunnels of my ear. In
fact, I felt nothing, no threat at all. My heart beat faster but the
ruse was quick and successful, and I hung up with a thrill. I didn't
fear Quinn, and I relished the thought that he might come to
fear me.

He lived around ten minutes away from Greenwood, in a part
of Sherman Oaks populated by small families and young profes-
sionals. I verified his address and parked the car across the street
from his house. It was a small gray house with a short lawn, on the
corner of the block. There was a burgundy Civic with a promi-
nent spoiler parked in the driveway.

I turned off the engine and sat listening to my respiratory
rhythm, my eyes attached to the house. In that moment, as I
watched the unfamiliar home of a practical stranger, I recognized
with vicious clarity that I had never done anything quite so crazy
before. Quinn made sense as Iris's secret lover, but I had taken a
strong hunch and given it the respect due to sacred fact. I was no
Marlowe. Where he was ever composed and competent, I moved
in response to jolts of love and fury.

I rang the doorbell and stood with my hands balled and my
feet digging into the ground. I heard slow, shuffling footsteps
coming to the door, the soft unhurried sound of socks on wood
flooring.

The door opened, and a powerful whiff of marijuana went
straight into my nose. Across the threshold was not Mr. Quinn,
but a scrawny Asian man in his late twenties, with bloodshot eyes
and a buzz cut, wearing cargo shorts.

I tried not to look surprised, and waited a beat for him to ask what I was doing in his doorway. He was looking at me with a blank expression, his mouth slightly open. He was starting his Saturday morning high as the moon.

"Sorry," I said. "Is Quinn here?"

He contorted his face into what was technically a smile, wry and vague. I wondered if he thought I was a romantic prospect. "He's not home right now, but you can come in."

"Will he be here soon?"

He shrugged.

I hesitated for a second before I figured out that this was a fortunate opportunity. With my suspect gone and his roommate inattentive, I could rummage through his things for something to retrace the dotted lines of my suspicion in ink.

As I entered the house, my heart started to pound with such obnoxious force that I feared it would give me away. But at the same time I let myself savor a small feeling of relief. This was not the living arrangement of a family man. I had prepared myself in case I ran into a wife or even a child, but I had not yet begun to deal with the idea of my sister as home wrecker.

It was a modest house, with two bedrooms and a large living room and kitchen. The roommate padded back into the living room, where he sat in a beanbag chair that already carried the mold of his body. A heavyset Asian girl sat on an armchair and looked up at me as I came into view. I waved meekly and hoped no one would ask for an introduction. No one did. While I stood studying the house and planning out my next move, the room-mate turned his head from within the beanbag. "Elliot's room is the one on the left."

I thanked him and let myself into Quinn's bedroom. If I was right, Iris had spent a lot of time in this room. The thought started to make me feel nauseous, and when I saw the outline of his twin bed in the corner of the room, I couldn't stop a flash of Iris's skin smothered by his from crossing my mind.

I switched on the light. It was ten o'clock in the morning and the room faced plenty of sun, but thick curtains kept it out, and I left them alone. It was a spacious room, with a desk and dresser and bookshelves leaving a fair amount of floor space unoccupied. On one wall hung a pair of samurai swords crossed in a short, wide X. Underneath it was a poster for an anime movie featuring colorful robots and busty girls in skin-tight body suits. A similar poster hung on the opposite wall. I took a look at his bookshelves and gathered that his study of history focused heavily on the Far East.

It was in high school that I first started hearing phrases like *Asian fetish* and *yellow fever*. They were tossed around lightly, with good humor, hot potatoes that no one wanted but that didn't hurt the holder. These were casual labels stamped onto any non-Asian boy who happened to show interest in an Asian girl. The reverse affinity was rarely noted and was, in fact, not very common.

But while most of the boys who dated Asian girls were also open to other races, there were a few who deserved the fetishist's label. The most extreme case knew all fifteen or so of the Asian girls in our class, and idolized each of us in turn. Once, I found myself behind him in the cafeteria line, and when I tried to pay for my sandwich, was told that he had taken care of it.

After that summer, I learned a lot about this indiscriminate worship of the oriental flower, a sickness that made itself known to every Asian woman in Los Angeles. I started to look out for the signs, and was quick to cut off suitors who showed symptoms. I was not a frequent target—the favorites gave off the exotic pheromones of submission with polite laughter and dainty walks, and they were almost always petite.

The Asian themes in Quinn's room made me uncomfortable, but I didn't jump to categorize it as a predator's cave. Instead, I made my way through his drawers in the same way I had combed through Iris's, in search of the stray love letter or token, any sign of my sister's place in her teacher's bedroom. I took my time, careful not to make a mess, but in less than ten minutes I saw that his desk drawers held only office supplies, and that there were no little notes hidden between polo shirts in his dresser.

I turned my attention to his bookshelves and scanned the titles with an aimless eye. He wasn't much of a fiction reader—his shelves were dominated by history books and a few dictionaries, including an English–Korean one. What little fiction he had was on the bottom of his three shelves. A few volumes by Haruki Murakami, and the silvery gray spine of *Lolita*.

I shivered when my eyes rested on that last book, tucked in the bottom right corner of his lowest shelf, adjacent to the floor. It was so out of place and so pertinent to my search that I crouched down and grabbed it. The book was in brand-new condition, the black lettering and smooth grain of the spine unbothered. When I flipped through the unread pages, something dropped from where it had been tucked inside the front cover.

I picked it up and nearly dropped it again. It was a four-by-six photograph of Iris.

Our school had no uniform, but she was dressed up like a fantasy schoolgirl. She wore a short pleated skirt and long socks, with a white button-down shirt open to the middle button. She was wearing a black bra underneath. Her face angled upward with an expression that was sweet and provocative, eyes wide and lips dewy and parted to show a flash of teeth.

Tears pooled in my eyes. I had come for verification, and I had found it. On the back of the picture Iris had written, "Happy birthday to my darling pervert," signed with a heart and a winking face.

I returned the book to its place on the shelf and put the picture in a flat pocket of my purse. I made sure my tears had not dropped onto my face, and left the room.

Quinn's roommate and his friend were still in the living room, in the middle of a slow, cheerful conversation. I had been in Quinn's bedroom for less than fifteen minutes.

"Hi," I said. "I think I have to get going."

The roommate stayed seated and looked up at me.

"Hey, do you guys know Quinn's girlfriend, Iris?"

They looked at each other and the roommate eyed me warily. "You're not a girlfriend? You are kind of his type." The girl snickered.

"Oh, no." I tried to fit in a good-natured laugh. "What do you mean by his type?"

He smiled and subsided into his beanbag. "You know, like, Asian. And young." He and his friend shared a long, hearty laugh. "You should see some of the babies he brings in here. God, do you remember that Bernadette girl? She must've been twelve."

I felt the hair on my arms stand up like frozen grass. "So what about Iris? You know her?"

"I've met her."

"Do you happen to know how she and Quinn met?"

"I think he picked her up at a bar somewhere. She's like, some kind of sorority girl. Pretty shy, though. Haven't talked to her much."

I nodded. "Have you seen her around lately?"

He looked at his friend and they both shrugged. "I guess not too much. She used to be here all the time, but last I saw her was a couple weeks ago, and she left quick. I guess maybe they're on the outs." He leaned forward on his knees and eyed me again with mock suspicion. "Hey, why are you so curious?"

"Like I said, just nosy. I left a note for Quinn, but you can tell him I was by if you want." I hoped he wouldn't bother mentioning my visit, but if he did, I didn't really care. "Thanks for letting me hang around. I'll see myself out."

I started my car and drove off in a hurry. I cried all the way home.

I hadn't seen Quinn in years, but I felt his presence everywhere. Over the city was the miasma of sexual predation, with submissive young Asian women as its eroticized target. Iris with her small feet and long, almond eyes was a fetishist's snack, and dollish Lori suited similar tastes.

When Lori came up on the screen, my initial reaction was a dry heave. My head lurched forward and my throat made a strangled, retching sound. Right away I felt Luke's hand squeeze my shoulder.

Marlowe knew the power of a photograph. The first dead body in Chandler's first novel showed up at a photo shoot with Carmen Sternwood in long jade earrings and nothing else. Her nude photos produced blackmail, heartbreak, and murder. A lot had changed since Marlowe's time, but the transfer from film to file did little to dull the impact of a cold image.

The kimono was an elaborate thing, all crisscrossed folds and drooping panels of fabric, a knife-cut hem brushing the tops of her feet, the toes of which just peeked out in clean white socks. A wine-dark obi clung to her middle, splitting a yard and a half of blushing cherry-blossom pink. Clouds, flowers, branches, and little birds painted and embroidered in soft spun gold and marshmallow white sprawled across the unwrinkled silk below her waist, and on the swingable sleeves that dipped near the ground.

Her hair was done up neat, bangs pinned away from her forehead with a fragile floral clip. Another flower bloomed in partial view over the back of her head in the form of a large comb or pin tucked into the quick of a relaxed bun. Her face was lightly made up, with eyebrows gelled into clean arches and lips wet with clear gloss. She smiled a coy smile, lips closed without pressing against each other, and she eyed the camera with just a slight, languid upward gaze from under a thin coat of mascara.

We stared at the screen in silence, eyes digesting Lori's strange gaze, for what must have been minutes. Eventually, Luke said the first three words that crossed my mind. "What the fuck?"

I nodded, the sick green feeling still swirling in my chest.

"Look at the rest."

IMG_1352 was Lori in the same kimono, this time hoisting the skirts to reveal the white socks that rode up to her lower calf, lacy ruffles adorning the ankles. Her eyes were wide and averted, and she stuck out her tongue under her protruding tooth.

IMG_1353 made me bite my lip so hard that I winced. Lori stood straight-backed in a sailor uniform, white blouse with a bow at the neck, pleated navy skirt reaching right above the knees. White socks and black Mary Janes on her feet. I tasted bile as I remembered Iris's costume, her flat, child's chest peeking out of an open blouse for consumption by a grown man. She made a picture of tarnished innocence that was more enticing than a real woman to a pervert's eye. Lori's picture, in comparison, was proper, but its existence was no less eerie.

IMG_1355 was the same as 1353, but she was curtseying this time.

IMG_1356. White T-shirt, Daisy Dukes. Pigtails.

IMG_1359. Pigtails. Watering can. No plants in sight.

"This is making me uncomfortable," Luke said. I could hear the strain in his voice.

I clicked on.

IMG_1363 showed Lori in a hanbok with a short jacket in key-lime green and a big poof of a bright magenta skirt that fell to the floor over a petticoat of equal size. I recognized the stiff, wrinkle-proof silk and arc-cut sleeves as kin to my own hanbok, which I wore once every few years when fancy struck on New Year's Day. The hanbok was far simpler than the kimono, a few blossoms swimming across the hem in tough clusters of off-white thread. Lori's hair fell thick and lustrous over her left shoulder in one long braid tied with the same magenta silk her skirt. But for this braid's light-molasses hue, she was the picture of a traditional Korean beauty. Her bangs fell lightly over her forehead and her complexion without its toasted July tan still had a smooth warmth in tone, like cake batter deepened with a good splash of vanilla. She stared at a spot below the camera, lips parted in a daze.

I clicked to the last file, IMG_1366, in which Lori sat in some undisclosed posture beneath the pond of opaque silk provided by her hanbok, and in the same motion slid my fingers off the laptop and dropped my arms, letting them dangle at my sides as I cocked my head and puzzled over what we'd just seen.

A few silent seconds later, I revisited the arrow pad and scrolled through all eight photos at a flashing speed, pressing down on the Up key until we were back up top. I shifted to the Down key.

Down again, then up again. I felt dizzy and closed my eyes. I crossed my legs and arms, all at once.

"Hey, are you all right?" Luke put a hand to my forehead and pushed back my bangs.

The photo I'd found in Quinn's apartment was one detail I hadn't shared with Luke. No object had ever held such power over me before, and I kept it hidden like some monstrous talisman. Out of sheer panic, I told Diego what I'd seen, but I didn't describe what she was wearing, omitted the doe-eyed expression.

"Thanks. I'm fine," I said. I took Luke's hand and brought it away from my face. I blinked and shook my head. I did my best to expel the old image and replace it with what was in front of me. I tried to think. "This was definitely a photo shoot of some kind."

"It looks like it."

"For sure. White-sheet background, outfit changes. Skipped file numbers make me think there were some reject shots deleted. And they were all taken the same day. February eleventh."

"For Valentine's Day?"

"That would make sense, wouldn't it?"

"She's so . . ." He paused, searching for it. "She's so clothed."

"I think that's the word I was looking for, too. That, and creepy."

"So what do we think?"

"She took these photos to give to someone. My hunch is that that someone wasn't Greg."

"Why not?"

"I gather that Greg had a thing for Lori, but it sounds like it went unrequited." I scrolled back to the hanbok photos. "I have one of these."

"Really? You?"

"Yeah, got it when I was in high school. Don't wear it much, but it's a traditional thing." I clicked back up to the first photo, and Lori changed out of her hanbok into a kimono in a lightning swap of pixels. "I do not have one of these."

"Right. Why would you?"

"Why would Lori? And why would she take pictures of herself in both a kimono and a hanbok?" I stretched out my jaw and let my tongue get some air, trapped as it was in a dried-out mouth. It made a thick, furtive sound when it moved, like a darting lizard. "This is making me want to throw up. These are the kinds of photos I might think to take if I wanted to whore myself to an Asian fetishist. Someone who just likes his women drowning in silk." I took another look at the kimono. "This thing is fancy. It belongs behind glass. She may have had the hanbok lying around, but I'm thinking the kimono was a gift."

"But she's Korean."

"A gift from an amateur Sinophile." The welt on the back of my head was starting to throb again. "Whoever it is, I despise him." I logged into my e-mail and sent myself the files.

"Well, she's clearly playing into whatever this is. These pictures make me feel dirty."

I felt my hands go cold. "Hector Lopez. Chaz's brother-in-law. He found these files and now he's missing."

I found Chaz's phone number and dialed it, only to get his voice mail. I left a simple message asking him to call me back.

"Wait, what are you talking about?" Luke's voice was shaking.

"That's why his wife thought he ran off with Lori—because she found these pictures." Greg Miller's dead white face painted itself in my head. "I hope to God he's hiding somewhere."

"But why would Hector have Lori's pictures?" His voice trailed off and his face turned white.

"He's a tech guy, and he might've seen something of interest that didn't belong to him. Shared drives, open e-mail—people aren't always careful about what they access at work. He might've seen it and decided it was worth something."

"Diego said Miller was in love with Lori."

"Not just that—he was in love with Lori and everyone at Stokel knew it. If Hector wanted a buyer, he didn't have to look very hard to find one." I folded my hands and looked at them instead of at Luke. "The thing is, someone had to access the pictures in the first place. The original, intended recipient."

We fell into a silence so thorough we might've heard an angel sneeze. Finally, Luke spoke up, and his voice cracked. "You think that's my dad."

I rubbed my thumbs together and ventured a look at Luke. It was a mistake—I could see him hoping I would shut him down as I had the day before. "He's the frontrunner in any case. There is something weird going on with him and Lori. And think about it—we're either dealing with a moron or someone from an older generation. Your dad may know how to use a computer, but when it comes to covering his tracks, I doubt he has the strain of paranoid caution that comes with growing up in the digital age."

He whimpered. "You said there was nothing in his office."

"I did say that, but I'm sorry. It doesn't absolve him. In fact, if I were involved in anything suspicious in his position, I would keep my office clean and its door open." I paused. "But again, we don't know anything for sure."

"My dad doesn't have an Asian fetish."

"Maybe it's a midlife longing for something exotic."

"Asian in L.A. is exotic?"

"You'd be surprised. Do you know how many times I get asked where I'm from? Or greeted by a 'Konnichiwa' or a simple 'Ching chong chang'?" I shook my head. It was pounding. "Maybe it's not an Asian thing. Maybe he just wants a delicate, soft-voiced girl, beautiful and obedient. Someone he can own and control." I remembered I was talking about his only father, and I saw the horror on Luke's face with some remorse. I changed the subject. "Do you have Lori's number?"

"I'm friends with her on Facebook. Let me check."

I navigated to Facebook and moved to let Luke log in. He pulled up her profile. Los Angeles network, a recent CSUN graduate. Her picture showed her in a deep-cut viscose jade top with butterfly sleeves, layered gold strands decorating the open expanse of her neckline. She was laughing with mouth wide open, painted red fingernails covering her eyes. Her hair stood out bright against a generic nighttime background. This was a picture for public consumption.

Her most recent update: "Lori just checked in @ Red Palace (Los Angeles, CA)."

"What's Red Palace?" I asked.

"I don't know."

"Google it. Because whatever she's doing tonight, I think we have to be there."

Nine

M arlowe never had the advantages of the Internet. He had to count on overhearing the right address, or stumbling on the name of a venue, written conveniently in someone's black book. I was happy to have the twenty-first century on my side. A search for "red palace los angeles" yielded a place called Red Palace Club on Western and Seventh, in the heart of Koreatown. I looked at the corner clock on the computer screen.

"It's almost eleven. We should go now."

"Now? We don't even know what this place is."

"It's a club."

Luke gave me a once-over and shrugged. I looked down at my gray T-shirt and jean shorts and frowned.

"Thanks. I have heels in my car."

"Okay. But I'll drive."

We traced our steps back to Luke's car and he drove us to mine on Lillian. I found my shoes from the night before among other like pairs—a passenger's side full of high heels was one mark of a single woman in Los Angeles. I swapped into the big shoes and found mascara in my purse. I gave my lashes a few swipes in the vanity mirror. We got back into the Porsche and reentered L.A.'s streets through the quiet-throbbing vein of Rossmore. "You know how to get there?"

"It's on Western past the Wiltern, right?"

"Yeah."

"I got it."

We rode east on Wilshire Boulevard, where brick condominiums gave way to strip malls and Korean lettering, block by block. The street was unclogged but alive with Saturday traffic, and each slow stoplight revealed the heavy breathing of cars headed into the night. We turned right at the Wiltern, a landmark theater with an ancient marquee, a place that had seen Koreatown sprout up and around it, leaving no lot unturned. Seconds later, we reached our destination. It was less gaudy than I'd expected, RED PALACE spelled out on a sign one could easily miss.

We pulled into a sloping lot behind a flashing-silver Mercedes sports car, out of which two middle-aged men in starchy dress shirts and designer jeans emerged from under gull-wing doors. A skinny valet in a black satin vest gave a shallow bow and took the car deeper into the lot. Luke pulled up and a stocky valet with spike-gelled hair took his place in the driver's seat and drove the Porsche to join in with fancy company.

There was no line of well-dressed clubbers peering in from the outside, and we followed the Mercedes men in through a pair of frosted-glass doors.

The first thing I noticed was that the club was well lit. Though it was lively with music and booze-tipped conversational noise, it was clearly not a nightclub. I took in the room—red carpet, high walls, and dozens of glossy wood tables surrounded by plushy red loveseats. On these loveseats sat men between the ages of thirty and sixty, and girls between the ages of sixteen and twenty-five. I scanned for Lori and couldn't find her.

"May I help you?" An Asian woman in a high-neck blouse and pencil skirt came forward, her soft hands folded before her. She was in her early forties, her complexion white and caked with makeup, her mouth drawn heavy with liner. Her short, black hair was pinned away from her face in tight, glossy lines. She spoke to Luke, her English weighed down by a slow, brittle accent, and she looked sideways at me through a fixed smile.

He started to extract his driver's license from his wallet and I did the same. He answered the woman, smooth-voiced and confident: "Yeah, can we get a table?"

"Have you been with us before?"

We shook our heads.

"Would you like a table or a private room?"

At the back of the room, I noticed a well-stocked bar, tended by two men in trim vests, with gelled hair. "Can we sit at the bar?"

"Of course." She looked at me again with a curious, evaluative gaze, and I remembered that I was dressed for the supermarket. Then she smiled again, conspiratorial, indulgent. "I suppose you will not mind that there is no hostess service at the bar."

She led the way through one side of the club, where we passed several closed, numbered doors. Those were the private rooms, then, where we might find Lori. When we reached the bar, she said, "Enjoy your evening." Then she bowed and padded away on light feet.

When she was out of earshot, Luke leaned toward me with his eyebrows. "Where are we?"

I studied the spread of men and girls, the keen, red-faced jollity of the former, the short-skirted pleasantness of the latter. The crowd was around 90 percent Asian, but the 10 percent that wasn't was exclusively male. The scene gave my insides a whirl.

"She said hostess, right?"

"Yeah, I was wondering what that was too."

"I think we're in a hostess club."

"What's that?"

"Look around."

He turned his head back to the room and started to nod. "It's weird, I'll tell you that."

"I think the way this works is that all the girls are hostesses. They're getting paid to entertain the men. Accounts for the uniform age disparity, right?"

"What do you mean, 'entertain'?"

"I've never been to a hostess club before, obviously. I don't think I know anyone who has, either. But they're fairly common in Asia. The understanding is the girls are like modern-day geishas."

"High-end hookers?"

He said the last word a notch louder than he should have, and the bartender chuckled. "No prostitution in the Red Palace. That's the party line. You guys want a drink?"

I gave him a curious stare, and stayed on him long enough that he might notice me lingering. He was about my age, with a look of hard luck in a thick, black set of unmovable eyebrows. He stood around six feet, and despite peculiar proportions, his wide nose, thin eyes, and taunting mouth formed a face with some appeal.

"Can I get a scotch and soda?" asked Luke.

"I'll have the same," I said.

He was quick with his hands and he presented our drinks with a white smirk. "I haven't seen you around here before."

"First time," I said. "Hey, what'd you mean about the party line?"

"What're you talking about?" He winked. "You didn't hear anything from me."

I took a swallow of my drink. "What's your name?"

"Albert. You?"

"You Korean?" I smiled. "Of course you're Korean. Albert."

"Hey, there are Chinese guys called Albert, too."

"Yeah? Are you one of them?" I took another gulp from the tumbler and blinked at him over the rim. "Didn't think so."

"So what's your name?"

"Take a cigarette with me and maybe I'll tell you." I felt Luke's questioning eyes, and I knew if I turned to meet them I'd blow the act. I motioned to the other bartender, who was listening in without much stealth. "He can take care of my friend a few minutes, can't he?"

"I guess I can take a few minutes."

As he came out from behind the bar, I gave Luke's shoulder a light tap. "I'll be right back."

I followed Albert to an outdoor patio through a rear exit. There wasn't much in the way of seating except a long red bench affixed to the wall, and clusters of patrons and girls stood around smoking and inhaling smoke. When the rest of the country gave up cigarettes in waves, only Koreans seemed to have missed the warnings. With half the bars in Koreatown flouting laws to allow smoking indoors, we would be the race that kept lung cancer relevant. The Red Palace kept things legal, and the patio was crowded. The space was mercilessly well lit, and every forehead around shimmered as if anointed with oil.

We settled, standing, in a spot comfortable enough that

eavesdroppers would have to be trying, and I withdrew my pack of Luckies and shoved it toward him, carton cap flipped down.

"Thank you." He pulled out a cig and I did the same. I fished around for my matchbook and brought that out, too. I'd sunk a whole afternoon a few years back learning to light matches with one hand. A sharp drag of calloused thumb gave us flame.

"So." I lit Albert's Lucky, suctioned between two lips and pinched like a joint where yellow paper turned to white. "If this is an establishment for horny men, how'd you end up behind the bar?"

He chuckled and exhaled a milk cloud of smoke. "Oh, I don't know. They like a man to pour their drinks, I guess."

"How long have you been working here?"

"Almost a year."

"So you know a thing or two behind the scenes, I take it."

"You could say that."

"I've never been to a hostess club before. I'm fascinated."

"What do you want to know?"

I smiled. "Well, how's it work?"

He moistened his lips and, to my delight, started to talk. "These men come in." He pointed vaguely at the men on the patio, the slack-bellied, stiff-haired men in business casual. "They have a lot of cash, all of them. You know a table costs something like two hundred dollars an hour, so you need to have a lot of cash. A lot of these guys are regulars, too."

"Jesus, two hundred an hour? For what?"

He smiled again, sly and conspiratorial in a way that started to look lascivious. "What do you think?"

"Why don't you give me the party line first?"

"They get table service. Their choice of booze and some

things to munch on. The girls serve them, and they sit with them, in or around their laps." He made a snorting sound. "The story is the girls just talk to them in high-pitched voices, laugh at their jokes, make them feel like big men. And of course, they throw money and booze around like some goddamn philanthropists."

"And what's behind the party line?"

"I probably shouldn't say, right?" He took another suck at his cigarette, still holding it like a blunt.

I studied his face and waited. He was dying to tell me.

"Well, isn't it obvious? Who pays that kind of money without a happy ending?"

"So you're saying what, this is a brothel?"

"Maybe not technically. But all the hostesses are gold-digging sluts. I know they're spreading their legs for money in a way that can't be legal."

And with that, I noticed he was suddenly ugly, his complexion sick and blotched with an angry shade of red. I took a heavy, scratchy sip of nicotine and tried to regain a flirtatious smile. "Is one of these sluts named Lori Lim?"

"Yeah. What about her?"

"Do you know if she ever entertains an older white guy?"

"She entertains a few of them, probably. It's her job. But you mean one in particular, don't you?"

I nodded. "You've seen him?"

"Tall ginger creep, about thirty. He's here a couple times a week. How could I miss him?"

I felt my pulse spike and did my best to hide it by tensing the muscles in my eyelids and staring at the lumined tip of my cigarette.

"When was the last time you saw this guy?"

"Actually, he was here last night. I just saw him for a second. Lori wasn't here, so he probably left quick."

I heard a cardboard click as that jigsaw piece fell into place. I could finally see that part of the puzzle well enough to know which way to orient it while I waited for the rest to come in.

"How about a guy in his fifties? Kind of tall, gray hair."

"We get a few of those, and I see Lori with them now and then. I can't pick out a face, though."

"And you think Lori's sleeping with all these men. Just all of them."

"Probably. I mean, you've seen her in action, right? She pretty much invites guys to unbutton their pants."

"Look, I could care less if she screwed every guy she ever met. That's her business." I didn't know how much more Albert I could tolerate, but I cursed myself as I heard the sharpness enter my tone. I made it sweeter and lowered my voice to a scandalized whisper. "Tell me, though. Do you actually know if she sleeps with men for money?"

He dropped his cigarette and snuffed it underfoot. "You still haven't told me your name."

"Oh, I'm sorry." I gave him the first name that came to mind, with a big smile. "It's Chastity."

"Why so curious, Chastity?" He smiled back, his eyes like two raisins folding into soft dough.

"It's interesting stuff." I shrugged and put out my Lucky Strike, scrubbing out the embers with platformed toes. The interview was over. "I'm getting thirsty again. How about you make me another drink?"

"How about I get your number first?" He touched my wrist, a gesture meant to make me comply.

"Maybe later." I shook him off and gave him my least confrontational glare. "I wouldn't want you thinking I was some kind of whore, Albert."

I made my way back to the bar while he stayed behind for another cigarette, which suited me. The moment I reentered the building, my eyes found Lori, her delicate figure softly presented in amber light. She wore a short dress of jade crepe de chine with spaghetti straps and a vertical ruffle falling down the bodice. A tall, curved heel on an oyster satin shoe combined with a messy up-do to bring her to a height from which she conversed with Luke eye to eye as he sat on a bar stool, with his back in my direction. The Chanel rested on the bar beside her.

I stood still for a moment, a spy in shadow. She leaned into Luke with the same dreamy look as the night before, lenses unfocused. Her small hand rested on his knee like it had every right to be there, and I could see her talking, mouth stretching brightly with each new syllable, tooth in varying degrees of exposure at the border of a well-curved upper lip. Her free hand flitted about her as she talked like a baby bird skirting the nest, and I wondered at the compulsion to reduce this strange and never-still girl to a 2-D image, no matter how pretty.

I walked up and slung an arm around Luke's shoulder like an orangutan. I turned my chin toward him and kept my line of sight focused away from Lori. "What're you drinking?"

"Gimlet."

I looked at him sideways. "Half gin, half Rose's lime juice, and nothing else?"

"I think it's just gin with a squeeze of lime, but sure."

"Got one for me?"

He turned to clone his order and I let my eyes wander and widen as they pretended to discover Lori.

"Lori! What're you doing here?" I pulled off the act with all the natural grace of a Hostess Twinkie.

She had been regarding the juncture between my armpit and the back of Luke's neck with pointed longing in a glassy eye that it took me a second to recognize as jealousy. It was like the cottontail of a fleeing rabbit—by the time I saw it, she was answering me.

"I work here." Her tone and expression were neutral, serene, without a defensive wrinkle.

"Here and Stokel?"

"I'm usually here on weekends. I just took last night off." She glanced at Luke.

He leaned against me applying pressure with his shoulder. "I was telling her you wanted to come meet a rich, single Korean guy and were too embarrassed to come alone. I can't believe you thought this was just a nice K-Town bar."

"Cute." I grabbed a taut wad of his cheek between thumb and knuckle. "Don't be tricked, Lori. Luke wanted to game some Asian girls and needed me to sneak him in. I guess we got a little mixed up. This sure is an interesting place."

She laughed and brushed my arm with the backs of two fingers, a touch so light I only felt it with hairs I didn't know were there. "Thanks for the ride last night."

"No problem. Why'd you have to get home so early anyway?"

"I live with my mom, and she's a little strict." Her lids shut halfway and her pupils gleamed dully at a spot on my shoulder.

"No shame in that." I opened my mouth to make a dig at Luke's father-dependent living situation, but bit my tongue before it could deliver that lick. But something else caught. "Don't take this the wrong way, but she doesn't mind you working here?"

She shook her head, her eyes hazy and still. "She's the one who got me the job. She's the manager here. You probably met her when you came in."

I turned to look back around the room and saw the woman who had greeted us at the door, carrying a large bottle of whiskey to one of the tables. She had an even, dignified walk. I hadn't recognized her from the glimpse in her car, with the sunglasses gone and the heavy maquillage in their place.

Korean music played over our heads and I looked from Luke to Lori to see if it was still my turn to keep the conversation rolling. Luke's nose in his cup and Lori's ever-glazed gaze said that it was.

I gave Lori's bicep a playful pat. "What did the bus driver say to the egg?"

Her eyes brightened with a lifting of lashes. "I don't know, what?"

"*Gyeran.*"

She giggled.

Luke pouted. "Korean joke?"

"Yeah. *Gyeran* is Korean for 'egg,' and it sounds like 'get on.' I've got plenty more I know you're dying to hear."

He swiveled on his nonswiveling stool and came back with my gimlet. "Put this in your face, will you?"

I took it and lifted it for him to clink against his own. "*Gun bae,* dude."

"*Gun bae.* Drain it."

I tilted the cup against my lower lip and angled my head to open up my esophagus. A little ice never hurt anyone, and I missed it as the room-temperature gin trickled in a prickly vein into my system. I swallowed half and came up for air. "Tastes sticky." I regarded the clear fluid. "And bitter as peel." I took another long tug at it and set the empty glass on the counter with a dry clack.

Lori was looking at me with quiet awe. Luke laughed. "She drinks like a three-hundred-pound man."

I noticed Lori's face was tan and glowing, with no more than a couple brushes of pink blush ruddying her cheeks. "You don't turn red either, huh?"

She shook her head with small whooshes. "I do. I take a Pepsid before I drink. It helps. You're lucky."

"Don't puff her up any. She may drink like a three-hundred-pound man, but she only has the tolerance of an unusually sturdy woman. Let's not have her get showy and end up over a toilet. I'm not holding her hair up, not tonight."

As Luke poked fun of me, I noticed Albert coming in from his break. "Speaking of toilets." I gave my right knee a convincing wobble and fixed on Lori. "I have to go. Will you come with me to the bathroom?"

She hesitated and looked at Luke, but only for a moment. "Sure. We'll be right back."

The restrooms were up a short duo of stairs at the other side of the arced bar. The men's and women's faced each other, doors open and separated by a mere five feet of floor. The approaching view showed girls reapplying lipstick, a man in a sweat-through shirt standing regal at a urinal. We walked in single file through the door, Lori guiding me with her small hand pulling mine with a grip so close that I felt the band of coolness from her cocktail ring crushed between my knuckles.

A short line of short dresses stood between us and the stalls. I was hoping for a little more privacy. I disengaged my hand and brushed bangs out of my face. I smiled meekly. I had her alone, but I couldn't boil up a roundabout line of interrogation.

She broke the silence. "Are you and Lucas going out?" Her voice was bright but her eyes were all nerve.

"Me and Luke?" I laughed. She was sweet on him like brown sugar on bacon. Her affections were conveniently placed, but not for her. "Why?"

She flushed a sudden peach. "Oh, no, just, you guys seem close."

"We're close, but no. He's more like a brother to me. The kind you don't make out with."

She hid her sigh of relief with the skill of an eight-year-old with a stolen cookie behind her back.

"Actually, Luke was saying he wanted to check out a karaoke place in a bit. Do you know of anywhere good?"

She thought for a second. "There's Bobos."

"Sure. Would you want to come with us?" I started to formulate my line of questioning for the dark karaoke box. "There isn't really anything for us here."

Her lips formed a breathless O. "I'd like that. I can ask my mom, maybe. She might let me go early."

A stall opened up with a forceful outward swing of metal door. A girl dripping with stringed hair and fringed cotton stumbled out in mock-croc heels. "You go ahead." I gave Lori a little pat on her shoulder.

"I don't have to go, actually."

"Okay, thanks then." I dipped in and out of the stall. She was examining herself in the mirror, head tilted, lips puckered, eyelashes batting slowly. I washed my hands and, faced with an empty towel dispenser, patted them dry on the butt of my shorts. "Let's get back to Luke, yeah?" She nodded and followed me out.

When we got back to the bar, Luke was gone. I edged in between bar stools and drummed the counter to get Albert's attention. He heeded my summons. "I see you found Lori. Drink?"

I felt myself flush. "No, actually. But did you see where that guy I was with went?"

"Yeah, sitting right here? He jetted a minute ago."

"Did you see which way he went?"

"That way." He pointed to the exit. "He ran."

"Ran?"

"Ran. As in, the opposite of walking."

I snarled at him. "Thanks."

"Where do you think he went?" Lori's voice was flavored with disappointment, but without urgency.

"I don't know, but change of plans. You're coming with me right now."

"Where?"

"Somewhere we can talk that isn't a bathroom."

"But my mom—"

I grabbed her by a wrist smooth and spare as bone. My lips found her ear. "Greg Miller is dead. I need you to help me figure out why."

Ten

It took me a couple of weeks to summon the courage to tell Iris what I'd found out. Our last fight had been dreadful, and I knew the potential for greater wreckage was all too high. I had started working at Stokel in mid-June, and I was grateful for the distraction. The commute from Northridge to downtown was a brutal series of car-choked freeways, and I lingered east of Hollywood after work to avoid the crush of rush hour in the other direction. Monday through Friday I left home before eight and was rarely back for dinner. I spent most of my time with Luke. We worked in the same office, and we fell into a routine of leaving together at the end of the day. There was no happy hour for us when we were not even twenty, but we ate a lot of Korean and Mexican, and we watched a lot of movies. On the weekends, I saw Luke and a few friends from high school who were already growing indistinct.

I kept Luke in the dark about my Iris investigation. It wasn't that I didn't trust him as a confidant. I needed a refuge from my home life, where I could forget about the silent evenings in our bedroom, the good-night wishes spoken into the fragile tension between Iris and me. When I needed to vent I called Diego, and he met me with an open ear and a saintly understanding, enough of an outlet that I could enjoy my Iris-less hours in peace.

When July came around, my family took a trip down to San Diego for the long weekend. The three of us had never felt so awkward and pasted together, and as we packed and loaded our luggage in slack, joyless quiet, I sensed that none of us wanted to go. It was a horrible realization. The Songs had never been a wholesome American family with soccer practice and pot-roast dinners, but we had had our own cohesion.

The Fourth of July trip was a tradition. We had made the two-and-a-half-hour drive down to San Diego every year since Iris and I were children. We'd been to Sea World multiple times, and my first memory of fireworks involved lying on the hood of our mom's car, with pillows taken from our hotel room. I built a lot of memories in San Diego.

By the second day of constant contact with Iris, I felt my suppressed emotions trying to seep out through my skin like a rash. I had tried to erase my visit to Quinn's house from my consciousness, to obliterate the dirty picture I knew I could never forget. But as the three of us lay in our two beds, watching television and waiting for meals, I could think of nothing but the task I had postponed. I would talk to Iris.

It was a hot Sunday, and while our mom relaxed, taking a long nap in the hotel, Iris and I went to the beach. It was crowded with bodies of different shades, different weights, a long continuation of flesh from shoreline to parking lot. Somehow, we managed to find an open plot of sand, and we lay down our towels and sat.

Iris was wearing a swimsuit I'd never seen before, three triangles of string bikini striped purple and blue. I was used to her body. We had always shared a bathroom, and when we were children, the two of us would bathe with our mother. Nudity was never an issue among the women in our house, and it was only later in life that I realized things were different in other families.

Still, I found myself keenly aware of Iris's body on that beach. She drew eyes as she walked, as naturally as the sun, and I saw men and women turn to stare at her as we made camp on the sand. At sixteen, I couldn't write her off as a child, but she was slight and narrow, with the fragile lines of a gymnast or a dancer. Her skin was pale honey, and it shone on the beach like something new.

She sat with her legs tucked beneath her and gave me her back. She handed me a bottle of sunscreen and said, "*Unni*, could you?" I moved her hair over her shoulders and noticed her roots had grown inches. She had dyed her hair a dark reddish color but hadn't bothered with a touch-up in months.

I rubbed sunscreen into her back, massaging the white into her skin. "Tell me about Quinn," I said.

Her shoulder blades went stiff under my hands and her head flinched, but she didn't turn to face me. I felt her try to calm her breathing. "Mr. Quinn? What about him?"

I rested my forehead on her hair and kept my hands steady on her shoulders. My chest hurt. "Iris, I know. Please don't lie to me anymore. I can't stand it."

She didn't say anything for a while, and I felt the greasy lotion between my palms and her shoulders start to mingle with our sweat. When she finally spoke, it was in a whisper that blended with sea noise and beach crowd, and I had to make her repeat herself. "What do you want to know?"

"Everything."

It was a long story, and to hear her tell it, it was, even now, an epic romance.

She found him difficult, at first, a strict and serious teacher with an infrequent smile. Their initial interactions were innocent, as far as she knew, and when she did poorly on her first exam, he offered to help her study.

They started meeting after school in the teacher's lounge, and in between quizzes, in between outlining notes, they learned about each other. She hadn't expected it, but he made her laugh. He had a dry, teasing humor that seemed so much easier and smarter than the bawdiness of boys her age. She started to find Paul dull.

She confided in Quinn. He emitted an aura of wisdom, and when she was with him, she felt protected. She could be herself around him, a stripped-down, new version—not the fragile sister or the stupid daughter or the quirky friend, but just Iris. And she thrived in those sessions. She became silly and sardonic and when he looked at her and laughed with her she felt brilliant. When no one was around, she tried calling him Elliot. It made him smile. It wasn't long before she dumped Paul and set her heart on Elliot.

One day when the teachers' lounge was empty she held his hand. He looked startled, but they continued to hold hands for most of the session. At the end, he walked her to her car and told her he had fallen for her. They gave up the pretense of teacher and pupil and scheduled their next meeting for his house.

She hadn't told our mom about her breakup with Paul, and she realized she'd anticipated the need for a cover story. She and Quinn met a couple times each week outside of school, and always on Sundays, during church hours.

He didn't pressure her into a physical relationship, but he didn't have to. She went to Planned Parenthood and got a prescription for birth control before sex even came up. She knew he would have more experience, and she wanted to be ready.

"I knew you would think it was weird, and that you would worry about me. But he's just this wonderful person, *unni*. I've never felt the same way about anyone before, and I'm not sure I ever will again. You have to understand."

I heard the clichés spill from Iris's lips with an earnestness that made me ache. "If he's so wonderful, why are you so sad all the time? Why isn't he here for you?"

She still had her back to me, and I saw her neck straighten toward the ocean. "It was my fault I got pregnant. I was stupid and forgot to take the pill a couple times. When I told him, he freaked out. He wasn't mean to me, it wasn't like that. But he panicked. He would lose his job, his friends, and he might even go to jail. So I told him I'd take care of it. And that seemed to make him feel better."

I sighed. "Shit, Iris. This is the kind of stuff they warn you about."

"But I knew we couldn't be together after that. I knew how much he was risking to be with me, and I knew that if we kept going, someone would find out. So I broke up with him. He didn't abandon me."

"Did he try to stop you?"

She hesitated, and I could hear her sniffling. "No. He didn't."

We didn't go into the water that day. When we left the beach, our eyes were swollen, and I had the beginnings of a bad sunburn on my back.

We left the Red Palace and Lori led the way up Western to a coffee shop she knew between Fifth and Sixth called, cute enough,

Mr. Coffee. I let her stay ahead of me while I dialed Luke. I got his voice mail four times along with a violent urge to smash my newborn iPhone into a mound of plastic and glass seeds against the pavement. The pins of my stilettos fell uneasy on the sloping sidewalk and my knees wobbled like a baby goat's. I stepped harder on the balls of my platforms and we made the three long blocks to the café in a harsh and unpleasant silence raided by the background buzz of a city sliding into intoxication.

My phone, now back in my good graces, showed 12:36 A.M. I hoped Luke was keeping his nose clean.

Mr. Coffee took the most conspicuous spot in a strip mall boasting all sorts of Koreatown–specific goods and services. A small Hispanic man in his late thirties played valet to a cheerful overabundance of automobiles. A new car entered the lot, and he spoke to the driver in Korean. The inside of the café was decked out in hollow wood and cheap red velvet. It was small and busy enough, thick with the mingling scents of smoke and pastries. I chose a circular table for us in the deepest pocket of the little space, with two oversize armchairs.

Lori sat in one chair and I pulled mine as close to hers as I could manage while leaving room for my knees to exist. I faced the last corner of the café, close enough to see the cracks in the vertical line separating wall from wall.

I had one elbow up on the table and concentrated my vision on her compact frame. The coffee shop was dimly lit, but no shadow could hide her from my gaze. I took one look at the crowd and knew no one was watching us, and that no one cared if I smoked. I lit a cigarette and watched her squirm. We sat still in this bully-and-bullied posture for a good minute before she spoke up.

"Did you say Greg Miller was . . ."

"Dead."

"Dead?"

"Uh-huh."

She nodded slowly, her curls suddenly heavy as sailor's rope.

"You didn't know?"

She shook her head with the same pendulous awe.

"Are you surprised?"

Again she nodded, switching the angle of her neck without surrendering a moment's motion.

"Do you have any idea why?"

Shaking her head again. Like train tracks changing. I was starting to get tired of it.

"Look. What can you tell me about Greg?"

Her bobblehead finally lost some steam and she parted her lips with some hesitation.

"You may speak ill of the dead tonight. Don't worry, I'll write you a note."

She gave me a malnourished smile. "I don't like him. I mean, I didn't like him."

"I hear the feeling wasn't mutual."

"He was really creepy. We met when I started working and at first I thought he was really nice. He would bring me coffee and make a point of chatting with me at my desk. I was new, and most of the lawyers were too busy to be friendly."

It was my turn to nod.

"But he asked me out pretty soon after I started. And he didn't just ask me to coffee, he sent me roses and asked me to be his girlfriend."

"Not your type?"

"Not so much, no." She said it quick and turned a sad shade of guilty at her targetless disgust. "I mean I thought he was sweet and all, then at least. But I said no."

"And that wasn't the end of the story."

"He wouldn't give up. It started with e-mails and phone calls, which I put up with more than I had to because, I don't know, I felt bad. He was so nice to me. But then he started following me around."

"I gathered as much. What'd he do?"

"Somehow he figured out where I hang out, where I work, where I live, and he'd drive by, show up, stalk." She grimaced. "There was this one time a few months ago, I was with this guy I met out, and we were walking around the Grove. I don't remember what it was but I said something and he got really mad and started yelling at me, calling me bad names. People were staring and I was about to start crying, and then Greg came out of nowhere."

"Did he knock him out?"

"No, he just put a hand on his shoulder and said, 'Hey, leave the girl alone.'"

"How very gallant."

"Well, the guy went away and I was thankful for a second. But then he asked if I was alright and put an arm around my shoulder and I felt icy as soon as he did that, because I thought, what was he doing here?"

"When did he start coming by the Red Palace?"

She bit down on her lip. "It's been a couple months."

"How did you deal with that?"

"It freaked me out when he first showed up, but it's not like it's a secret that I work there. I tried my best to treat him like any other customer. I drank with him, made conversation." For a second she looked like she might burst into tears. "But a few weeks ago he made a move on me. He said something like in the movies,

that he knew he would get me to love him, and then he just . . ."
She closed her eyes tight and pinched the skin above her nose,
like she was chasing away a migraine. "I had my mom throw
him out."

I felt a drop in my store of pity for the dead man with a strange
sense of relief. I put out my cigarette with a tight-wristed squash.
"This isn't going to make you feel better, but he died outside
your house."

She shuddered like her insides were yanking at her outsides.
"How did it happen?"

"I was hoping you could tell me. I can tell you he was probably strangled, but I don't know why. No guesses? Who knew
that he was stalking you?"

"It wasn't a secret, was the strange thing. He didn't seem to
think he had to hide it, and people at work teased me about it all
the time. They thought it was funny." She let out a sad, breathy
laugh that was mostly a sigh.

"What did Mr. Cook have to say about him?"

She paled. I pushed.

"Last night you said you weren't sleeping with him. I don't
believe you."

She was silent, staring at a ringed and laminated menu lying
on the table.

"Take your time. I'll get us some coffee." I pressed the service
button. A ponytailed and aproned waitress came and took my
order for two six-dollar coffees and, when I realized I hadn't had
dinner, a ham and cheese sandwich. I leaned back into my chair,
crossed every limb, and kept my eyes barnacled to Lori's nervous
head.

The coffee came dark and fuming in kitschy ceramic mugs.
She stayed motionless and I lit another cigarette. Smoke swirled

from its tip, steam rose from our coffee, and the air hung with the chatter of fellow patrons, noise so close and so irrelevant.

I nudged her shin with the bottom of my shoe. "Have some coffee. Are you drunk?"

She looked at me as if she'd forgotten I was there. "A little, but not too." She emptied two packets of Splenda and a full three-second stream of cream into her mug. She lapped at it suspiciously.

I was still smoking, watching, when the waitress brought my sandwich. I took a few thoughtless bites and turned back to Lori. "So what's the deal with you and Cook? Don't say 'nothing' 'cause I won't hear it. That clutch." I nodded at the Chanel where it rested on an arm of her chair. "Is that from him?"

Her features grew tight and for a moment I thought she was gearing up to shout. Instead, she let out a pained breath and said, "Why?"

I smirked. "Why? As in, why do I want to know?"

"I like you," she said, her voice high and quiet and bold. "But I've only known you since yesterday. Why do you get to know everything you want about me?"

She looked at me with shaky defiance and I stared back at her with all the heat my two eyes could bring. "Do I have to spell this out for you? A man was killed—"

"But I didn't kill him. I didn't do a thing to Greg Miller. If anything, *he* hurt *me*." She was expressive, and her tone carried the indignation of the falsely accused.

I leaned forward and bowed my head toward her. "Give me your hand," I said.

Her fingers were cold despite the coffee, and as they alit on the tender bump on my head, I felt them vivid against its rawness. I let go of her hand and she pulled it back slowly.

"What happened?"

I looked at her again and took a softer tone. "I'm in trouble, Lori, and you're the only person right now who can help me get out. Please."

Her shoulders dropped and her mouth quivered but she didn't speak.

I looked back at the clutch. "Is that from Cook?"

She pulled one arm across her chest, gripped her neck, and nodded—just the tiniest grade of a nod, but it was enough.

I felt no triumph, no vindication. Only the solid, dead weight of a suspicion confirmed. "Jesus. Luke was right."

Her eyes filled with terror. "What do you mean?"

I felt sorry for her. "Tell me something. When did you develop a taste for the son?"

She blushed and opened her mouth. "How did you know?"

"Were you trying to hide it?"

She nibbled a finger at the second knuckle and nodded.

"I guess you would have. I don't envy whatever you have going on with that family."

She sighed and took a swallow of her coffee, lifting the mug with both hands. She put it down and the strings that bound her lips fell with it.

"I don't know if I can explain my relationship with Mr. Cook. It isn't . . . romantic."

"Some men give you flowers, some go for luxury goods. I wouldn't knock either."

"No, that's not what I meant. I mean, it's very friendly."

"Lori, middle-aged married men don't have 'friendly' relationships with attractive young girls. Not if their wives can grow fingernails."

"I know. I know that, it's just—" She tilted her mug and looked without looking into its center. "I don't know."

"Does he hang out at the Red Palace?"

"No." But her eyes darted and she saw that I noticed. "He came once. He didn't know I would be there, but we started to get to know each other that night. We've been friends since then."

"Does he know Greg made himself a regular?"

She nodded. "He knows the bouncer who made him leave."

I sat up. "What do you mean he knows him? He put him there himself, to look after you, didn't he?"

"I don't think it's like that." She dragged a nail across the tablecloth, and her eyes followed the motion. "He told me he had a friend who could use the job, and I asked my mom if she could use him."

"This bouncer—is he a white guy, medium height, blondish, in his thirties?"

"How did you know?" She looked up and her eyes went wide. "What does he—"

"Is he there tonight?"

"He usually is, but I didn't see him."

"What's his name?"

"John."

"Last name?"

"Something with an *L*. I don't remember."

It was better than Humphrey Bogart.

I decided not to name a murderer to Lori just yet. "Why would Cook install someone to spy on you if you guys are just 'friendly'?"

She said with surrender, "It's complicated."

"I can help you simplify." I leaned forward and rested my chin on an easel of thumbs. "Are you guys having sex?"

She opened her mouth fast and let out a gasp that was the

beginning of a protest, but thought better of it. "I'd rather not get into it."

I didn't push the issue. It didn't seem to require pushing.

"How about Hector Lopez? Are you involved with him any?"

"Who?"

I fiddled with my iPhone until the screen showed my interlocutor in her heavy Japanese formalwear. I curled it across the table.

She leaned forward and crooked her neck to look at the screen before taking it in her fingers with sudden and startled recognition.

"Where did you get this?"

"What wouldn't surprise you?"

She blinked several times with muscular effort, slow and tense. "I'm not sure. It wasn't just this one, was it?"

"No."

"I don't know where you would've gotten them, or what they would have to do with anything. My mom took them to send to relatives in Korea."

The contours of a new twist hardened as I read the honest puzzlement in the echo of her voice, the ridge between her brows.

"So . . . your mom took pictures of you wearing a kimono to send to your relatives in Korea? Why?"

"I haven't been back to Korea since I was a baby, so she updates the family once in a while."

"With photo shoots?"

"News, pictures, sure, whatever."

"And how about the kimono? Where did you even get that thing?"

She bit down on her lower lip with the crooked tooth and a shade of apology. "It was a gift."

"So if your mom took these pictures for people who don't live in this country, how did the files end up in Greg Miller's office desk?"

Her lower lip gave a dry, stuttering tremble as she said, "I don't know. I've never—" she paused to verify in her head, "I've never even touched the files."

I remembered the flash drive, hidden away at Stokel, and I remembered that Hector Lopez of IT had gone missing. "Someone thought Greg might want them. He didn't find them. Someone gave them to him. You said everyone knew he was obsessed with you? Did you mean everyone?"

"It was well known."

"So all that had to happen was for one person to find them and give, or rather sell them to Greg. But they had to get found first."

Relief rippled her features as her cell phone sang something peppy and manic. She made a ceremony of extracting and answering her phone, fingers pointed and deliberate.

I gave my coffee some attention. It had lost every last hint of scorching heat, but I knocked it back bean-black. I looked at the remains of my sandwich but had no appetite. I kept one ear keyed in as Lori apologized to her mother. Her voice was drunker than she was, running sweet as plum wine in a dribbling stream of Konglish.

She shut her phone with a gentle click like she was turning it off in a movie theater. She gave me a mask of apology that lacked every shade of the requisite emotion. "I have to get back to the club. My mom is furious." She tapped her tongue to her tooth and played with the curls.

I smiled, indulgent as a grade-school teacher insisting on first-name basis. "All right, I'll walk you back. But don't get silly. This is just the beginning of a very long conversation."

I remembered that Luke had abandoned me in the middle of Koreatown and I called for a cab. I gave the company the address for the Red Palace.

I left a twenty-dollar bill on the table and Lori and I made our way back to the hostess club. I pulled two new cigarettes from the carton, shoved one in my face, and held the other out to Lori. "Smoke?" I asked through the side of my mouth. She waved hand and head in unison with coy earnest and I stuck the loner in the pocket of my shorts. "It's a nasty habit. You get yourself in enough trouble as it is."

Her voice came out high-pitched and gaspy. "Am I in trouble?"

"I don't know." I struck a match, lit up, and shook it out. "Is there anything you haven't told me?"

She shook her head with ingratiating vigor.

I thought about bringing up Albert's story about prostitution in the Red Palace. But there was no way to put that without losing her altogether, and I didn't put that much stock in the words of a slut-shamer.

"You haven't told me much." I gave her head a light muss. "I like you alright. I can't help it, you remind me of my sister."

I tried Luke again. His automated secretary didn't sound any happier to hear from me. I finished the Lucky with a peripheral view of Lori's moping brown head turned to the sidewalk.

When we reached the Red Palace, my cab was waiting.

"I'm sorry to drop this on you all at once," I said. "But you're right in the middle of something serious, whether you know it or not. I'm going to need your number."

She mumbled her phone number, and I noticed she was shaking. She curled her fingers around mine and locked them together with twitchy strength. "Are you safe?"

I smiled. "I sure hope so."

"Please be careful." She squeezed my hand and disappeared through the Palace doors.

I slid into the cab and asked for Rossmore and Beverly. The clock over the radio read 1:46 A.M. I slumped in one corner of the car and watched the light and dark of the city run by. I kept my mouth shut until we hit Rossmore, where I asked the driver to turn and directed him to my car on Lillian.

I drove to Park La Brea, as sober as I had ever been. I steeled myself against the dread of entering my home. I had to believe I could sleep in my bed, and I remembered I had a deadbolt I didn't always use, and good ears, and a decent set of kitchen knives. I pulled into the parking lot and drove through it slowly, but it gave nothing away. The elevator in the lobby was still broken and I took my time with the stairs. My studio was the right kind of quiet, and I bolted the door and grabbed the bat. I slipped out of my shoes and picked up my laptop on the way to bed.

I propped two pillows against the headboard and sank into them with a creak. I brought my knees up so my thighs made a cool bed for the computer and burrowed my feet under the covers. I checked my e-mail. Among the junk mail from various names selling various things was a whole lot of nothing from Luke and an e-mail from Jackie. It was time-stamped at 12:15 A.M. and asked, "Do you know where Diego is?"

I felt myself straighten, my shoulder blades pushing up on wood behind the pillows. I had enough to worry about with one rogue friend on the loose, and it would have taken a lot of worrying for Jackie to reach out to me. Diego unaccounted for and away from a fully charged cell phone with e-mail access after 8:00 P.M. was not quite as alarming as a confirmed terrorist attack, but it wasn't unworthy of the comparison. I tried his cell. It was becoming a night of courting voice mail. I sent three e-mails. The first was an angry inquiry to Luke as to his whereabouts. The second was a gentler missive to Diego, letting him know his wife was worried and that I would call him again later. The third was to the worried wife, declaring my utter uselessness. All three were signed with a bad taste hounding the back of my tongue.

I called Luke and Diego once more each, just to get it through my head that they weren't about to pick up. I tried Chaz again, with the same result. I googled a couple of gossip rags to subdue my brain waves, but it was no use, and all that was sordid just made me think of Lori's strange pictures. I closed the laptop and placed it on the other side of the bed. I thought about washing up, but suspected I was on a path that ended in slumber and felt disinclined to disturb it. I wormed out of my shorts, cuddled a pillow, and drifted. It was no steady raft, but somewhere it evened out and I slipped asleep like a stowaway on inky waters.

Eleven

My dreams were miasmic tarantulous things full of sticky voices and glinting teeth, but they dissolved in the morning sun without aftertaste. All things considered, my unconscious got off light. I hadn't moved more than an inch in my sleep.

My day lay before me, a balled-up tangle of delicate chains that I didn't know where to start yanking. I pushed down on the mattress with my shoulder and craned my neck to look at the clock. It was 9:40 A.M. and the sun poured through my window like it had been knocking impatiently for some time. I looked at the door. It was undisturbed.

I let my head fall back onto the pillow and let myself believe for just one second that I didn't have to get up to face this day. I filled my chest with hot air and sprang to postured attention. I slumped my way to the kitchenette and brewed myself a cup of drip strong enough to paint my nostrils black. It tasted like punishment and I took it like medicine, standing all the while over the counter. My head ached and a hand to a jellyfish scalp confirmed that it hadn't done a lot in the way of healing. I took a cup of yogurt and a triple dose of Advil for breakfast.

I brought my computer and my iPhone to the coffee table and sat forward on the couch. I set about evaluating my tasks.

I roused my laptop and refreshed the e-mail screen, and for a moment I felt a screaming gleam of hope flash behind my eyes. It lasted for the second it took me to scan the lonely, bolded newcomers in my in-box. Sunday morning meant even the vendors were shy in knocking, and the lack of response to any of my personal e-mails was unmitigated by the usual spam cushions.

I dialed Diego. I dialed Luke. I thought about dialing Chaz, but decided he could wait until I'd collected my friends.

I tried Jackie. After four long rings I heard the end of a quick and earnest inhalation followed by a voice that was tired, gasping, unfamiliar.

"Hi, who is this?"

"Jackie? It's Song. New number."

Silence pounded in my ear.

"Is something wrong?"

I thought I heard a hiccup from a hundred yards away.

"Where's Diego?"

And with that, the girdle came undone and she started to cry.

"Where is he?" I heard a voice that was barely mine.

"He—he—he—"

"Jackie, where is Diego?"

"He—he—he—"

"Dammit, Jackie, talk to me. Where is he?" The voice that wasn't mine was yelling. "Jackie, where are you? I'm coming."

"I'm at a police station." She sobbed like a woman on the verge of drowning. "Juniper, my husband is dead."

✦

I dropped the phone. It fell to the wood floor and made the sound of a tree falling in an empty forest. Jackie's wails were swallowed in the wormhole between me and the rest of the world.

I sat for a while, still and barely breathing. After some time, I stood and slunk into the shower and turned the water to scalding. I went through the routine—shampoo, conditioner, soap— with a drawn meticulousness like I was being watched and graded. I made the mistake of shaving and gave myself a savage nick at the kneecap. With the water beating down, the blood didn't have time to bead and it ran ruby and dilute down my leg. I stared at it and felt my cheeks tense and my eyes burn. In the confusion of running fluids and of the muddle of my mind, I couldn't count the tears but I cried.

I'd forgotten to draw the curtain and my floor was flooded but I didn't care. I patted myself dry with the wilted energy I might use to clean an overripe fruit. I threw on new underwear and a T-shirt and slumped back onto the couch. My eyes felt beat and my mouth felt dry. The silence sounded more like static than absence of noise.

Jackie was at the police station. Diego didn't die in his sleep. And the way things were going, I would've eaten my hat if he wasn't involved in whatever mess had sprouted around me since Friday night. I ground my teeth and sent Jackie a text: "What's the address, I'm coming."

I set the iPhone on the table and pushed myself up with all the strength in the heels of my hands, which didn't amount to much. I forgot for a moment whether I'd brushed my teeth, but a quick taste of my mouth answered that for me and I scrubbed the whole cavity short of bleeding. I felt my contacts like a thick film in my eyes and I doused them with a few drops of solution and a lot of hard blinks. I picked yesterday's shorts off the floor and put them on, then fastened a bra on under my baggy black V-neck. I was sitting on the couch, looking at my shoes, when the phone sang out with the notice of a new text.

She was at the LAPD headquarters downtown, at Second and Spring. I could make it there in twenty-five minutes. I texted her: "Don't move." I put on my flip-flops, grabbed what I needed, and flowed to my car quick and heavy as floodwater.

Sunday morning. Slim traffic. I turned the stereo on and my brain off. Third Street took me there smooth and undemanding as a conveyor belt.

The station stood eleven stories tall on the western border of Little Tokyo. Scant palm trees played nice in front, dwarfed by the station's height, darkened by its dark glass. I parked illegally, blinkers on.

It didn't take me long to find Jackie, and when I did, I wished I hadn't. She had never warmed to me but when she caught my image among the unfamiliar bustlers, suits, and deadbeats in the station, her features melted with the yield of cold ice hitting cold water, and I was her raft, her crutch, her best friend. She threw her arms around my neck and plunged her nose into my shoulder like she was searching for the scent of suffocation. Her sobs pulsed through me in currents. I put a hand in her hair with all the knightly reassurance I could gather.

"Can we go outside? I need air."

She nodded. When she lifted her head I felt the cotton of my T-shirt stick to my skin where she had left a puddle of tears.

We sat outside the station like a couple of lost kids. What I really needed was a cigarette, but I remembered the ultrasound, the last and only recipient of Diego's DNA, fatherless now.

"Have you seen him?" I asked.

She wheezed as she nodded.

"How did it happen?"

"Shot. Diego." She almost laughed, a limp flutter of irony shaking her lower lip. "Shot."

"What do you mean he was shot?"

"I don't know. He was shot. It's what they said." She was sobbing.

"Where? How?"

"They said he was downtown outside some abandoned warehouse. Skid Row, Juniper. And they said . . ." She sobbed again. "They said they found drugs in his pocket."

"Drugs? What, he was carrying a doggy bag of crack?"

She bit the inside of her lower lip and convulsed in the shape of a nod.

I stood up, anger smoking from my ears and eyes. "Jackie, you know Diego. This is bullshit."

She nodded again. "I know." It was the voice of a girl admonished, so soft it nearly squeaked. It made me feel pretty sore.

"Jackie, listen to me. Total bullshit. And not because I couldn't live with it if it were true. I could. But I know Diego. He treats the law like it birthed him, nursed him, and saved him from a burning building. So quit it with your questioning." I heard the acid in my voice and cut it out. "You know better than anyone how he is."

"I know, and you're right. I just—" She hiccupped. "It's just, why was he there? And why would he have drugs on him? I mean, these are facts. They need explaining."

"When did you hear from the police?"

"Just this morning."

"When did you last see him?"

"We were with my parents at the Grove. We ate dinner at the Cheesecake Factory and were walking around after. All of a sudden, he said he had to go. And he left. He just ran off. Then he didn't pick up his phone. All night. I didn't sleep. I was going to call the police this morning, but they called me first."

What did Marlowe do when he heard that Terry Lennox was dead? He mixed himself a mourning drink, lit himself a mourning cigarette, then started to ask questions. He was threatened, beaten, even incarcerated along the way, but he didn't rest until he knew what happened. I understood now, what that meant for Marlowe, where that drive came from. If a few threats from a glib psychopath were enough to restrain me yesterday, they were nothing now.

I stayed with Jackie until her parents came. When the Blumenthals showed up, I watched as she ran to her mother, and I bowed slightly in their direction before I took my leave and indulged in a cigarette. It wasn't my place.

And as the phrase crossed my mind, I asked myself, *Where is my place?* In a matter of hours, I had lost one of my best friends and misplaced the other. Nothing was right about the way Diego was found, and the gnawing hunch that it had something to do with this tangle made me so nauseous I was scared to breathe.

One loose strand of links peeked out from that thick ball of chains. I drove to 432 South Citrus to give it the best yank I could muster.

❦

It was just past noon when I got there. Lori's Jetta was parked on the street, flouting the conventional wisdom and law that demanded no more than eighteen inches between wheels and curb. The driveway was empty.

I parked on the street and hustled to the front door, where I rang the doorbell to the sound of a discount Christmas tune. Not a creature stirred, and a peek through translucent lace curtains showed no light.

I sat on the front curb and dialed Chaz. At the fading end of the sixth ring, I got through. When I heard his flabby voice, it felt like a small miracle.

"It's Song. Has anyone bothered you since last night?"

"Who's supposed to bother me?"

"Look, Chaz, I don't know where Hector is but I have a bad feeling about it. You should be careful."

There was a pause at the other end of the line. "I have a bad feeling too."

"Did you find something?"

He started to whisper. "I went into his computer. Really went in there."

It figured that Chaz Lindley was a hacker. These days, knowing his way around a computer was probably part of his job description. "And?"

"The guy has dirt on everyone at Stokel. You would not believe how much he dug up. He's got the seeds for a dozen divorces and ruined careers right there on his hard drive. These lawyers are morons." He snorted. "And they all watch porn at work. Weird shit, too."

I listened as I hoped against hope for Hector's life. "I think he may have blackmailed the wrong person."

He cursed under his breath, in a quiet, angry string. "Do you know?"

"No. But I'll keep in touch."

❦

I found Ross Macdonald's *Black Money* in my purse. Death and police meant more to me now than they had the day before, and I put it away after a couple of paragraphs. I smoked a cigarette, then another, trying to make that familiar act fill every corner of my consciousness. I thought about my health and my youth, I thought about the filter and the nicotine and how I'd always wanted to roll my own. I thought poundingly about Diego.

When the Lexus came up the driveway my iPhone said 1:14 P.M. I hadn't moved more than an elbow in over an hour.

The Lims slid out of the car and onto the sloping cement. The mother came out first, and this time I got a good look at her.

She looked much prettier without the thick, white makeup, and my quick glimpse of her profile in the car proved more accurate than the version I'd seen last night. She wore a fitted white blouse over fitted black slacks and closed-toe pumps in clean black leather. She cut a slim figure and looked to have at least a couple of inches in height on Lori, which made her almost average with heels. Her face was not young, but it was wrinkle-free and attractive, and it was impossible to pinpoint what it was that gave away her age. She wore her hair short, like many older Korean women, but it was stove black and unpermed, with the air that it might grow back into a commercial-ripe cascade if she only willed it.

She had Lori's little nose and full mouth, but her eyes held a fierce focus that her daughter's would never imitate. They glistened in the sun like dark stones under rippling water, and they were fixed on mine.

Lori walked with the molasses gait of a sunbathing seal. She wore a raspberry cap-sleeve cotton dress with a full skirt and

Peter Pan collar with tan ballet flats. Her bangs were curled in a dramatic puff across her forehead and her long, light hair bounced loose about her shoulders. It took a few seconds more for her to notice me, and then only because her mother had stopped and she bumped her nose on her shoulder blade. Her lower lip went slack and she said, "Juniper."

I stood with all the steadiness of a rumpled straw straightening to length without help. I slouched a limp bow toward the mother and greeted her in Korean.

She didn't move, but she responded in English. "Hello. I did not know you were a friend of Lori's. I hope you were not waiting long. We are just returning from church," It was a voice like stained-glass windows after dark. Perfect Ls, perfect Rs, stiff as rods. I remembered her broken accent from the night before—an act, then, for the English-speaking patron.

I nodded. "My name is Juniper. I need to talk to you both."

Mother Lim looked to her daughter, who stood so close behind her that their faces nearly collided with the turn of her shoulder. Lori stared at me with her lips parted and I realized that her haziness was never a product of alcohol alone. Her eyes, perfectly aligned as they were, lacked direction and clarity, as if some mischievous thing had taken a candle to her pupils and smudged the ashen remains about each iris.

She squeezed past her mother, tucking an arm toward herself to pass her by. When she was a couple feet away from me, she put out a hand and grazed my fingertips in an offering of empathy. "Are you okay?"

I felt the sore swelling of my tear canals and the taut dryness of the skin on my cheeks, showered and shrunken like poorly done laundry. I snapped back my hand at her touch without meaning

to, but she didn't seem to notice. "Yeah. I mean, could be worse."
I shook my head. "No, it couldn't be worse. Can I come in?"

I addressed Lori, but it was the older woman who answered.
There was no warmth in her tone, but she said, "Of course."
She stepped past me with a jingle of keys and opened the front
door.

It opened into an entrance-cum-living-room, with a couch
and an armchair in a black leather L on one end and a TV on the
other. The floor was light wood, and the shelves lining either side
of the doorway holding sundry footwear told me my varnish scuf-
flers were not welcome. I slipped them off my feet and tucked
them into an empty cubby, a practice amply familiar from my own
shoes-off upbringing.

I took a seat in the armchair without being asked and beck-
oned the Lims to take their seats on the couch. Under normal circumstances, it was no way for a twenty-six-year-old Korean girl to
behave, but I was in an ornery mood, to say the least. The mother
looked at me with a wary puzzlement that brought about the first
shadow of a wrinkle, just a ridge showing dark an inch northeast
of her right eyebrow.

"Would you like an apple?"

"No. Thank you."

The two of them sat on the couch. I brought my elbows to my
thighs and washed my face in my dry, upturned palms before
looking back up.

"Mrs. Lim, I'm guessing?"

"My name is Chung, actually. Yujin Chung. But yes, I am Lori's mother."

"Oh." I gave her a foot-eating look but she didn't seem offended. "I have to ask you about Greg Miller."

A rapid change came over her features, a darkening under her skin, calm and feral.

"The name sounds familiar."

We blinked at each other in silence until I told her what she probably already knew. "He worked with Lori until Friday. Friday he was murdered. Outside of your house. I have to say, I'd be very surprised if Lori hadn't mentioned this little anecdote to you between last night and this morning."

Yujin Chung put a hand to a stray lock of hair that dared fall over her ears and pushed it back with a reprimanding gesture. "That was his name, yes. Yes, okay, Lori told me. Most unfortunate. The man was not well."

I couldn't decide on the appropriate address for Lori's mother, so I looked directly at her as I spoke. "From what I understand, he was a regular customer at the Red Palace. He was there Friday night looking for your daughter. Just hours before he died."

"I wouldn't know anything about that. I was at home that night, waiting for Lori to come back from her party."

I remembered my mother's vigilance when I was younger, the background checks she'd run against parents of friends when I was invited to sleepovers. But Yujin Chung was shaping up to be the strangest overprotective mother I'd ever met. "I don't get it. You take off work to monitor your daughter, but you let her work in that seedy place? How's that fit?"

Her lip stiffened into a cold smile. "The Red Palace is a legitimate establishment and it puts Lori's best gifts to use. How is it that you presume to judge my decisions for my own child?"

I didn't shrink. "Greg Miller had pictures of Lori at his office. Pictures I think you took. To give to relatives."

At this Lori turned her head to her mother with a look of kittenish curiosity that turned over to surprise at what she saw. The head of Yujin Chung displayed the slow clouding of a bad omen in a crystal ball, stormy behind sturdy glass. She turned to Lori with a flash of something yellow gleaming behind inky eyes.

Yujin Chung looked back at me with her hands clasped, a primness that might've worn cute on a schoolgirl but that made me think of a villainous nun.

"What pictures are you referring to?"

"Lori done up like JonBenét Does Asia."

Her steady stare blinked blank.

"Sailor suits, kimonos, pigtails. I can show you. I have them."

She straightened her shoulders like some massive bird of prey posturing to spread its webbed wings. Then she relaxed, slumping with a sigh, looking wretched for a cigarette.

"I know the ones. It is a long story. Are you sure you would not like something to eat? I am going to make some tea."

I waved a hand with a floppy wrist.

"You know, you are very rude."

"I don't mean to be, but this has been one of the worst days of my life. You have a front-row seat."

"Well, I am going to make some tea, if I may be excused."

"It's your house."

She stood with such marked silence that I wondered whether the fabric of her slacks touched the couch cushions at all. As she walked to the kitchen, her feet stayed hidden in the slight flares of pooled polyester accustomed to draping over heels.

Lori gazed with crooked neck at a crisp copy of *The Economist* squared too perfectly in the middle of the coffee table. I kept my eyes on her. Her temples pulsed and she took in every letter written on that cover.

Yujin Chung returned with a plastic tray patterned with impressionistic flowers, heavy with three glasses and a ceramic plate holding cubed watermelon. She set it down in front of me, leaving a careful sliver of space between refreshment and magazine. I recognized the picture—the hospitality of the Korean mother, a pretty still-life I'd seen numerous times in my own home, in another era.

"Hyunmi-cha. My cousin sent it from Korea. Very good."

Thick, cracked half-moons of ice crowded vase-tall glasses filled with the cool amber tea. The sliced watermelon glistened, black seeds peering out like bright, wet, hungry eyes. She took a dwarf fork and stuck it into the grain of a large chunk and handed it to Lori. She took another and gave that to me, the fruit dripping juice into her cupped hand.

I took it with a quick thanks. My teeth made a satisfying scrape as they bit through sweet red flesh. It was phenomenal watermelon, the kind of stuff I'd ravish over a sink in the comfort of my home, cut up nicely for public consumption. I kept a stern face and discarded the slimy black seeds into a small, empty bowl she had brought out for that purpose. "You were saying, though, about the pictures."

"Juniper, right? Let me tell you a story." She took a long sip of tea. I nodded and Lori and I ate more of the fruit as she spoke.

"Lori and I, we are doing okay now. We are both working, and we can pay the bills. Her father is a selfish man who neither Lori nor I have seen in fifteen years. It has not always been easy for us. I wanted it to be easy, at least for my daughter.

"I came from Korea with my little brother when I was twelve and he was eight. My mother had come two years earlier to pave the way for our arrival, working hundred-hour weeks as a seamstress. By the time we saw her again, her hands were worn with scabs and blisters that never went away.

"My own father left us when I was just a little girl. I remember he liked beer and dried squid, and I remember the sound of him sucking his teeth after he ate. I do not remember much else about him. In any case, when our mother left, we stayed with her brother's family." She sipped at her tea.

"They were a family of five, with two girls and a boy. The boy was the oldest of us children, at thirteen, and the two girls were twins my age. My brother was just six at the time."

Lori's eyes grew half hooded like a stuck camera lens. She hadn't said a word since we entered the house.

"They were poor. We were poor, but they were not much better off. There were a lot of mouths in that house, and I have never forgotten how hungry I was in those days. I am grateful to my uncle. He took us in when we had nowhere else to go. But I was hungry in that house."

Lori slumped forward, her cheek on her mother's shoulder. Yujin Chung didn't miss a beat.

"We ate millet. Have you ever had millet?"

I shook my head. Slowly.

"Of course you have not had millet. You have rice. You know, I never had rice once the two years we were in that house. But my brother did. And my cousin. They were growing boys. You have it good here. Watermelon this red and this juicy, just for showing up at a friend's doorstep."

I remembered that, showing up. It felt like hours ago. I remembered, too, that I wanted to know—the pictures, what about them.

My lips fell apart to let words fall out. "Mrs. Lim, I don't get where is the point is where are you going, Mrs. Chung."

My tongue felt like a dead oyster in my mouth and my voice passed through the thick sieve of air around my ears like piano music smothered by a stuck pedal. A paralyzing exhaustion washed through my body, unsnapping every sinew, and I thought I felt myself go limp, though I couldn't be sure.

Twelve

It was different this time. I blinked slowly, eyelids creasing as they moved against their will. A gummy film of sleep caught on my lashes.

It was naïve of me to take Yujin's offerings and put them in my body. But then again, even Marlowe took drinks from strangers. Sometimes they put him out for a while.

My lenses focused on a man and a woman embracing in the rain. A poster for *The Notebook*. This was not my bedroom, and this was not my bed.

I lay still for a minute, not quite thinking, sloshed brain working its way through my surroundings with the boneless posture used for sorting out Magic Eyes. My head was on a pillow and I lifted it to note that I was lying on a white comforter dotted with orange five-petal flowers. The room was small and square with walls painted the sherbet tone of blended peaches. The bed was against one wall, opposite light wood dressers with surfaces like jewelry junkyards. To its left wall, a closed white door with a gold handle curved like a treble clef. To its right wall, a white bunching of lacy curtains layered heavily over a small square window, letting in the modest, honey rays of a waning summer day. A ceiling lamp hung overhead with lights off and slow fan whirring.

To my left lay Lori Lim, a Snow White and a dwarf in her own right.

I snapped my shoulders off the bed and noticed for the first time that my right arm hadn't been flung over my head by happenstance. Cold metal kissed my wrist and a tin clamor rang behind me. I twisted my head past my shoulder and saw where the handcuff clung to an aluminum headboard painted a cheap off-white to imitate something finer.

The prelude to a shout formed in my throat, but I thought better of it and whispered through nostrils and a gate of teeth, "You've got to be fucking kidding me."

I rolled over on my right side and landed knees to hard wood. I gave my wrist a halfhearted yank—the handcuffs looked about as pliant as an anvil. Pivoting around my wrist, I climbed back onto the bed, knees sinking slightly into the mattress, and regarded the little sleeping nymph.

She rested in a pose of perfect death, fingers locked snug on her slow-rising, slow-falling chest. With her tooth and her flat-Coke eyes tucked under lips and folds, she was pretty and unerotic as a poisoned princess. In one respect she was better off than I was—her wrists were free as the day she was born.

In other respects, my heart bottomed out with empathy for this poor girl. I knew what it was like to grow up without a father, and I knew, too, the agitated, compensatory watchfulness of the mother who remained. But my mother had never tranquilized me like some unruly beast.

"Hey." I poked her knobby shoulder, but she lay unruffled. I shook her with my free palm pressed against the peak of her clavicle, gently at first, then with the vigor of a washerwoman scrubbing at a creek. The bed frame gave a rusty moan and Lori came to life with confused languor.

I held a finger to my lips with a quick one-*h* "Sh."

She blinked at me, her eyes spending double the time closed that they did open.

"*The Notebook?*" I smiled, favoring my right cheek in an attempt to look winsome.

She scraped herself half upright with small-animal agility. The sheets rustled clean and starchy as they bunched under her elbows. She scanned the walls like a curious, anthropomorphized periscope before landing on me, her drugged and impotent Prince Charming. She blinked her way to the appearance of wakefulness with a rhythmic quickening.

"Hi," she said.

"Hi, Lori. This is your room, right?"

She nodded. "I love *The Notebook*."

"I think your mom might have knocked us out."

She nodded again. She was no longer looking at me.

"Why aren't you more surprised by this?"

She sighed. It was a voluminous sigh, noisy as it collected through her nostrils, noisy as it let out through limp, pouty, parted lips. "My mom . . ."

". . . Is crazy?"

"She means well. She only does things like this when she's trying to protect me."

"Well, that's all peaches for you, but I'm not her daughter." I blinked back at Lori. "Wait, does this happen often?"

"Sometimes."

"Why?"

I realized the moment I asked that there would be no good answer, and so I waited for the bad one. Lori gave her lower lip a long chew, revealing that wayward tooth, and then she gave me her eyes. "I'm not the smartest fish in the sea, you know? She does it for my own good."

"You're not a dog, Lori. You can make your own decisions."

"My mom—she made a lot of mistakes when she was my age. Younger, too. She used to run with some crazy *kkangpae* before she had me."

"Oh, so what, she *used* to be a criminal?"

She kept twisting her lips, worrying them with her teeth. "She isn't usually like this."

"You mean she doesn't usually drug perfect strangers? That is very criminal, you know that, right?"

"She's been more, I guess, unstable lately." Her voice grew quiet. "I think she met a man."

"A man like William Cook?"

"No, not Mr. Cook." She flushed. "I don't know who. But she's always influenced by the men she's with. She gets very dependent."

"So wait, you're trying to tell me that some dude's sweet loving got me in these handcuffs?" I jangled them against the bedpost. "Did you notice I'm in fucking handcuffs?" My attempt at an inside voice as I spit profanity resulted in a wheeze that in any other situation I would have found funny.

She curled her knees to her chest and pivoted on her tailbone to face me completely. The hem of her dress cascaded to her waist, revealing a shy patch of underwear, Bo Peep pink.

With nimble movements she bent forward, and snatched at the cuffs. She examined them with touching concentration and let them go with a soft clang. She fell back on her wrists and shot her legs out over the edge of the bed and walked over to her dresser, where she picked up a single long earring.

She came back and knelt on the bed. For around the eighth time since I'd met her, I marveled at how very tiny she was. She licked her jutting tooth and made a sucking noise as she straightened out the hook of the earring with the delicacy of a fisherman handling a worm.

"You can't pick handcuffs with that."

"I can try."

She lowered herself and lay propped diagonally across the bed. The cuffs rested at the corner of the mattress in a stiff loop about the bottom of the headboard. I watched the back of her curly head not without curiosity, not without a doubting but undeniable degree of hope. She fiddled with the earring, jamming it sideways, frontways, backways into the slot designed with a more specific key in mind. Her legs changed tracks toward the ceiling at the knees and she hooked her ankles and swayed them gently as she worked.

We were close enough on the bed that I felt her hesitate. Without looking at me, she asked, "Why were you crying?"

All at once, I was flooded with Diego's death, and I cursed Yujin's poison for its weak effects. I gasped, and my hands tensed in their chains.

Lori stopped working and looked up at me with her vague, sad eyes. For a moment, I let myself hate her, this quicksand girl who had started it all. If she had never been born, then Diego would have lived, and I savored the sweetness of this easy blame.

I glared at her. "Diego was murdered."

She dropped the earring and her eyes grew wide. "How—"

"I don't want to talk about it. Not with you."

I was aware that my tone was harsh, that it was unjust to place the weight of another death on her shoulders. When she cast her eyes down, I felt chastened. She picked up the earring and re-tackled the cuffs without a word.

I watched her hung head, its cloud of wavy hair fluffed with unsolicited sleep. I decided to change the subject. There was plenty to talk about. "If you were to guess, why are we here?"

She tinkered in silence for several seconds. "I wish I knew."

Her voice came up muffled, but somewhere around the second syllable of *wish* I heard the unmistakable hiccup of a snot globule obstructing the windpipe.

I sighed. For all my grief, I didn't want her to cry. "Hey. What's a robot's favorite food?"

She shook her head.

I cleared my throat and delivered the punch line in my best robotic voice. "BI-BIIIIM-BAP."

She nodded and let out two weak laughs, breathy *eh*s couched in sounds of sorrow.

"You know what they say." I sang the line of popular Korean wisdom passed down to me from my mother when I was a child. "If you laugh when you cry, you grow hair on your asshole."

We sat like that for several minutes, Lori sniffling and working at my freedom, me sitting useless and tired with the puzzle before and around me, a ten-thousand-piece jigsaw of endless black. We held that posture until the doorknob rattled.

Yujin Chung appeared in the sliver of the opening door. She seemed to hover there, watching and leaning without entering, for days.

When she came in I was relieved to see that she was wearing the same clothes as before. Over these was the suspicious covering of a styled black coat ending at midthigh. I dipped my head in a short bow. "Thank you for your hospitality. I'd like to get going now, if you don't mind."

She smirked in the way that all villains smirk when they no longer have identities to hide. And I the slippery hero with nothing to run with but my mouth.

She walked over to the bed, never losing the smile, a glassy hatred icing her eyes, and she delivered a smack to my right cheek so clean and musical it was its own soundtrack.

I brought my hand to my cheek. Yujin Chung shook out her wrist as if the effort had strained it. Lori's soft sniveling turned to steady, strangled sobs. Yujin Chung spoke first.

"Lori, be quiet. You are embarrassing me."

I glared at her with such force that I felt my eyeballs test their lidded walls and a twitching in my forehead where some nerve winced from the exertion.

"Before I let you out of those cuffs, I will advise you against doing anything unwise. We have an errand to run."

"Are you going to strangle Lori to death if I run away?"

She smiled bright as rigor mortis and opened her coat to reveal a cut-out pocket and a harsh-veined hand holding a short kitchen knife, gleaming a wet mercury silver from handle butt to tapered tip.

"We will walk outside together, holding hands."

She led the way, and her hand felt colder than the touch of death. Lori climbed after me into the backseat, and her mother waited until we had buckled in before taking the wheel. I sat, obedient, wondering whether Yujin Chung would throw the knife into my brainstem if I attempted to try my luck and tumble out of the moving car. The sticky smell of lemon air freshener tickled my sinuses with sharp fingernails, inflaming the headache holding congress around the soggy, swollen patch on my scalp.

Yujin drove at the speed limit. We wound down La Brea and rode the 10 west through the Sunday traffic loose as an un-cinched belt. We rode it until it narrowed into the ribbon of the Pacific Coast Highway by the ocean at Santa Monica and with a seasick smirk I knew where we were headed. For the rest of the climb up to the Cook mansion in the Palisades Highlands, I pre-dicted each turn with a lean of my neck.

A week after our beach trip, I left Iris at home and drove to Sher-man Oaks to see her molester. This time, Quinn answered the door. He looked different from the way I remembered him in high school, and I realized it was because he wasn't dressed like a teacher. He wore a plain black T-shirt and loose, faded blue jeans, and his feet were bare. His hair was shaggy and likely unwashed.

I froze up at the sight of him, with fear, disgust, and rage. No matter Iris's convictions that this man was a helpless Romeo, a pawn of the powers of love and fate, I knew what he really was—a pervert, as she had called him in jest, a child molester, a criminal.

Quinn gave me a long appraising look, and I wondered if he recognized me as Iris's sister. I had expected he would. I'd shown Diego pictures of Iris and our parents, and if Iris saw Quinn as her boyfriend, it was natural that she would talk about me.

He gave me an inscrutable smile. "Can I help you?" he asked.

I smiled back, though it was at least half sneer. "Let's talk, El-liot." I pushed past him through the doorway, my shoulder bump-ing his chest, and found my way to the living room. I took a seat on the couch.

He came in behind me with a scowl. "Hey, who do you think you are, barging into my house like that. I don't know you."

"Elliot." I leaned forward and crossed my legs. "Don't bother playing innocent. I have you in a corner, and you probably have a good guess as to who I am."

He studied my face from where he stood, and, to my pleasure, a stiff look of fearful recognition spread into his features. "What do you want from me?"

"I just came to tell you in person that you won't get away with raping my sister."

His face colored in splotches and in seconds it was a uniform Coke can red. He balled his fists and I could almost see smoke come out of his nostrils and ears. "Get out of my house. I don't have to listen to your lies."

"Lies? I would hope that you had the presence of mind at some point to look up the law on statutory rape. Because I have, and it doesn't concern me nearly as much." I bored my eyes into his and he stared back, unblinking with angry defiance. "How old are you, Elliot? Because it doesn't matter if she said yes. It doesn't even matter if she somehow convinced you she was eighteen—not that that one's likely, her being a junior and you being in a position to learn her date of birth if you were interested. Unless you're under twenty years old, you're a rapist before the law, sure as any."

"Get out of my house."

"You're missing a photo. Aren't you worried about where it went? Come on, just sit. I told you we needed to talk."

His body folded onto the other side of the couch in sharp right angles. "You? You were in my room?"

I nodded. "I was let in and it wasn't hard to find. You don't stock much in the way of literature, and *Lolita*? Must be Iris's idea of a joke, because I don't think you've ever read it, Humbert. You might've learned a thing or two."

His head was in his hands, bent forward with his face dipping toward the floor. "What do you want from me, Juniper?"

I smiled. I had won, and despite my hatred and anger and Iris's despair, the feeling was euphoric. "Nothing. You will pay for what you did to my sister. I'm going to make sure you regret it for the rest of your life."

"Listen, please. I love Iris. I never meant to hurt her."

"Wow. Did you come up with those lines all by yourself?"

"She loves me too. Listen, she flirted with me. I didn't just pursue her like some animal. We fell for each other." He swallowed. "But you're right. I regret it. I never should've laid a hand on her. There's something deeply wrong with me. When I was younger, I—"

I put my hand out in front of his face. "Stop. I'm not interested in your psychology. I know you're fucked up. You seduced a sixteen-year-old student. There was never a question of whether or not you have some kind of baggage. I don't care." I paused. "Was Bernadette Loo eighteen when you slept with her?"

He didn't look at me. "What?"

"You remember her. Couple years older than me, so, lucky for you, Iris wouldn't know her. I hope Bernadette turned out okay, but I'm angry with her. If she had gotten you fired and prosecuted like she should have, you would never have touched Iris. Which is why I have a responsibility, knowing what I know."

He sat up straight and gave me a pleading look. "She was eighteen. Look, I don't know what or how you heard about Bernie, but please do not say anything to Iris. It would only hurt her."

A cold tingle went up my spine and ended at the back of my head. I had no real proof on Bernadette, who I only knew by name, and the confirmation that Quinn's affair with Iris was not an isolated case born of a unique and burning love clung to my skin like a layer of sweat.

"No, it wouldn't only hurt her. It would hurt you. You want

her to see you as the love of her life, as some brooding, romantic older man. As long as she thinks she's special, she'll protect you to the grave." I stood up. "Well, I've done what I came here to do, and I'll see myself out. If I were you I'd resign while I still could."

I started to walk past him but he grabbed my arm. "Wait," he said. He was pale.

"Don't touch me, you fucking predator." I wrenched my arm from his grip and headed out the door.

The house came into view around the last curve, and Yujin Chung pulled into the entrance. She rolled down her window and slipped in the security code with thin-boned alacrity. Luke's birthday, naturally. The grand wooden gate opened and we rode patiently up into its yawning jaws.

The Cook mansion was smaller than the Buckingham Palace, but it might've given the White House a run for its mint. The driveway led up to a space large enough for a motorcade, cobbled with stones so smooth and shaven they were almost tile. Yujin stopped the car and the three of us walked to the front door. In another life, I had been a welcome visitor, armed with wine and high heels for this or that holiday soiree. Now the huge white doors themselves seemed to eye me with suspicion.

Not so much as an "It's me" came from Yujin's mouth before the door opened to reveal the big man himself, dressed in a clean green polo tucked into belted khakis pleated perfectly down the middle of each leg. He emanated musk from a fresh spritz of co-logne and his sandy cheeks glistened with aftershave. He'd been expecting us.

He smiled at me with good nature written across bright, bared teeth. "It's been too long, Song."

I wanted to smile back, just to show him I could. I couldn't. Not without shaking. "I might have borne it a bit longer."

"Still funny, I see."

"Not trying to be. You murdered one of my best friends, Mr. Cook. One of your son's best friends. And now you've gone and kidnapped the other."

His smile snapped shut faster than a Venus flytrap. "I had nothing to do with what happened to Diego, Song."

"We're going to have to have a long talk if you expect me to believe the first letter of that lie." I looked around the marble foyer and the four empty rooms it led into.

"Let's sit down."

The four of us shuffled into a parlor with lush couches between a fireplace and a seven-foot grand piano, expensive oriental rugs decorating the floor.

Cook led the way inside, where both Yujin and Lori waited prim as buttons for the man to take a seat before settling onto the couch cushions themselves. I sat on the piano bench some feet away and knuckled a couple of notes on the polished keys of the Schimmel. They rang round and dewy and golden in the chapped silence.

"I'm sorry we had to bring you here like this, Song."

"Me too. I'm going to smoke. Mind if I smoke?"

"Go ahead."

I made a show of patting myself down. "Actually, I don't have a cigarette. Could I get one from you? It looks like someone stole all my shit."

"Would you like a cigar?"

"Only if it's expensive."

He stood up with dignified leisure and retrieved a cigar from a cedar box on the mantel over the fireplace. His brown leather loafers looked new and they patted the floor with rhythm and secrecy as he walked back to me with the cigar in one hand. I took it from him and gave it a showy sniff. I didn't know the first thing about cigars. They were social currency for men like William Cook, and this would be the last I ever smoked. He cut the tip and lit it with a wood match before taking a seat on the empty cushion of the couch nearest to me.

I puffed at the fat tube of tobacco with squinted eyes and a stiff wrist. Its width splayed my smoker's grip to full V. I was almost certainly holding it wrong.

Yujin and Lori sat quietly on the couch. Yujin put a finger in Lori's spine and Lori straightened her shoulders.

"I've always liked you, Song. I'm sorry I had to bring you in like this. I'm glad to see you're taking it all rather well." His voice was smoother than usual, like he'd practiced each line before it left his head.

I didn't have that luxury. "Do I look that way to you? 'Cause I'm wretched and scared out of my mind."

"Of me?"

"Of you, of her." I pointed at Yujin Chung. My heart thumped in my ears. "Are you surprised? I've found a corpse, I've been threatened, I've been knocked unconscious twice in the past forty-eight hours. One of my best friends died in what can only have been a sloppy setup. And incidentally, your son is missing, though judging from your serenity, you know exactly where he is."

He looked at Yujin, holding his fingers in a loose lock between his knees. His eyebrows pushed well-fleshed wrinkles into his forehead, deep enough to hold lengthwise number 2 pencils. "Yujin, can you take Lori outside?"

She nodded and laced white fingers around Lori's browned wrist. She rose, then she rose, and daughter followed mother out the front door and into the dying heat of a dying Sunday afternoon.

I nodded toward the door. "Are they going on their merry way?"

"I doubt it. But in the meantime, it's just you and me, Song."

"Who's the audience?"

"I'm sure you have a thousand questions, but I have a few for you too."

"Can I assume that you have a better, let's say, macro understanding of the situation than I do?"

He hesitated.

"Come on, boss, or I'm going to assume everything else you say is a lie."

He smiled, teeth hooded by a sneering upper lip. "Yes, if you know very little."

"Well, I know very little."

He leaned back and crossed his arms, then leaned forward again. He ran a hand through his hair and let it come to rest on the back of his neck. His Adam's apple showed a swallow.

"Yujin mentioned that you came by certain photographs. Can you tell me how?"

I took another puff at the cigar and decided I'd had enough. "What should I do with this thing? It's an awful nice rug to scrub it out on."

He took the cigar from my fingers and left the room, returning so quickly that I had no time to take clever advantage of my seconds of privacy.

"So you were saying?"

"Before I answer that, why don't you tell me why those photos exist. I already know they were taken for you. Tell me why."

"Why do you assume they belong to me?"

"Don't insult me, Mr. Cook. We both know I wouldn't be here if they didn't."

He grimaced. "I don't have to answer to you."

"No, I guess not. You can let me think the worst of you, and believe me, I do."

"Look. I'm not some kind of pervert. I'm a family man."

"And Lori—she's the Soon-Yi to your Woody?"

"I took an interest in her. She needed someone to do that. I care about her a lot."

"Oh my God, so many snide things to say, I don't even know which one to go with."

"She means a lot to me. So what if I wanted pictures of someone I care about. Like I said, I don't answer to you."

"Fine. What about Luke?"

He reddened. "What about Luke?"

"You wanted to know where I found those pictures, which means you haven't gotten it from your son. I—or we, rather—found them in Greg Miller's office." I called up all the defiance in my reserves to look him in the eyes. "Know the name?"

He looked like he could use a smoke. He screwed his lower lip off center and sighed across it.

"He was a troubled young man, but I was sorry to hear of his death."

"Is this you disavowing the handiwork?"

"Do I look like a murderer to you?"

"Do I look like a naïf to you?"

"Why—"

"For a thousand reasons? He was a creep? He was stalking your girlfriend? And how about this one—he was a piece-of-shit first-year associate with the gumption to blackmail a named partner of Stokel, Levinson and Cook, L-L-fucking-P."

My voice quivered at the end as my chin wobbled and my volume increased. Mr. Cook looked hard at the ceiling, and I found crisp satisfaction in the observation that he was visibly stunned.

When he spoke, his voice had lost its studied gloss. "I didn't kill him."

"But I'm right, aren't I? He knew about you and Lori. I mean, of course he did. He was obsessed with her, after all. He must've made it his business to know who she went to bed with. And it must've killed—ha—it must've just murdered him when he found out it was you." I slapped my knee. I was feeling high. "And then he came by some pictures he must've known were destined for your personal spank bank. So how much?"

He hesitated, but not for too long. He spoke fast. "A lot. But do you really think I would've killed some cheap blackmailer? Even if he was getting a little expensive?"

"Add to that the fact that he was on Lori's lawn when he got dead, and I think we have a motive. I'd even venture that he wanted you to cut things off, that maybe an ultimatum was on the horizon."

"You're right." For the first time since I'd known him, his voice was out of his control, booming with misery. "He threatened to go to my wife."

The admission struck me silent for a few seconds, and before I could say a word, he continued.

Softly now, pleading and humbled: "You've known Luke for a long time. Do you know much about Erin?"

"I know some."

"I knew when I met her that she'd never make things easy for me. It's not like she was this put-together person who fell apart after I married her. I went in with my eyes open." He clasped his hands together. "I loved her so much, I just had to hope she'd get better."

I knew this much—she never did. I kept quiet.

"She tried to kill herself when Luke was a boy. Did you know that?"

I nodded.

"But I'll bet you don't know why."

"Luke said—" And then I remembered that Luke had never confronted his father about the alleged infidelity. "Why?"

"She thought I was having an affair. I wasn't. But she'd heard this and that and gathered her own evidence, and by the time she asked for my version, she'd already decided on hers. When I denied it, she took that as further proof of my treachery." He clutched at his heart. "What do you think she would've done if Greg Miller had gone to her with those pictures?"

I had never seen Cook act vulnerable, and in a basic human way I felt for him. Then I remembered why I'd come. I remembered the pictures, the presents, the suffocating force of the Red Palace. I remembered, too, that he was the same kind of man as the one who had raped my sister, plugged into the machinery that gave men license to possess the exotic woman. I remembered that in his pursuit of perversity, he had left men dead. I had no room to pity him. "People are dead because you couldn't keep your hands off that girl. You're a murderer, Mr. Cook."

And as I uttered the words, I saw him harden. When he spoke again, he no longer seemed to care what I thought of him. "I'm a murderer because you think I'm having an affair with Lori?"

"Are you denying the affair?"

He leaned back on the precious stitched fluff of cushions behind him and pushed both hands through his hair in quick succession.

"Well, I didn't murder anyone over it."

I felt a chill as I remembered Quinn's nervous manners, pro-claiming his good intentions and sincere apologies. I never thought I would hate Luke's father, but I knew that I did.

"Who's your friend John?"

He lifted his eyebrows as if to say, *John Who?*

"Blond, around yay high, dresses like a screen actor from the wrong decade. You made him a bouncer at the Red Palace to watch over your prized possession, remember?"

"How do I explain this?"

I waited.

"John is a very troubled young man." This appeared to be his euphemism of choice for *turbulent, dangerous,* and *insane.* "He used to work for me and we were fond of each other, but he was a little, well, unstable for law-firm work. So I took him on as a personal assistant."

"Someone who does your dirty work."

"The thing about John is that he takes liberties. He thinks he knows what I want before I ask, and he does things to please me that are not always pleasing."

"Are we talking about excessive dry cleaning or murder? Are you telling me that John took out Greg for a scratch behind the ears?"

"If that's how you want to put it, I can't say it's inaccurate." He perched his brow on the heel of one hand and rubbed both eyes, side to side. "He was only supposed to intimidate Greg. I knew Lori wouldn't be working Friday night—"

"You sent her to Luke's party."

"I suggested she go."

"And what, you knew Greg would show up at the Red Palace to stalk her?"

"As he has done every weekend for all these months."

"So you told your henchman to put the scare to him. Or maybe you were vague—maybe you told him to get Greg to leave you alone." I looked at him coldly and wanted to spit. "Your troubled sidekick. You were hoping he'd go that extra mile, solve all your problems."

"Greg Miller was a son of a bitch and I'm not sorry he's dead," he snapped. "But I had no intention of seeing him killed. Jesus Christ, Song, do I look like all my problems have been solved?"

I thought about bringing up Hector Lopez, but I had a feeling it wouldn't serve me well to mention a missing person whose identity Cook had no reason to believe I knew. "Well," I said.

"Well."

I swirled that around in my head for a while, and he let me do so in airtight silence. I cracked my knuckles and let the dry pops resonate in our ears.

"I'd say, what now? But when I met Greg Miller he was a bit cold to me. Diego, on the other hand—I may be obliged to avenge him. Was that John too?"

"I don't know what happened to Diego. I'm having a hard time figuring out what he has to do with this whole situation."

"I will eat every cushion on this couch if you're being straight with me."

"I hope you like the taste of down."

"Look, all I know is that Diego does not hang around Skid Row looking for trouble. He does not try to score crack for the first time in his life on the day that I find a dead body in my car. That was a clumsy setup."

"Don't forget that I also knew Diego. If I were planting illicit substances on him, I would not have chosen crack. The man was an attorney. Powder would have been more convincing."

"But then I would've known it was you."

"Are you operating under some delusion that Diego's killer was thinking of you, Juniper Song, overeducated bum and bored civilian, in orchestrating the scene of the crime?"

"It's not that I don't notice you insulting me, understand. I just don't have the energy to care."

"I'm telling the truth, in any case."

"I guess that's all I get, then."

We sat there like two people who've taken care of the check and missed the natural window to get up and leave.

"One more thing. Is Mother Dearest on your unofficial payroll?"

He stiffened. I had my answer, and it filled me with disgust.

"I had to wonder why your protégé hasn't put her on ice just yet. I guess that would probably piss off your girlfriend, huh? But the woman is crazy—you'd be doing Lori a favor. In any case, what happens now? I'd rather not leave in a box, if I can help it."

"I really need you to understand that I am not the villain in your little adventure."

"Stop talking to me as if I asked for any of this. I'm a reader, not a player. I find no pleasure in taking blows to the head, in being tailed and blackmailed, in losing people I love. There is not one painted fingernail of glamour to this entire enterprise."

"Then stop. Go home. Convince Yujin that you'll mind your own business, then follow through. Remember it was you who showed up at her doorstep with a bundle of questions."

"I can't do that, you know I can't do that. One of you psycho pieces of shit murdered the best person I've ever known. I wish I could believe you on this point, you know? It'd mean I didn't have anything to do with it either, but I'm not as blind as we wish I were."

"Then I can't help you."

"I didn't expect you to, but you're a fucking liar. Your crew of crazies would do whatever you asked them to. Now. Do I get a head start or am I riding home with your femme fatale?"

A shuffle of socks on tile and a cough that wasn't a cough announced my ticket out of the castle.

"Hey."

Luke stood at the entrance to the room in yesterday's jeans and a green T-shirt. He looked like shit, eyes scarred red and chin spotted with dark wheat stubble.

The piano bench made a loud squeaking sound that provided the sole soundtrack for the next several seconds. I jerked up, walked over to Luke, and wrapped my arms around his chest. He brought one hand to the back of my head and we stood still as his shirt pocket filled with whatever tears I had left.

"Dad, I'm taking Song home."

Thirteen

Marlowe never counted on anyone for rescue. Mona Mars saved his life in *The Big Sleep*—he hadn't expected her help and he fell half in love with her for it. Marlowe was a lone wolf, too dismayed with the world to make a lot of friends. It was only in *The Long Goodbye* that he ever found one, and that, like everything else, had ended in sadness.

Luke's car was parked in the massive garage between his dad's silver and black Ferraris. Cook didn't say a word and we turned on our heels with speed and silence. He didn't follow.

Yujin and Lori were standing in the driveway at attention, and as Luke's Porsche slipped by them with me in it, the older one flashed an expression of panic so pure and exquisite, I would've given her a gleaming smile or a straight-knuckled finger if I'd had the energy.

I was limp as a beanbag suspended in air and slashed down the belly, all of its insides dry and rattling on the floor.

The drive down the Highlands hummed with the retreat of

menace into the breathing of evening palms. The clock read 7:42. I hadn't been unconscious more than four hours, but if four hours is enough time to watch *Citizen Kane* twice, it's enough to sap plenty of joy out of one girl's leaking life.

"Luke."

"Uh-huh."

"I have a thousand and fucking fourteen things to ask you."

"Yeah."

"But not now. Take me home with you. Please."

He drove and I reclined my seat and curled up with my shoes off. I dreamed something foggy and stinking with cheap symbols. It evaporated when I woke up in Luke's garage to the approaching footsteps of my name.

"Song. Song. Song." It was a metered chant, soft, dry, and withered. "We're here."

And we were, back at the Marlowe, a turnstile at which some incompetent karma conductor had put me on the wrong train. For all my admiration, I never wanted to be Marlowe. He went around getting his heart broken every day, and I wanted none of it.

The elevator, etched with a giant, matte silver fleur-de-lis, pinged twice as it opened, pinged twice again as it dropped us off on the third floor, a brassy gong in an echoless hall.

He let us into his apartment and I walked to his bedroom door.

"I'm tired, Luke. Aren't you?"

He nodded.

I waved him into his room and labored under the covers with the slow, intuitive movements of the first person to happen upon a bed and know just like that to lie in it.

He followed like Adam, and we fell asleep chaste as children, dreaming of Diego and darkness and nothing at all.

✦

I woke up at midnight with Luke's arm across the side of my face. My eyes snapped open like eyes sometimes do in first scenes and moments loaded with premonition. I tossed the arm behind me and got out of bed. Luke snored with the gentle susurration of a fairy-tale princess. The bedroom door was open and I stole out into the living room, aching for a smoke. I canvassed the room before wakefulness caught me like a wet blanket and I remembered that Luke didn't smoke cigarettes. I wandered to the fridge. He had stocked well for the party, at least. I opened a cold beer.

The next thing I needed was something for the headache, that new tenant in my brain, the one that played loud music at every hour, subwoofer barking. I made my way to the bathroom and opened the medicine cabinet. Next to the Advil was a white-capped container of candy-clear orange plastic filled with small white pills. It had no label.

I torqued open the Advil, washed down four capsules with beer and steady eyes, and closed the cabinet door. I had no idea what was in Luke's medicine cabinet and it wasn't any of my business—his cell-phone history over the last twenty-four hours, on the other hand, might just qualify.

He'd fallen asleep in his jeans, on top of the covers. He lay on his left with his arms in front of him and one leg curled into his stomach. The light washing in past me from the living room showed the bulge of a wallet in his right rear pocket, flat fabric on the other. His phone would be in his front pocket.

His breathing stirred the quiet, its volume increasing as I walked over and sat by him on the bed in the indentation I had left minutes before. I took a long drink and studied his face. He smacked dry, sleepy lips and moved an extended hand across the covers until it found one of my folded knees.

"Wake up, Luke. I need to talk to you."

He groaned, a sound that turned from playful to mournful as waking up became waking to reality.

He stood up and switched on the light. When he came back, he sat with his legs crossed, elbows burrowed in knees, the heels of his hands supporting his eyes by their lids.

His voice rasped thick with sleep and sorrow. "Song, Diego—"

"Don't. It isn't real."

"Song, he—"

"No, I know, I'm not naïve. I'm not saying there's some conspiracy and he's actually not—but you know. It happened offstage and I'm still running on whatever fumes are left from when I knew he wasn't. So I won't accept a damn thing until I figure out how and why he was killed."

He slid his face in his hands and regarded me over tented fingertips.

"Okay." He nodded. "Okay."

"So." My foot was falling asleep. I stood up and put the beer down on Luke's desk. I stayed standing, looking down at him on the bed. "Where the fuck did you go last night? Do you have any idea how many times I called you?"

"I'm sorry." His apology hung in the ensuing silence like a single sheet on a long clothesline.

"You didn't answer."

"I know, I'm being an asshole."

"Luke, I need to know. I deserve to know. You left me alone on one of the worst days of my life. In a hostess club." I sighed.

"I was this close to snooping into your phone, but decided to be a good friend and give you a chance to tell me what's going on."

"Thank you?"

"You're welcome."

"I'm sorry I left you there."

I stared at him and felt anger stir inside me like the pointed end of a feather poking around my nerves. He looked at one or another blank spot of cotton on the rumpled blanket, his green eyes the dry dull matte of old Christmas lights. We sat in ear-searing silence for over a minute, searching for the exit.

"I went home. My dad texted me, said it was an emergency, and I went home."

"Why didn't you tell me? I was fucking scared, Luke."

"I don't know, what if you'd followed me? Look, I know there are bigger things going on than my Daddy issues—"

"I have never used that phrase."

"—But I had to talk to him alone. I wanted to give him a piece of my mind. I was so pissed off and confused, I just had to do something about it."

"Incidentally, I asked your dad point-blank if he was sleeping with Lori Lim."

He nodded.

"Like I said, incidentally."

He nodded again.

"So you confronted him? What about, exactly?"

"I mean, what not about?"

"He didn't seem to know you were with me when I found those pictures."

"I might have left out some things he could get on my case about."

"What did he tell you?"

"Not a whole lot."

I clenched my teeth. "Do not hold out on me, Luke. Don't even dare. Your dad is a criminal, and he would love it if I disappeared. Don't help him make that happen."

His eyes were moist and miserable. "I'm on your side, Song."

I sat back down on the bed. I had to believe him. I had no other choice. "Do you know John?"

He hesitated, and when he answered he looked past me. "Yes." It was a chastised *yes*.

"Did you know who he was when I told you he showed up at my apartment? Did you know he was the one who threatened my family, who broke into my home?"

"No, I didn't know." He sighed. "I mean, maybe some shadow of a shadow of a shadow? But I only saw it, you know, glimpsed it, like I didn't know until I really knew. You know?"

"No. I don't."

"Look, if I'd really realized who it was that was putting you in danger—Song, listen—of course I would've said something. I think at most something tugged inside my head, like one of those itches you can't get at because you don't know where it's coming from."

I leaned back and locked my arms around my knees.

"As it turns out, I can't really afford to put you in the doghouse just now. I'm not sure what would've happened to me if you hadn't shown up when you did."

"My dad wouldn't have hurt you."

"Maybe not with his own hands, but I didn't have a whole lot of say as to who was going to take me from his house and where I would be dropped off. The roads are dangerous, and many a ditch would love to have me, I'm sure."

He shuddered. It was a real shudder, shoulder to shoulder, the likes of which I had rarely seen rise to the description.

"So can I ask you—until this all, I don't know, blows over—can you stay in my sight?"

"You think—"

"I guess more, I'd like to stay in yours."

He grimaced and found a choice piece of blank wall to fix his gaze on. "Why's that?"

"Your dad dotes on you, and I'm assuming you'd never forgive him if he had my head transferred to any silver platters in your presence."

"Hah."

A tickle of neuron fire and I frowned at him. "Would you, then?"

"Never."

"He knows that. Stay with me."

"Okay."

We sat without speech, without eye contact, for several long minutes.

Luke broke the silence, his voice weighted and grainy. "What are we doing?"

"Well, let's start with John. Does John have a last name?"

"Lawson. You can google him if you want, but I don't think it'll get you anywhere."

"What's his deal?"

"He—" His shoulders rose and slumped like a marionette's. "He's crazy. You were right about that."

"Never doubted it."

"He's unpredictable, really a broken human being. But the one thing that's always been true is that he's—how do I put it—I guess he's obsessed with my dad."

"Like, sexually?"

"Oh, no. He just, well—John didn't have a father of his own, and somehow my dad became the closest he could get. He wants his approval. All the time. And he's pretty single-minded about it."

"And your dad puts up with it?"

"He doesn't really have a choice. And anyway, he has a soft spot for him."

"The male ego and its never-ending tolerance for worship."

He shrugged. "Sure, something like that."

"Well, I don't like John."

"You think I do? How do you think he feels about me?" He shook his head, looking suddenly and physically hurt. "He loves my dad. He fucking hates me. For being my father's son."

"You know, your dad isn't my favorite person right now either. Did you hear what we were talking about when you came in?"

He nodded.

"'I can't help you'? Give me a fucking break."

"I'm sorry."

"It isn't your fault. I'm sure this sucks for you too. I mean, being alive isn't that cool when your family is executing your friends."

My cheeks tingled as I remembered John's voice talking about Iris. This man was a murderer, and I had crossed the object of his deepest adoration. My head pounded, running worst-case scenarios drawn in blood.

"I need to use your phone."

He looked at me with clouds in his eyes.

"If I were going to search it, I would've done so while you were conked out. I need to call my mom."

"Of course." He pulled his phone out of his pocket and handed it to me.

I walked into the living room. It was 12:36 A.M., 2:36 in Texas. I dialed my mom. The phone rang brash and unheeded. I hung up on the answering machine's dull recital of digits and tried again. This time my mom's voice answered in a slurring "Hello?" caked with sleep.

"Oh, *umma*."

"Yoon-Kyung-ah." Her voice came alive with a sharp angry pitch. "Are you crazy? What time is it?"

"*Umma*, listen to me."

"What time is it? Is something wrong?"

"*Umma*, listen to me and trust every word I say."

She paused. "What's wrong?"

"There is a murderer who might be trying to kill me, and I'm afraid he might find you and do something."

"Yoon-Kyung-ah, what are you talking about?"

"Just get out of the house. Go stay with Uncle Min and don't let anyone else come near you."

"Song Yoon-Kyung. You—have you lost your—what time is it? Are you drunk?"

I groaned with a shrill crescendo. "I'm so sober it hurts. Have I ever done anything like this before?"

"Okay. Okay, I'll go."

"Thank you, please, now."

"But you have to—"

"I'll call and explain tomorrow. But please, hang up and go. Don't call ahead, just go."

I heard her start to cry, a bewildered, sniffling sound. "I don't know what this is, but be careful, daughter. I love you so much."

The day after my visit to Quinn, Iris told me she hated me for the first time since we were children. We fought for hours, both crying and sometimes screaming, our mom keeping a vigilant distance from her bedroom next door.

Quinn had called her after my visit, had showered her with the urgency of his love before launching into accusations of betrayal and lack of affection. He told her I was out to ruin him, and that she was turning a blind eye while it happened. He said I was turning him, her Elliot, into a pervert, and that by letting me have my way, she was rejecting him, nullifying all that they'd ever had. He knew just what to say to make Iris hate me.

I told her about Bernadette, said to her breaking face that she was not as special to Quinn as she had thought. He had not counted on my silence, and Iris spit back at me that he told her I'd say that. He'd confessed to her, abject and heartsick, that he'd had an affair with a student before he'd met her. She hated to share his history with another girl, but he assured her that she was different, special, that Bernadette had seduced him, while he and Iris had fallen in love as naturally as earth and sky. The more I insisted that Quinn was a sicko, an incorrigible predator of girls, the more she retreated from me and took his side. I had never dealt with anyone so irrational, and it was the first time that I came face-to-face with the destructive power of love.

So I did what I thought I had to do as a loving sister concerned for Iris and out for revenge. I told our mom everything.

It was a scene. Our mom cried and cursed and wondered how such a thing could happen. To her credit, she didn't give in to her anger with Iris. She fumed about the things she wanted to do to Quinn, and she held my sister like the teenage child she was, spilling tears for her heartbreak and the pain that she'd gone through without sharing the burden with her mother.

I insisted that we see Quinn fired from the school and that he be taken to court for molesting an underage girl. Iris was firmly against it, and when I appealed to our mom, I was surprised to learn that she agreed with my sister. She was delicate, but in the shadows and crooks between her words, I knew what she had on her mind. Reputation, disgrace, the Korean community. Iris was only sixteen, but her choices took her out of the locked world of mischievous teenagers and into the wider, thicker network of adulthood, where wrongs led to lawsuits, and lapsed discretion left permanent marks. If the affair was made public, it would follow her forever.

But one thing our mom could not do was keep Iris in that school. Our uncle and grandparents all lived in Houston, and over the next month our mom found a new job and arrangements were made. The Song family was moving to Texas, and Iris would enroll in a new school. Iris protested, but her efforts were wasted—her very objections led our mom to believe the move was necessary.

I didn't tell them about the picture or my resolve to make sure Quinn never taught again. I didn't have to go through the school—I was not above blackmail. Quinn would not be allowed to claim another victim.

Iris waited until I was back East. She called me one night and told me she loved me, and that she was sorry for what she had put me through on account of her stupidity. I was grateful, and I went to bed that night feeling like the nightmare was over.

In the morning I woke up in Diego's arms with a smile, and we made love without brushing our teeth. I went to class and turned off my cell phone. It was my favorite class, on American detective fiction, that genre I had always loved. As I listened to a lecture on Arthur Conan Doyle's acknowledged debt to Edgar Allen Poe and his man Dupin, I doodled a magnifying glass in the margins of my notebook.

After class I had lunch with Diego and Luke in our dining

hall, baked ziti with a lot of cheese and a stale piece of garlic bread. It was a warm day, and we wandered to the lawn by the library and lay out on the grass. We spent a couple of hours in idle conversation, and I mentioned my phone call with Iris. I was in a blissful mood. Diego played with my hair while I talked.

It was past four in the afternoon when I remembered to turn my phone back on and found a desperate voice mail from my uncle. I called him back with only the faintest sense of untargeted worry.

Our mom had found her that morning, hanging from a curtain rod by a long silk scarf, her body lying against cloth and wall. She had been dead for hours, and where her heels had damaged the thin material of the drapes, her feet dangled, toes pointed at the ground. My mother, in her grief and anger, spared me no detail, and she could never forget the scuffed curtains. She never let me forget them, either.

Iris left a short note saying she loved us and that she was sorry. That was all. There was nothing she could have said to save me, but what she did say was not enough.

I flew to Houston for the funeral—it was my first time in the state, a place that had no home or meaning to me or to Iris. It was my mom's decision to keep her there, and I didn't argue. She decided to stay on in Texas, where she had a new job and family nearby, and she wanted to make sure Iris always had fresh flowers.

She moved out of the two-bedroom apartment she'd rented with Iris. She couldn't bear the place, and she stayed with her parents until she bought a small condo for herself. But new building or not, I could never bring myself to look forward to visiting my mom in Texas. When I spent Thanksgivings and spring breaks at school or with Luke and Diego, my mom didn't protest. I loved her and didn't blame her for anything, but over the years I put distance between her life and mine. And she did the same. She rarely called, and where before she had always been interested in my grades, my future, my life, she no longer asked.

In a literal way, my life went on. I ate, and I slept, and in a mechanistic way I continued to function. My grades dropped—for the first time ever I saw Bs on my report card, even the occasional C. I took up cigarettes and I drank a lot, often alone. I had never been outgoing, but I lost interest in people almost completely.

It was in this hour, the longest of my life, that I turned back to my old friend Marlowe. I always loved Chandler, but as I read more and more books, I'd drifted away from the mystery genre. It seemed too shiny, fake and cardboard, with implausible plots and ciphers for people. But after Iris died, the bitter vision embedded in noir struck me as truer, barer, than anything I'd encountered before. For days at a time, I kept myself locked up with my books, eating granola bars when I had to in the dark warmth of my bed.

Diego and Luke dragged me out of the most abysmal stages of depression. They sat with me for hours, while I said nothing, did nothing, catatonic. I didn't talk about Iris, and they learned quickly that I wasn't waiting to be asked. But in their persistent support and ongoing vigil, I found a small salvation.

I broke up with Diego a few months later. We hadn't slept together since Iris's suicide, and the very notion of being in love started to feel disgusting and foreign. I remembered Iris's accusations, that I had become so absorbed in my own romance that I'd stopped listening to the outside world. I thought about what love had done to her. I spent the next eight years in the shallow end of the dating pool, without much desire to swim.

My life smoothed out over time, but Iris's death changed everything about it. I lost my ideals and ambitions, my teenage optimism. I graduated without issue, but with middling grades and unexciting prospects. When Diego studied for the LSAT, I studied with him. We both scored well, but when the time came to apply to law school, I found I lacked the motivation to go back to school and build a career.

Marlowe was a man without a past—no family, no childhood, nothing to his life but what happened in his books. But we the fleshed were nothing but crippled agents, moving forward with the merciless current of time, the burden of memory chained to our ankles, dragging us every day under the water. I would never escape my little sister, her silk noose, and I'd given up hope of finding anything else with enough weight to replace that episode as the defining moment of my life.

I'd been surviving and existing for years, but now, for the first time since Iris's death, I felt an awful, momentous sense of purpose. The same people who had in all likelihood murdered Diego were also responsible for drugging and exploiting a young girl. I found, with a sense of dread, that I cared.

I hung up the phone and went back to the bedroom, where Luke was sitting at the edge of the bed. "So, what now?" His voice was dead.

"Ideally, I'd like to save my ass. How do you feel about selling your dad's favorite psychopath to the cops?"

Luke stood up and paced diagonally across his room, like a slow-roaming Break Out ball glancing at angles off the walls.

I walked over to the empty bed and sat on its springy corner. "You don't like that idea."

He sat in his desk chair, a solid, vertical plop that barely provoked the wheels.

"It's okay. I didn't think it'd be that popular, just throwing it out there. Of course it would probably, you know, lower the chances that the police find me dead tomorrow, having apparently choked on some dangerous combination of chow mein and acupuncture needles." I patted his knee, dry and stiff-palmed.

He postured arms akimbo on his thighs. "Song, I don't really know what to say to that."

"I know. I said I was just throwing it out there."

We sat staring at each other's ears.

"I don't want you to think— Here, let's put it this way. If I weren't confident nothing would happen to you even without going to the cops, I would call right now. But I'm not going to let anyone so much as touch you, got it?"

"My hero." I clasped my hands together beside my cheek and swooned back on the bed.

"Can you trust me?" A warmth entered his voice like iodine spreading yellow, threadlike and fingered through water.

I looked up at the ceiling and stretched my arms straight toward the light in a pointed gun. I let them crumple and sat up again.

I thought about Luke, hiding in the shadows of his father's mansion; Luke, disappearing from my side without a whisper. I thought too of our years together, of the undeniable fact that he had just saved my life. But none of it mattered now in any practical sense. I knew I needed him. "What choice do I have?"

He bent forward and pulled me into a quiet hug. His eyes sat warm and motionless in the shelf of my right shoulder. I palmed the back of his head. His hair wanted washing.

It was just me and Luke now, and I knew that the two of us would have to see this thing through. We owed it to Diego, and without closure I would never make it out of the weekend. But Diego wasn't the only one on my mind. At the core of everything was a girl. The femme fatale. The one I wanted to save, and who might give me answers in return. There was only one thing that we could do next, that we had to do. I spoke into Luke's ear. "We have to go to Lori."

Fourteen

He didn't argue with me, didn't point out what happened to the last two people who loitered about 432 South Citrus, the first murdered in the street, the second a hunted woman going back for more trouble.

It was 1:24 A.M. when we left, and the streets were low-lit and sleepy, preparing for Monday morning. The Porsche tore through the quiet, a revving bullet, slippery, skimming the ground.

"So what are we going to do with her?"

"We're taking her from that house. And while we're at it, we're going to clarify a few things."

"What things?"

"I haven't written it out or anything, but I have a list. I figured we'd get her first, then go from there. I mean, I don't know, don't you have some questions?"

"I guess."

"Like—what's the deal with her and your dad? I kind of gather that they're like, you know, but how the hell did that happen?

And those pictures? Why didn't she know about them? Why is her mom in on the whole thing? I sense some twisted shit, Luke."

He nodded.

"Did you know your dad's been paying Lori's mom to keep quiet?"

"What?"

"Yeah. But it's fishy. I'd feel more comfortable if she at least acted hostile towards him. Like, if she were blackmailing him."

"What do you mean, 'if'?"

"I mean I don't get the sense that she is. She went straight to him when I showed up, and you should've seen how incredibly deferent she was in his presence. Like a goddamn courtesan."

"So?"

"So, I don't think she's blackmailing him. I think she's pimping her daughter."

"That's kind of sick, don't you think?"

"Absolutely. It doesn't make it impossible. The woman drugged Lori along with me, and it wasn't the first time she'd done it, either."

"In any case, what's the difference? Isn't that just another way of phrasing *blackmail*?"

"It's more friendly. I don't like the friendship."

We drove up to the corner of Fourth and Citrus and parked on Fourth by the Stop sign. We got out and rounded the corner on foot.

Lori's house was in the middle of the block, vaguely awash in dusty yellow light. The Lexus was perched up the driveway. The Jetta was parked on the street. My roving Volvo was nowhere in sight.

We whispered, windlike on a windless night.

"If I'm not back in fifteen minutes, ring the doorbell. It won't be ideal, but you are the crowned prince. You can at least get me out of there."

"This feels shady."

"And what world have you been living in all weekend?"

"Be careful."

I stared at him and crossed my arms.

"What, are you kidding me? You're helping. I don't have the hops to clear that fence alone. Not without making a lot of noise, anyway."

We walked up the driveway, past the nose of the gleaming Lexus. A wooden gate with peeling paint separated us from Lori's backyard. A quick, tight push satisfied us that it was locked. Luke made a platform of his palms and with that lift I climbed over the top of the gate, clutching at all possible supports, pushing my feet to the adjacent wall and belaying myself with the care of an amateur mountain climber down to the other side.

I stepped onto a mossy patch of garden growth trickling over concrete. The backyard was several shades darker than the front, and I waited, breathing with my mouth open wide, for my eyes to adjust to the cut light.

The yard was deeper than it was wide, fenced in by three walls running the perimeter in sallow bouclé plaster. Dark grass followed the wall by the fence in a narrow stream that overflowed its banks, and halfway into the yard fed into an undecorated expanse of lawn, kept glistening and inky by a rogue sprinkler swirling with lopsided rhythm under the moon. I walked to the border of the grass on plain concrete and turned to face the back of the house.

The view startled me, and it took a few moments for me to realize why. Except for the absence of warmth and light and the smoking of a brick chimney, the back of Lori's house looked just like the house every kindergartner learned to draw. Sloping roof, centered door, and two small, square windows peeking like unblinking eyes at the back-door visitor in the yard. Both lights were off.

I chose the one with the princess curtains, approached it on cat feet, and knocked. I rapped gently and took it on a slow crescendo, but Lori came to the window faster than I'd hoped, and pushed aside the curtains. She opened her cell phone and shone the faint light on my face. I pushed a finger to my lips with urgency and indicated her bedroom door with the other hand.

She looked back through the halo of light with wide eyes asking questions. I pointed a finger forward and then left, indicating the path from her bedroom to the front door of the house. I fanned out the fingers of my shushing hand to make a megaphone and mouthed, *Outside*, slow, wide, three times. She pointed at her heart and mouthed, *Me?*

A few more volleys of gestures and mouthed words and one final warning to hush and I watched her flit soft and easy to her door. I made my way back to the gate and went through it the old-fashioned way, with a latch and both feet on the ground. Luke was waiting on the other side, watching the front door open.

Lori appeared in a long, plain gray T-shirt that reached a few inches down her thighs. I couldn't tell if she was wearing shorts underneath. Her face was clean and pretty without a spot of makeup. She closed the front door behind her with a degree of care that shot me through with gratitude. We padded toward each other, Luke treading lawn behind me, and she bounded into me with her arms wrapped like an infant koala's around my neck. I stooped over, moved her hair aside, and whispered in her ear.

"You have to come with us."

I felt her breath move as if to say something, but she nodded instead, her head rolling against my chest.

We walked back around the corner to Luke's car. The house remained blissfully dark and quiet, and we kept our tongues stuck on Mute until we were well inside the Porsche with all doors locked. I installed Lori in the front seat and sat behind her.

Luke started the engine. "Where are we going?"

"Somewhere we can talk," I said. "Your car isn't ideal."

"My apartment?"

Lori was leaning forward in the seat, her head facing the empty street. "My mom will look for me soon," she said. "She's a light sleeper."

"Then we should avoid the Marlowe," I said. "I don't think she'll spend a lot of time guessing who took you, and she knows more or less where I went."

"Okay, then where?" Luke asked.

"Just drive. We'll figure something out."

Over the last two days, my life had taken an unlikely turn. I, Juniper Song, was a chased woman.

I couldn't say for sure, but my guess was that zebras didn't stop to graze with lions and hunters on their tails. But at one forty on this particular Monday morning, I found my stomach was pained and hollow. Bars and coffee shops were closing, and once I gave it some thought, I told Luke to take us to Canter's.

We pulled into a dreamboat parking spot in the neon glow of the green-and-yellow letters marking Canter's Restaurant Bakery

Delicatessen, Open All Night. The clean, consecutive thuds of shutting doors rang a percussive triplet clear and solo in the humming street. We went inside and a bored, pretty blonde just a shade too bland for the big screen gave Lori and her pajamas a once-over before leading us into the main dining room.

Canter's had the self-assured air of an institution, with black-and-white photos hanging like diplomas and accolades on beige walls. Light came filtered through kaleidoscopic colored glass fixtures in a grid on the ceiling. Cylindrical lamps hung at intervals about the room cast white light on nut-brown Formica, but the space was washed with the warm old yellow of nicotine stains and well-read books.

Even at two in the morning on what was technically a Monday, Canter's was at 90 percent capacity. I couldn't say what slice of Los Angeles made up the clientele, but it was generously cut, with patrons ranging in age, respectability, wealth, and sobriety. We passed a drunk, noisy table of three boys, the one quiet one sitting with curly head hung limp and hands stuffed into the marsupial pocket of a USC hoodie. I put them at twenty years old, sophomores or juniors, enjoying a nameless night in a summer of undifferentiated unemployment. The sentient two looked at us. One was Asian, likely Korean, with thick-rimmed plastic glasses and a beginner's scruff of a goatee. The other had solid charcoal eyebrows and an olive tint to his skin that made him ambiguously ethnic despite a long, pointed Anglo nose. Eyebrows nudged Goatee and waved to us as we walked by.

"Can we get that table, please?" I pointed to a booth in a deep corner pocket of the room. The waitress nodded with a swing of her hips. We sat on squeaking sepia leather and took our menus. I sat next to Luke on the inside, across from Lori.

"Order whatever you want. It's on Luke's dad."

She looked at Luke. He smiled with one side of his mouth and nodded.

"What're you guys getting?" she asked.

"I'm not really hungry." Luke shrugged.

I looked up from my menu and jutted my chin out at him. "You've got my life in your hands, and I know you didn't eat dinner. Have a fucking sandwich."

He flapped his menu, pulling it taut, plastic and nylon whooshing with the sound of sheets relieved of dust by strong arms.

"Fine. Do you just get to boss me around now?"

"I kind of think that's fair."

"The sins of the father?"

The waitress came back with a pad and a ballpoint pen. "Are you guys ready to order?" The shadow of a southern accent lay chastised under her measured speech.

As soon as she left our table, Eyebrows slid into the booth next to Lori.

"Mind if I sit here?" He addressed Lori but turned to Luke and me in afterthought.

"Your ass moves faster than your mouth," I said.

He cocked one gnarly eyebrow. It bristled with living energy.

He turned back to Lori. "So my friend over there, see the Chinese guy with the glasses?"

Goatee eyed our table through splayed fingers, like a moviegoer negotiating fascination and fear to the tune of building suspense.

Eyebrows turned to Lori and continued. "He thinks you're cute, but he's too much of a pussy to ask for your number." He said *pussy* with enough volume and length to cross the room. Goatee folded down the index and ring fingers of both hands.

Lori shot a glance at our side of the table then faced her suitor's proxy. "Oh. I don't know."

"Come on, just give it to him." He fished out a phone.

A corner of her mouth receded where she bit the inside of her lower lip. "I, I guess," she said.

She shot me an uncomfortable look and I interrupted. "I'm sorry, kid, but she has a boyfriend."

He glared at me with teeth locked together and lips flared in a comic snarl. "Hey. I wasn't talking to you, woman."

I looked at Luke and threw my hands up. He swallowed the beginnings of a laugh. When our eyes met, we saw the illusion of normalcy pooling with opportunistic hope in their tired corners and looked away.

Lori spoke up, measuring her words with the care of a pastry chef piping cream on her first day of work. "I'm sorry, but I do have a boyfriend. Tell your friend that he's very sweet." She stuck her tooth out at him with a crescent smile.

"That's too bad. I'll give you his number anyway. Do you have a pen hiding under that T-shirt?"

She shook her head. We were shaking ours before he even got around to looking.

Goatee shouted across the room, "Come back here, Greg."

I felt a tightening in my shoulders at the sound of that name, and I felt it in Luke, and I felt it in Lori. Greg shrugged. "Well, it was nice to meet you all." He stood up and rejoined his table, where Goatee was waiting with a closed fist.

"I don't have a boyfriend." Lori tied her lips together and looked from me to Luke. Her voice came fuzzy and quiet, like padded bunny slippers navigating a long hallway.

"Not in the traditional sense, anyway." Luke regarded her through dry, glassy eyes. "Do you give your number out to anyone who asks?" I'd known Luke long enough that I heard the sneer in his voice.

Lori didn't seem to pick it up. She nodded. "It's easier that way."

"It's easier until you get a stalker, and the stalker winds up dead outside your house."

Her eyes filled with hurt and pleading and sought the ketchup on the table. "I'm sorry."

"Don't be," I said, glaring at Luke. "What the fuck are you saying, Luke? That somehow it's Lori's fault that Greg was obsessed with her? That your dad's henchman killed him?"

"I didn't say that." His voice was sheepish, defensive. "But maybe if Lori didn't have men following her around like she was the Pied fucking Piper, none of this would've happened."

"Be very careful, Luke. That sounds a lot like, 'She was asking for it.'"

If there was one thing I could never like about noir, it was the story of the femme fatale. A woman could never be beautiful without a taint of evil. The men who fell for her were only victims, helpless sailors tempted by the siren's song, flies zapped by bright lights. Odysseus was a hero for plugging his ears with wax, and Marlowe showed his virtue by resisting seduction. Women were, in the end, traps to be avoided.

Our waitress came, bearing our food with the poise and silence of a mime. When she presented Lori's plate, she said, "And you had the cheesecake," as if she had been speaking all along. She retreated in long-legged strides.

I picked up my fork and knife and laid a napkin on my lap. "Don't listen to Luke. He's had a rough day too and he's being an asshole. But we do have to talk. Go ahead and eat, but when we're done eating, I have a lot of questions I need you to answer. We didn't kidnap you for kicks."

She gulped down a small bite of cheesecake. Her face said *I need milk* with more clarity and persuasion than any commercial I'd ever seen.

I set at my food like a starved lion attacking a plump and hapless martyr, with prejudice and marginal enjoyment. I took a long drink of water, put down my glass, and turned to Lori. "Look, we need to get some things straight. I don't know how much you've figured out, but I'm in something of a jam. I've been tossed and dragged around town all weekend and if you're not honest with me now I will flip out."

"Okay."

"I'll start easy. Where is my car?"

"It's at my uncle's shop."

I made a mental note to call Chaz. "Do you have the key?"

"No."

"My phone?"

"No."

"Your mom."

"Yes."

I paused and pushed my hands against the edge of the table. "Did you know your mom was getting money from Mr. Cook?"

She bit her lower lip, hard, and shook her head. "No."

"You didn't know until just now, when I told you."

She nodded.

"Do you know why?"

She shrugged and shifted in her seat.

"Come on, Lori. This is an easy one. And for the record, you lied to my face the other night. I think I deserve more than that."

She lifted her eyes to mine and they gazed wide and unfocused, the dark pupils shivering, so black they held the blue of night sky, the blue of deep ocean. "When did I lie?"

"About Mr. Cook. You told me you weren't sleeping together."

She shook her head about the pivot of her eyes. "I didn't lie."

"You mean—"

She nodded. "Mr. Cook is very kind to me, but that's all."

I felt Luke rustle in his seat. "Are you really telling me that you and Cook aren't sleeping together?"

She nodded.

"And you never have? Not even once?"

She turned a uniform, fiery red.

I looked at Luke and turned back to her. "Lori?"

"You're going to laugh at me."

"Try me. I could use a laugh."

She put a hand to her face and spoke quietly, her voice obstructed by her palm. "I'm saving myself. For my husband."

"What?" I cocked my head and looked at her bright red face through the tawny blinds of her spread fingers. "Really?"

She nodded again.

"I have to ask—why?"

"It's a religious thing, I guess."

I remembered her in her Sunday dress with the Peter Pan collar, coming back from church, just over twelve hours ago. "No judgment here, Lori, I'm just curious—are there a lot of virgins for Jesus working the Red Palace?"

Her face flushed darker still. "I'm not perfect. I know it's a weird job. But my mom is always there to watch me, and I just, I don't know, I guess I flirt, but I don't, like—"

She'd given herself all these excuses before, but they still fell clumsily from her tongue. "You don't sleep with your customers, then."

"Of course not." She was relieved to be interrupted, and to deny dishonor rather than defend her innocence.

"Your friend Albert seemed to think it was standard operating procedure."

She glowered at the sound of his name. "He's not my friend."

"I'm going to take a wild guess—he tried to sleep with you."

"Me and every other girl there."

"Well, that explains a lot." I shook my head. "Still, I can't believe you're a virgin. I mean, don't take that the wrong way—it's just, this whole thing started 'cause Luke told me you were sleeping with his dad. And somehow I'm the sluttiest one here." I looked at Luke. "Sluttiest girl, anyway. So if you and Cook aren't having an affair, can I ask what in Christ's sweet sacred name you are doing? 'Cause I will throw you to those undergrads if you try to tell me it's strictly professional."

She cleared her throat. "We have lunch every Saturday and dinner every Wednesday after work."

"So, what, all you do is grab meals together?"

"Sometimes if he has no one else to go with we watch movies. One time we went to the Getty. That was nice."

"Has he ever made a pass at you?"

"Never."

"You just go on these dates. Like a couple of regular normal healthy people."

"They're not dates, really. He's a lonely man and I keep him company."

Luke's fist hit the tabletop with a loud thud and a tinkle of disturbed silverware. "How would you know?"

She startled, and in a nervous pricked tone she asked, just to say something, "What?"

"How would you know that my dad—*my* dad—is a lonely

man?" He stood up without waiting for an answer. "I'll settle up. Meet me in the car."

Lori's lips started to form Luke's name and I touched her hand and said, "Let him go."

"I didn't mean to—" She sighed. "Is he okay?"

"Be realistic, Lori. Why would he be okay?"

"His dad never cheated."

"Maybe not in every sense of the word, but we're past that now anyway, aren't we." I watched Luke leave the diner, his back long and sullen. "So Cook confides in you, then."

She nodded. "I'm his friend. I mean it."

She did mean it, and I wondered how firmly she believed it. "When did this start?"

"I don't know. About a year ago?"

"Did you know your mom knew about it?"

"Of course. I don't hide things from her."

"Well, she doesn't extend you the same courtesy." I shook my head. "Why didn't you tell me this yesterday? You sure have been acting like you had something to hide."

"I'm not supposed to talk about it."

"Says who?"

"Mr. Cook. My mom," she said softly.

"Did Greg know you weren't sleeping together?"

She nodded. "He cornered me a few months ago and he kept asking and asking until I told him we weren't. I thought that would make him go away."

There was a moment of silence, unscripted and eerie, for the dead man. "Cook buys you things, doesn't he?"

She nodded.

"Nice things?"

She nodded.

"Did it ever occur to you why he might do that?"

"I've asked him before. He said he had enough money and that he wanted me to have nice things. I don't know, I used to feel weird about it but I guess at some point that stopped."

I scratched the back of my neck and squinted. "Did he ever ask you for anything? Like, oh, locks of hair or maybe pictures of yourself gussied up like a geisha?"

She reddened. "I didn't know those were for him."

"Lori, I think you need to have a long talk with your mother."

We sat in tight silence, grabbing for our glasses, taking slow gulps and looking about the room. After a while, Lori spoke up. "She isn't a monster, you know."

I decided not to point out what Yujin Chung had done to me that day. I could tell Lori wasn't done talking.

"My grandmother brought her to the States to give her a better life, but she couldn't follow through. She drank bleach and died when my mom was thirteen. My mom found her." She looked at me with a plea in her eyes. "You never forget something like that. It changes you."

I swallowed the thick dryness in my throat.

"And it wasn't just the trauma. She was a thirteen-year-old girl with a nine-year-old brother, no mother, no father, and she didn't speak English." Her voice welled with pity. "Please understand her. She's had it hard her whole life."

I was sorry for Yujin Chung, and I was sorry for Lori, but I kept my mouth shut. I didn't tell her I knew a couple good sob stories of my own; that I had a mother, too, who had been through the ruinous episodes of a hard damn life without emerging cruel and weaponized against the world.

We left the diner in clunky silence and found Luke waiting in the car as promised.

I got into the front seat and asked, "You okay, man?"

He nodded. "Fine. Where are we going?"

Before I could answer, Lori spoke from the backseat: "I can't go home."

"I know. Taking you back was never the plan." I didn't point out that her mom would be waiting with knives. I looked at Luke. "We can call Jackie."

✦

Luke handed me his phone with Jackie's number on the screen. I took it and put finger to touchscreen to call my ex's widow just a handful of minutes shy of 3:00 A.M.

She picked up after two rings. "Luke?"

"Hi, Jackie, it's Song."

"Goodness gracious, Juniper, it's almost three in the morning. Are you okay?" Her voice came through with the thin transparency of crinkling cellophane. It carried the weight of exhaustion and the tormented keenness brought by long, wakeful hours.

"Are you at home?"

"No, I'm at my parents' house. Why?"

"I need to ask you a favor. A pretty big one."

"What's going on?"

"It's a long story, and I hope to God it's in its last chapters, so look, at some point, soon, I hope, we'll you and me get a cup of coffee and I'll tell you the whole thing. But first, can I drop off a . . . well, a person, at your parents' house? She needs a place to stay."

"What? What person?"

"Her name's Lori, she works for Stokel. You'll hardly notice her. She's very small."

"I'm not even—"

"Jackie, please? I wouldn't be asking you now of all times if it weren't important. I'm in trouble, and she can't go home right now without me getting into more trouble." I hesitated. "I'm getting to the bottom of what happened to Diego. It's like swimming down a jar of mayonnaise, but I'm getting there, and I promise you'll be the first person I call when my nose hits the glass."

"Okay," she said too fast, with a tremble. "Okay."

"What's the address?"

"It's 2515 La Mesa Way. Santa Monica near Brentwood. Are you coming from the Ten?"

"We'll figure it out. We have GPS." I dictated the address and Luke plugged it in.

"The code to get in is 1492."

"Columbus sailed the ocean blue."

"Park on the street and buzz yourself in. Text me from outside and I'll meet you at the front door. I don't want to wake my parents."

Luke looked up from the GPS. "Tell her we'll be there in twenty."

"Did you hear that, Jackie?"

"Yeah. See you soon." She hung up without noise.

"Where are we going?" Lori asked.

"Jackie's Diego's wife. I would advise against talking to her about Diego or anything that might upset her. But she can babysit you overnight and I'll get back in touch with you in the morning."

We took Beverly past the Beverly Center and rode down Santa Monica Boulevard, through Century City, west, west, west. The street signs turned from blue and white to blue and white and striped with yellow, and soon enough we hit Twenty-sixth Street and hung a left. We turned onto La Mesa Way a few uphill yards past San Vicente and found 2515 on the right.

We parked on the street under a tall, leafy tree with a bifurcated trunk and muscular, sprawling roots. The Blumenthal house peeked out at us through a thick, bushy hedge that gleamed lush and licked in the dark. We followed the sidewalk to the gate and hit 1492. The gate buzzed and I grabbed the knob and pushed.

We walked into a front driveway four times the size of my apartment. A soft light turned on by the front door and pooled the view with a nectarine glow. This house was a house like the Louvre was a gallery and the *Mona Lisa* a painting. There was beauty in the Spanish architecture that murmured through the dim light, cut-out silhouettes and soft contours gasping out of shadow.

I borrowed Luke's phone and texted Jackie.

"I'm sorry for everything." Lori squeaked. She was crying, like a child lost for the first time, with hiccups and an open mouth.

I patted the top of her head. "Stop it, kid. You don't even know what you're apologizing for."

"Everything."

"No, you can't fault yourself for everything. You're at the eye of a rotten storm, but you aren't rotten, not as far as I can tell."

She looked up at Luke with swimming eyes puddling moonlight. "I'm sorry about your dad. I'm really, really sorry."

Luke looked back at her with a weary hardness and I couldn't tell if he was going to say a word, but Jackie came to the front door and thereby changed the subject.

The door opened by inches and Jackie came outside and closed it to a slim crack behind her. She stood ensconced in a man's shirt with light blue stripes that I recognized as Diego's. She was barefoot. Barefoot and pregnant, I remembered.

Luke walked over and wrapped her in a long hug. He mumbled something into her hair and she started to nod and cry. Jackie had never connected with Luke, and I suspected she saw him as an airhead and a waste of her husband's time. I thought back to that morning, when she clung to my chest and soaked my shirt. Each shared friend and each shared space and each shared moment must have touched the tap of her tear ducts and hurt her anew. The poor woman's face was gaunt and angled, blotched and red from the wet and dry of grief. Diego was my ex, my friend, but he was her husband and the father of her child. It might have been better to leave Lori in a basket on a stranger's doorstep than to bother this woman at this time.

It was too late for that. Jackie would take Diego's place in my confidence, if not tonight then sometime soon. She would heal the circle without expansion, and she could keep Lori safe. I looked up at the Blumenthal mansion and saw echoes of turrets and towers. Cook was a man of money. He knew its power, and he knew how to use it. But he was also a lawyer, and if I knew lawyers, he would be too cautious to reach wrist-deep into a place like the Blumenthals'.

Jackie's sobs dwindled to silent swells and she and Luke separated. "Sorry," she said.

"Don't apologize. It makes me a shitty person." I hugged her. "Thanks so much, Jackie. I didn't know where else to go. This is Lori. Lori, Jackie."

"Hi," Lori said with a small wave.

"Run away from home?" Jackie looked Lori up and down.

"Sort of." Lori spoke meekly and looked at me.

I coughed. "I needed to borrow her for a bit."

"Juniper." Jackie put a hand on my shoulder. "What sort of a mess have you gotten yourself into? Does it have to do with what happened to Diego? He was acting very preoccupied after you left, and then . . ." She trailed off and stared at me, wide-eyed. "Sorry. I didn't—don't, please."

I looked up at the stars, blinking hard. They whispered small comfort, bright dots of overwhelming significance speckling the infinite dark. I gripped at my shirt, fist full of fabric like some desperate patriot. "Don't apologize. I'm in a huge mess, just an unbelievable, like, I don't know what historical catastrophe I should be belittling with a comparison, but for me, it's along those lines. And I don't know, maybe Diego was standing too close to the edge of the whirlpool. I don't know, Jackie, I think it's really likely. You know I would never have put Diego in danger if I'd known better. I'm going to find out what happened, I promise. And if at the end of the day I have to come back with my own head on a spike, I'll do that for you. Hell, I'll do it for me."

There was a moment of quiet until Luke spoke. "When's the funeral, Jackie? What can I do to help?"

"We're still working that out. Ana and Jorge are flying in tomorrow."

"How did they take it?"

She smiled bitterly. "Darling, how do you think they're taking it?"

There was another silence, one that lacked tautness and energy. It was as if Jackie had been holding one end of a jump rope and Luke and I the other, and the three of us had been thwacking it rhythmically against the playground floor, loop after loop, until we noticed that the kid for whom the rope swooshed had moved to another part of the playground, leaving us with too much rope, too much slack. I almost forgot about Lori.

"Jackie, Luke and I have to get going. Thank you so much for taking Lori. If there's any way you can keep this whole thing quiet, at least for a couple days, I'd really appreciate it. I'm sorry I haven't been all that forthcoming so far but I'll fix that when I find some slower waters."

She nodded. "I'll watch her for now. Be safe, Juniper. Luke." She hugged us in turn, with real warmth in her skinny arms. I had been half prepared to have Jackie attack me and blame me for Diego's death. There was plenty of time left for that, but for now I was grateful.

"Lori." I mussed her hair. "Be good. Don't call your mother until you hear from me. And do not talk to Mr. Cook."

She stuck herself to me again, her arms in a circle around my lower back, her cheek spilling warm breath on my chest. I felt true affection for the girl, this tiny, unbroken reflection of Iris. She looked at Luke with her tooth biting down on a glistening lower lip, a plea in her eyebrows.

He bobbed his chin at her. "Good luck."

We exited through the iron gate and climbed back into the Porsche. It was 3:33 A.M. and we were not quite close to home.

Luke turned on the ignition. "I need to stop for gas."

"Perfect. I need cigarettes."

We stopped at the corner of San Vicente and Twenty-sixth at a 76 that charged a small fortune for every gallon. Luke walked into the station and put his gas, a lighter, and a pack of Lucky Strikes on his card. Spending Cook's money gave me petty satisfaction until

I remembered the cigarettes wouldn't cover a tenth of the tax on Lori's Chanel or on Yujin Chung's hush money.

I leaned against Luke's car while he filled it up with gas. "So what do you make of everything?"

"What do you make of everything?" He reflected the question back to me with varied inflection, an overrounded *you*, like a drama-class exercise.

I sighed and watched the numbers rolling on the pump. "I sort of believe Lori. I don't think she's sleeping with your dad. It fits, somehow. I mean, I think she's cut herself a lot of slack to keep herself feeling innocent, but I buy it. She likes church, she likes flirting, she likes attention. She let the attention go too far, but she ignored that line as long as there was nothing physical."

"I don't know." He put a hand to the pump and squeezed the trigger back and forth. The numbers stopped and started, stopped and started. "I don't know. I asked my dad pretty much pointblank. As did you, didn't you? I mean, wouldn't he have denied it if he were being faithful to my mom?"

He let the numbers climb steadily again and a minute later the pump let out a dry click. We got back in the car. As soon as we left the station, I lit a cigarette. It hit me like a blessing, a familiar warmth that spread from my lungs to my fingertips and the roots of my hair.

"Well, here's what we know. Miller was blackmailing your dad, and your dad was worried enough about what he had to send John to silence him."

"But if he wasn't sleeping with Lori, what was he afraid of?"

"Well, for one thing, he didn't seem to think your mom would believe him. But even if she did . . ." I closed my eyes and spoke automatically, like a medium for my own thoughts. "When you saw those pictures, Luke, I'm not sure you saw the same thing I did."

"The weird photo shoot? I saw it for what it was, and I didn't like it."

"I know. It was just that, a 'weird photo shoot.' But when I saw that picture of Lori decked out in that awful kimono, I felt, I don't know, sick."

"As did I."

"But I felt sick 'cause . . . I don't know, it was like, I felt exploited. Uprooted. Violated. And personally, too." I grasped for words. "There was—look, I tell you everything, pretty much, but there is something I've never told you. I only told one person, and, well, he's dead now."

He nodded, his eyes concerned.

"I know I don't talk about my sister a lot, and it's not because I don't think about her. It's just that in a lot of important ways, everything that happened with her feels so fresh it hurts to breathe on." I shut my eyes tight and felt their lids quiver. "But you know that Iris has been here since Friday, living her last months in my head, scene-by-scene."

He nodded again. "I'm sorry."

"But what I'm telling you is, I didn't put Iris's teacher to the wall without any proof." I wet my lips—they were parched. "She gave him a picture of herself, and I found it."

"Jesus," he said.

"That photo has some kind of power over me. I mean, I still have it, in a place where I will never see it by accident. I've thought about cutting it up, burning it, but it feels too important. Iris poured a lot of herself in there, and I'm not superstitious, but the thing seems too essential to my sister to destroy. I think about her taking that picture, thinking about Quinn and how much she loved him, and it just wears me down."

"Is it . . ." He trailed off and I knew what he was asking.

"It's not a naked photo, but it wasn't taken for public consumption, either. She was wearing a schoolgirl outfit, and you know Greenwood doesn't have uniforms. Her blouse was open a button or two too deep, and you could just see that she was wearing a black bra under the white blouse." I paused and thought about how to explain myself to my white male best friend. "When I first found it, I dropped it on the floor like it was something cursed. It made me feel inside out, just defenseless and even personally violated. But it wasn't the bra that got me. I didn't like that at all, of course, but you know what? People take naughty pictures. I mean, I sent bikini pictures to Diego the same summer, and Iris was more covered than that. It wasn't the skin, or even the lingerie. It was that costume."

"I think I get it. I mean, schoolgirl is weird. When that picture of Lori came up with her in uniform, it made me feel pretty gross, too."

"It's not the same for you. When I found that picture, it was like someone pulled a string somewhere in me, just yanked at it without warning, and I didn't know where it was coming from. I knew, in a vague way, what a fetish looked like, and Iris was dressed up to please a pervert. She was so young, and she was putting herself on display as this Asian-schoolgirl archetype. It made me feel sick, as her sister, of course, but I felt like it reached and grabbed on to the Asian girl in me, too." I swallowed the drying saliva in my mouth. "But my point is, when I saw Lori's pictures, I got that same messed-in-the-organs feeling, groped and undressed by proxy, and unable to defend myself because the attack was on the inside."

"What are you saying?"

"I'm saying that maybe I could've handled them sleeping together—creepy, but at least this time it would've involved two consenting adults. Affairs happen every day without anyone getting killed. Maybe this whole freak-show charade is worse. And maybe your dad feels the same way."

"I disagree."

"I know, but think of it this way. An office affair? That can be described and condemned with a choice word or two. What Lori told us about? That's harder to sort. It's the kind of thing that you can't dismiss because you keep trying to make it look one way or another. Eventually all you can know for sure is that it's twisted."

"Sure, it's hard to classify, but how could that be worse than cheating?"

"Do you know how many married sleazeball lawyers fuck secretaries and HR girls? Your dad sleeping with Lori would've been a pretty standard story. Sure, people might have talked about it, but it would've fit. It wouldn't have fucked with their perception of the universe and they would've forgotten about it, confused him with another lawyer, whatever. But not this. This would stick. It would ruin him."

We were slipping down Beverly now, cutting the miles back to the Marlowe like so much silk ribbon. I watched Luke drive, looking straight ahead, but the corners of his eyes told me they felt mine.

"It bothered him enough that Greg Miller was a major problem. Blackmail only works when the target has a secret worth keeping. What Greg had was explosive enough to take out his family and his career in the click of a mouse." I swallowed again. "And I'm worried about Hector. He was collecting dirt—Chaz found it on his computer, and there was plenty of it. He may not have had the gumption to go after the boss directly, but if I'm right, he got a piece of the punishment just the same."

We took the road in seasick silence. Luke's Adam's apple

quivered now and then like a shy student raising a hand to just below the desktop.

He piped up, his voice uncertain: "But where does Diego come in?"

"I don't know. I don't think we have all the info we need. I'm terrified we never will."

"I don't feel like talking anymore. Can we stop?"

I heard the pleading note in his voice. "Okay."

We parked in the Marlowe garage and rode the elevator yet once more to the third floor. Luke keyed us in and flipped on the light as we took off our shoes.

Then there was a sound I'd never heard before. It was dry and metallic and decisive.

"Hello, children." John smiled as he pointed the barrel at Luke.

Fifteen

He was sitting with an ankle resting on the opposite knee, loafered foot rotating slow and smug as a rotisserie chicken. His suit was a coffee-nut brown, lightweight but wrinkle-free, newborn. The shirt underneath was beige linen, the necktie rouge textured silk. One hand cuddled a felt fedora on the table, but his hair held the same stiff crest as the other day. It was past four in the morning.

The other hand held a handgun. Marlowe would've identified the make and model, but all I knew about handguns was that they could kill. This one was small, probably five, six, seven inches long. It was jet black from nose to tail, hard and without luster. It took the humor out of his old-time costume.

I was about to comment on our reunion when Luke stepped toward him. "How did you get in?"

He reached into his breast pocket with his unarmed hand and withdrew a set of keys. He tossed it to Luke, underhand. "Like a civilized man."

His face was calm and, despite a jovial tone of voice, utterly lightless. I couldn't see Luke's face, but the back of his head was expressive enough. "Why are you here?"

"Look, Luke. The girl's mom called your pop. Your pop called me. So I came. See?" He gestured with one hand, wrist turning, explaining, reasoning. The other held the gun steady.

"You can't hurt Song. You can't do it."

"Son, you have to see it from your father's perspective. He doesn't want to hurt her, and he even told me to stay away, he really did. But he can't very well have her stealing Lori from her bed in the middle of the night, can he? Everyone is very worried."

"I won't let you." His voice came out choked and shaking and I saw the wobble in the backs of his knees.

"Careful, junior. I may not have the okay to kill you, but your father will forgive me if I take out a knee."

"I'll go to the cops."

"Your father has chosen to take that gamble. The stakes make one a bit hot around the collar if you ask me, but your friend seems to have made things difficult. And besides, what's one more secret among family?"

Luke was shaking all over now, a volcano on the verge. "I'll fucking kill you, don't think I won't."

I touched the narrow part of my hand to Luke's shoulder in a light karate chop. "I didn't think your dad would let you see me die, but I must have miscalculated."

His shoulder tensed. "Nothing is going to happen here."

"Look. If he's going to kill me anyway, there's no sense in you being heroic. There's no one to impress here. Anyway, he has a gun. I'd say that narrows down your options."

I turned to John. I felt suddenly drunk, like I was experienc-

ing the scene through layers, like Tom Sawyer watching his funeral, all truth and all farce. I knew there was real fear somewhere,
but it was on ice, dredged in alcohol or morphine, to be dealt
with later. The man with the gun was just a character in a play,
and I was standing stage right, remembering my lines. "Well, hi
again. What do I do?"

"I'm going to need Luke's phone."

Luke took his phone out of his pocket and approached the
table. As Luke took slow steps across the carpet, John moved the
gun just a few degrees to the right. It was only a couple of inches,
and his hand moved steadily, with aching, deliberate speed. But
even in those few moments, the intention was clear. As Luke
moved closer, the gun moved from his face to mine.

At the same time, John's expression shifted. The change was
quick but unmistakable, like a last gesture seen through the shrink-
ing screen of closing elevator doors. A tightness came over his
features, a tightness and a wild mirth. One corner of his mouth
lifted, then the other, and the lip in the middle leaned toward his
nose like a flower to the sun.

Luke snatched for the gun, but John was too fast. He snapped
to his feet and as Luke reached him he grabbed his wrist and
twisted him backward. I had seen that move before, in a women's
self-defense seminar somewhere. Now Luke was facing me and
his eyes were wide and bright. Then the hard sound of metal
on bone, and they went half shut, like the rocker eyes of a por-
celain doll. He folded forward, an empty shirt sloughing off its
hanger.

"Tsk-tsk." John shook his head. I watched as he gathered all
seventy-four inches of Luke's body in his arm as if Luke were the
diminutive Christ in Michelangelo's *Pieta*. He placed him on the
couch, on his back with one arm dangling over the edge and

bent where the wrist kissed the floor. As he did so, he knelt, and he stayed for a long minute on his knees.

I watched him in profile, staring at Luke lying there unconscious. He was still shaking his head, heavily, like the pendulum of a very large clock. He lifted one hand and moved it toward Luke's face and I felt myself go stiff, but he only brushed the blond hair off his forehead.

He got to his feet and picked up the phone where it lay on the floor. He looked at it with interest before dropping it into a jacket pocket.

When our eyes met, he seemed almost startled to see me. He straightened his tie and the dark glinting green of his eyes went smooth, like the sea unwrinkling at the end of a storm.

"He'll wake up soon enough. Though I suppose you'd know better than I would."

"We're not taking him to the local chicken joint?"

He picked up his hat and held it to his chest. "He'll stay home. Now, Miss Song, if you would please come with me."

There was nothing else to do. I followed him into the garage. He'd parked and walked in just like any of the residents.

I pulled a Lucky out of my back pocket and lit it. I breathed it in and tried to taste every strand of flavor. I cherished the harsh orange glow of the embering tip.

Survival had never been such an urgent and difficult project. Marlowe could get out of a situation like this. Marlowe had a gun, the experience to use it, and physical prowess to boot.

I thought about it—the big sleep. It wasn't the first time, but it had more shape and more promise than it ever had before. Rimless, dark, silent, like the spaces between stars, shorter than staples from the ground, longer than planets once you left Earth. Maybe it wasn't so bad. I pictured the scene of Diego's funeral, Jackie sobbing, clutching her womb, hating me, blaming me— and I remembered, too, without context, struggling, drunk, with the buckle of a shoe, when Diego bent down and undid it for me. If there was ever a time to punch out early, it might just be right now.

On the other hand, if I were to choose a last face to see before dying, John's was only preferable to Freddy Krueger's because I preferred his bone structure.

"You're really going to kill me this time, aren't you."

"That depends, Miss Song. It won't hurt you to do as I say. For instance, don't try to run away from me."

"Do you see me trying?"

"Wonderful. Now." He produced a familiar car key.

There was my Volvo, smiling at me, and for a moment I felt true affection for my prodigal machine. "My car." My lips spilled the words like dribble, chewed, watery, and discolored, dumb.

"Your car." He nodded and pulled a pair of handcuffs out of his breast pocket, a clean, cold pair of metal jaws. "And when you're done with that cigarette, which you'll note I haven't begrudged you, I'm going to ask you to loan me your wrists."

"Do they just let anyone buy these fucking things?"

He smiled.

I shimmied a spare Lucky out of the pack and handed it to him, mouth-side forward. "Do you smoke?"

He took it between two fingers. His nails were clipped short and square but the cuticles were bitten and red. "That's friendly of you, Miss Song."

"What's my angle?" I flipped on the lighter and he took it from me without disturbing the flame.

"Something like that."

"I'm curious."

He nodded and let out a spiral of smoke.

"I don't think you have a damn thing against me, not personally. What's in this for you?"

He frowned. There was something genuine in the brownness of this expression, a sudden shadow, even surprise. "I realize you think you're in the right here, but you've been a great source of stress to Bill, which makes it personal. For me."

"Why? Because he's your boss? Because he lets you run around in your get-ups wreaking havoc with his money?"

"I don't—" He peered at me with curiosity, like one might stare at a "spot the difference" exercise. The affect was exaggerated, with a tilt in the neck and stress in the brow, but it struck me as more pure and less theatrical than everything else about him. He dropped his shoulders. "Bill is my brother."

I slurped smoke down the wrong tube and coughed. My throat felt thick and slathered with grit, and it spit out with a hacking, cacophonous sound.

"William Cook? Luke's dad?"

He nodded, slowly.

"So Luke is—"

"My nephew, yes."

"And he knows this?" I regretted the words as soon as they left my mouth.

He laughed, short and humorless. "Of course he knows. Why wouldn't he know?"

"Because—" I was about to say, *Because he didn't tell me.* The logic didn't hold.

"I'm surprised he didn't tell you."

"*You're* surprised?"

"No." He shook his head, big swoops like a child. His hair didn't move. "No, I suppose I'm not."

"No one told me. Not Luke, not his dad. You're his brother by blood? How old are you?"

He took a greedy drag at his cigarette and gleeked out the smoke through closed teeth. "Thirty-nine. Forty this year."

"And Cook is fifty-five? Fifty-six?"

"Fifty-four."

"So you're closer in age to Luke than you are to your brother." Luke said John hated him. There was, then, a breed of sibling rivalry. "Same father?"

"Same father. Different mother."

"Right. Of course. What's the story?"

"Bill is a good person, Miss Song. He didn't know about me until I was thirteen years old. My mother drank herself to death. It was just the two of us, and then it was just the one of me. I found my father. He didn't care—but Bill did."

Against my will, I felt his words pierce my sympathies. "And then what, he took you in?"

"He wanted to. Erin said no. They were married just a year or two, and she was pregnant."

It was no wonder he resented the privileged son, born guilty to his father's love. "Where's the happy ending?"

"Bill looked out for me. Took an interest, is the word. I went to college because of Bill. He found me my first apartment. He gave me my first job."

"I heard about that. I also heard you were fired."

He tugged at the hem of his jacket. "It wasn't Bill's fault. And it didn't matter. I only work for him now, and that's okay."

"He called you troubled. A troubled young man. Like you were someone unfortunate. Unfortunate to someone else."

He sighed and fixed me with a smile that was downright magnanimous, like that of an adult too tired to indulge a child. "Well, that's enough chitchat, Miss Song. If you think you're going to ruffle my feathers and run away, you'll find I'm less stupid than I am troubled. Now are you about done with your cigarette? I'm afraid I rushed through mine."

He dropped the stub to the concrete and crushed it out with a quiet turn of the heel. I took in the last length of cigarette with the bitter love of a last kiss and followed suit.

He took my right hand in his and held it between us. His palm was warm and dry. He looked straight into my eyes. I saw the green-black eyes, and now they were familiar, a dark-forest version of a pair I knew so well: lush, wet vibrancy crossed with branches and spiderwebs, wide, trembling pupils caught like flies.

I didn't like any of it. I looked away.

Still holding my hand, he arced around me and stood just short of a foot from my back. With the solemnity of a prom date, he looped my wrists in the cuffs. I heard the grind of metal and felt it cool against my skin. I thought I might cry.

He took me by the shoulder and led me to the passenger side of my car. He opened the door. He even buckled my seat belt.

He walked away from my car, and for one stupid second, I thought he had changed his mind, that a witness had come to my rescue. I craned my neck to watch him as he walked to the Dumpster and threw Luke's phone in with the week's trash. I looked away before he could see the hope in my eyes turn to cinders.

I heard him walk back to the car and slip into the driver's seat. He whistled as he pulled out of the spot. I didn't know where we were headed, but it was nowhere good.

✦

I thought about the word *hard-boiled*. Marlowe was hard-boiled. Spade was hard-boiled. Was I? I felt fear deep in my chest like a living, yellow yolk, sloshing this way and that, bound and whole but runny and unbound. The yolk of a hard-boiled egg was just as real, but gray and solid. Maybe they were scared too, then, these heroes of mine, scared, but with their fear kept separate and suspended from everything else.

Unless of course the egg got cracked. Who knew what would happen then.

If I had any chance of escape, it would have to come from inside my car. Without moving my head, I took a brief survey of the front half, looking for a key to this locked-room riddle. My car was as I had left it. A twice-read copy of *Red Harvest* in the driver's-side-door compartment, four pairs of shoes in the passenger foot well. I turned to look in the backseat, casually, quickly. A summer sweater I wore the middle of last week, crumpled up to one side. Beside it was a black leather box with its lid removed, revealing a short stack of notes and letters, a scatter of dried rose petals. I hadn't seen it in years.

The car moved steadily as I watched the mist condense on the scratched screen of my tired mind, revealing loops and shapes, maps and plans. As far as the bastard Cook was concerned, I was making my exit at the end of this ride.

John hadn't broken into my apartment just to make my bed. He'd done a thorough search for my sources of human vulnerability, and he'd found the mementos from my time in love.

I leaned my head against the window and shut my eyes. For all his mental problems, John lacked imagination. The degenerate

Hispanic shot in a drug deal; the sentimental woman a love suicide. It made me pretty mad. It made me feel hard-boiled.

We were driving down Third, with K-Town on the right. To
the empty warehouse where he killed Diego.

John's gun was behind him, tucked between his back and the
driver's seat. My seat. His left hand was on the wheel, his right
on the stick. If I only had my hands, I'd be home free.

But I didn't have my hands. The cuffs chafed like teeth and I
was losing sensation in my fingers. I knew it was possible to get
out of handcuffs—if you had time, opportunity, keys, or bolt
cutters. I had a moving car and an armed kidnapper. Any way you
cut it, I was pretty well doomed, trussed up and ready for the
oven.

I couldn't die without knowing the truth. It was a feeling I'd
watched and read about often enough, this eleventh-hour greed,
of rogue reporter, abandoned son, but the weight was real, clus-
tered and thick. It swelled in my lungs and caught in my throat
like smoke turned to plastic.

I tried to remember everything I could about Diego's last day.
I saw him in the early afternoon. He went to lunch and hung out
with his in-laws until he took off, sometime before nine. Right
around then, he called me and I missed the call. No voice mail.

Jackie said they had been at the Grove. Walking distance from
my apartment.

I remembered Diego's face as I told him about the man in my
trunk and the man behind my steering wheel. It was worried and
shocked—but it was something else, too, and as the newness of
the news wore off, this was what remained.

Determination. And suddenly I had a hunch, and within seconds the hunch swelled inside me like a sponge in water. With a
full turn of my head, I looked at John. I narrowed my eyes and

stared with every seeing part of me at his profile. He was watching the road with a little too much interest. A tautness at his ear said he felt the pins of my gaze. I spoke slowly, words like water drops from a leaky faucet, small and gathered and heavy.

"Diego called me. When he was following you. It was the last time I heard his voice."

I was staring at him so hard his head became small and blurred and half transparent, so that I had a full view out the window, of weird shapes in lifting darkness. A muscle twitched behind his ear, rustling the hair like an animal in brush—but that was all. I was drowning, and it was a straw.

"Look, I already know you killed Miller. Your lovely big brother went and told me. I'm willing to wager you've killed others, too. I'm in the palm of your hand right now. Will you just be kind and tell me what happened to Diego?" It was hard not to whine. I tried to keep steel in my voice and weed out the tin.

"You seem to 'know' a lot, Miss Song." I heard the quotation marks as sure as if they were written.

"I know he was tailing you just before he was shot. He told me so."

"He told you he was following me and that he was about to get shot, do I have that right?"

I flushed. "It was late, and he was dead in the morning. Don't patronize me."

"I would never. A regular old sleuth like you."

"I told him about you. He followed you because he thought you were going to hurt me. You led him somewhere you could kill him. Why? Did you even know who he was?"

His lips parted just a centimeter and let out a short, dry laugh that was half nostril. His face softened, and when we hit a brief red light, he looked at me with eyes slimed over with pity. "I knew who he was. Diego Diaz. Twenty-five years old. Married. With a child on the way."

I felt whiteness scar the backs of my eyes, dizzying and hot. He kept me locked in his unctuous gaze even when the light turned green. He smiled sweetly as he played with the stick and only looked forward again when I broke my wet eyes from his.

City twilight passed us outside, video without sound. I turned my head to my window, but as it came to rest on the glass I glanced back at my shoes in the foot well.

There were four pairs. Three black, one red, all with four- to five-inch heels. These were the shoes I could never drive in, that years of experience in L.A. taught me to leave in the car. They were all stilettos, beautiful and deadly.

I had a semblance of a plan. If it didn't work, I would be none the worse. If it did, I might die anyway. Given the circumstances, it was low-risk.

The seat adjusters in my Volvo were the old kind, with sudden locks on a slide rail. As far as I could tell, my seat was all the way up or close to it. The seat could fall back as much as a foot, maybe a foot and a half.

I would have to be quick. The whole thing couldn't take more than three or four seconds. The space between his arms and his gun was a gift, but not a generous one.

I slouched my head against the window and slumped deeper in the seat, bringing my wrists behind me to the right. I shook off my left flip-flop and chose the left red stiletto. It was a sling-back pump with an open toe, and it boasted a platform and a five-inch heel that was just thicker than a knitting needle. I slipped into it and bobbed my heel up and down twice to secure the back strap. John watched the road.

I waited for my breath to even out. I counted silently to three.

I lunged backward and sideways and hooked my right foot under the metal bar of the seat adjuster. I yanked up on the bar as hard as I could and my seat rolled back and snapped into place. As it did I pulled my high-heeled foot out from the foot well, raised my leg as high as it would go, and slammed the pointed heel straight down into John's groin.

The lack of resistance felt sickening, like stepping in very thick mud.

He screamed. It was high-pitched and terrified, blood-dipped and metallic. It filled the space in the Volvo like Alice filled the rabbit's house. It was the worst sound I had ever heard.

A second later he was still screaming but his right hand left the stick shift to go for the gun. My foot raced his hand and shoved the steering wheel left, left, left. He tried for the wheel as he slammed the brakes, but he was in too much pain, and we were too close to the streetlight.

The crash came quick, and with it the sound and scrape of shattering glass. I kept my head down but the impact snapped me forward, where I met a deploying airbag. Parts of me stung, but they stung like parts of someone else.

My gamble had paid off and John had gotten the worst of it. I didn't know if he was dead, dying, or not even close, but his eyes were closed and his face striped with blood. I didn't want to find out.

Sixteen

I tossed off the shoe and unlocked the car with my toes. I pulled the driver's side handle and pushed the door open. I bent my knee to lower my foot behind John's back. My first two toes found the trigger guard of the gun. They worked like a crane to get a good grip, and when I had it raised in the air I chucked it outside. It didn't go far, but it was out of reach.

I pulled myself back up, all limbs on the passenger's side, and opened my door with my fingers, facing the inert villain as I negotiated the handle. I stepped onto the street. The sky was the color of miracles.

We had crashed on the corner of Fourth and Olive, en route to deeper downtown, where I was to plant a goodbye kiss to the world, following my one true love. It was a pretty idea.

I wobbled, but my legs were in walking condition. My right had fallen asleep despite all the excitement and the shivers went up and down as I made each step around the car.

The car was in bad shape. It had crumpled hard into the

streetlight, and whatever force was opposite and equal to a car driven in no traffic had shot straight through the left headlight.

I walked around to the driver's side and found John slumped and unconscious, cheek to the steering wheel. Deep red stained a small circle in the crotch of his pants. The rest of him didn't look so good, either.

If he'd been planning to package my murder as a suicide, he had keys on his person. With a warm swallow of Los Angeles air, I approached his blood-let body to take inventory of his pockets. My chest heaved and pumped breath from my open mouth with a volume that surprised me. Now that I expected to live, this man terrified me even in his sleep.

"Juniper Song."

I jumped inches off the ground at the sound of my name, and it took me a full second to register that it came from behind me.

When I turned around, I was staring into the driver's side of a black Mazda, where private investigator Charles Lindley sat gaping.

"Help, please." I heard myself hyperventilating, my words long and bumpy. I had no idea why he was here, but I was relieved to see him.

He parked his car and bounded over. "What the hell?"

"I need you to search him and find the keys to these cuffs."

"Sure," he said. "Sure."

I watched as he manhandled John's limp body, and in a minute he produced a slender silver key and freed my wrists.

I stumbled to John's gun and picked it up off the concrete. I had never held one before. It felt cool in my hand, and heavy, far heavier than I'd imagined.

Chaz gave me a worried look. "Do you know how to use that?"

"Hopefully I won't have to."

I walked back to the car, wedging my way past Chaz to face the man who'd tried to kick my bucket. I kept the gun pointed at him with my finger on the trigger while I checked for a pulse. His throat was warm, with skin loose around the glands like an ill-fitting sock. It took me a few seconds to feel it, but he was alive. How alive was another story.

"Let's get out of here." I shoved the gun into the waistband of my shorts, the grip against my navel and the business end resting against my thigh.

Chaz was already talking by the time we entered his car.

"I went to check on Hector's car again. If they knocked him off like you said, I thought I could find something at that body shop. Instead I found your Volvo and I thought, well, that's funny. So I stuck with it, and sure enough that man came by and picked it up, and he picked you up, and— Christ, you're lucky to be alive."

I sat in Chaz's car in a daze, and his words barely reached me. I managed to say, "We have to go."

"We'd better call an ambulance."

"Do it driving."

He didn't argue, and we slipped deeper into downtown while I curled up in the seat and hurt. The hurt was everywhere. My left leg was bloody and glass-bitten, and my back was going to punish me for weeks. The headache felt like it would never leave. I thought about all that had happened in the last few days, and I dared to ask myself if it was over. The murderer was behind me, fighting for his life. I had found my answers.

But I knew it wasn't over. Sleeping in his mansion and dreaming of a young girl in a short skirt was the real villain, the master behind the subservient puppet with a convenient criminal profile. I still held the information that got Greg Miller killed, and my status as his son's living best friend assured me no safety. And I wasn't the only one still in trouble. There was the girl.

In the eight years since Iris's death, I had never come to terms with what she did. I tried to avoid thinking about her, never talked to her in that needy, epistolary way we address the dead. I couldn't forgive her for choosing Quinn and tragic love over the rest of her life as my friend and sister. And in a private chamber of my thoughts, where the door swung open at the hint of invitation, I knew, with the immovable belief that backs up fact, that what had happened was entirely my fault. There was no one else who could have saved her, and with my best intentions I had let my only sister destroy herself for the sake of a wrongheaded love, while I watched.

At least Lori was not in love. But she was in Cook's power, and her mother would do nothing to keep her out of his reach. I had done nothing for her yet but take her away from that place and leave her where she could not stay. For her sake, I had to follow this thing through.

I thought about telling the police. Chaz had 911 on the phone, and all I had to do was scream murder to bring the law crashing down. It was about time I handed over my problems and let justice do the rest. Then I remembered who I was, and who Cook was, and how much I had in the way of direct evidence.

Chaz hung up the phone and pulled over. "Looks like I got you out of a tight spot. I think it's time you filled me in."

I took a Lucky from my back pocket. "Mind if I smoke?"

He shook his head. I borrowed his car's cigarette lighter and fired up. I took a deep lungful of smoke and exhaled the whole story, letting it tumble out in fast, ugly sentences.

He listened, closing his eyes in solemn respect for the numbered dead. "You think Hector's a goner."

"You should tell the police what I just told you. See what they find. I hope I'm letting my imagination run away with me."

"We should go to the police right now. I'm not in the business of hiding murders."

I shook my head. "If we call it in now, Cook will get away with everything. I've got nothing but my word, and against him it won't be worth much."

"The cops have no reason not to trust you."

"Remember that part where I took Lori from her home in the middle of the night? I mean I doubt that's a kidnapping, technically, but it doesn't put me in a good position against her mother and a lawyer."

He scratched an itch high up on his inner thigh. He was thinking. "What would you rather do, then?"

I would have to negotiate my safety. Cook had lost his gunman and I had his gun. "I just need to get to Cook before I go to the cops. If you won't take me, I'll get a cab."

He protested for a few minutes, but in the end he complied. I could tell he was rattled, and that the sight of me, haggard and injured, left him unable to refuse me. Chivalrous Chaz, my knight in white tennis shoes.

The Mazda's clock said 5:14. The morning was coming and the sky knew it if I didn't. We drove into the thinning blue, through empty streets that would be clogged in another couple of hours.

We were outside the house by 5:35. I punched in the gate code and had Chaz pull into the driveway and stop his car where it wouldn't stick out to observers at the windows.

I looked at the house. "This should only take a few minutes. I'll grab Cook and then we'll take him to the police. Do you have the handcuffs?"

"I'm not staying in the car and picking my nose." He undid his seat belt and opened his door. "How am I supposed to look my daughter in the eye if I let something happen to a little girl like you? You stay in the car."

I felt a smile climbing on one side of my face. "That's not happening. Do you have a gun?"

He frowned. "No, I don't. Are you taking that with you? You'd better let me hold on to it."

"No, thanks."

I opened the door and hobbled out of the car. I went straight to the front door and leaned my fist into the buzzer.

I felt my hand go toward the gun in my waistband. It surprised me. I had never touched a gun until an hour earlier, but I had read about them and seen them so often onscreen that I had built a real-life response to cinematic danger. Marlowe kept a gun and he knew when to draw it, knew when to touch it in anticipation of its need. I was on the enemy's doorstep. I needed backup, and Chaz was neither intimidating nor capable of firing at will.

My plan was simple. I wanted to produce the villain when I presented my story to the police. It would take more than a phone call to get Cook in handcuffs, and once he learned that I had survived the night, he might find fifty ways to worm away. I knew the power of a drawn gun from recent experience. I had a thousand reasons to kill him in cold blood. He would do what I wanted.

It took him a minute to get to the door, but when he opened it I saw that he hadn't been sleeping. He was dressed as I had seen him the afternoon before, in a different polo shirt and the same khakis, a little more worn. His face was drawn and sallow, plagued with wakeful agony. It was a face that needed a drink. It fell when he saw me in his doorway, injured but alive, wearing my hate like a cape.

"Let's talk," I said.

He backed away from the door and cleared a path. I heard Chaz come in behind me. When Cook was five feet away, I told Chaz to close the door and drew the gun. My head started to pound and my body moved with nausea. I heard Chaz mumble a bewildered obscenity and felt myself separate, so that I seemed to watch this new scene from behind a curtain.

"What do you think you're doing, Song?" Cook's eyes started darting as I crept forward, leading us to the living room we'd sat in less than twenty-four hours earlier.

"Yeah, what do you think you're doing?" Chaz whispered.

I laughed, a bitter, breathless laugh. "What do I think I'm doing? Where do you think I got this?" I said, giving the gun a slight shake. I tried to stay focused, eyes open and hands steady. I was on the verge of explosion, and my voice came out in a trembling shout. "Aren't you curious, Mr. Cook? Aren't you curious at all as to why I'm here instead of your brother?"

His face turned white in the wan strands of morning light falling into the room. I felt my finger tense on the trigger and realized with revulsion how badly I wanted to cock the hammer and squeeze.

"You murdered my best friend and tried to kill me. Tell me why you get to live."

I could hear the thick, parched maneuvering of his tongue. "Please, Song. Put the gun down. I didn't—"

"Why the fuck should I? Your brother admitted everything. Gleeful, gloating. You—"

"I promise you, Song, on my life, on the life of my son—I had nothing to do with Diego's death."

"Bullshit."

He trailed backward and swallowed. "I swear to you, John acted alone. He thought he was doing what he had to do. Protecting me. Our family." He was starting to sweat. "When I found out what happened to him, I was sick. He was a good man. I didn't want him hurt."

I laid out the players in my mind—the two brothers, one powerful and fatherly, the other fatherless, unhinged, grateful, and obsequious. I knew it wasn't impossible that Cook was telling the truth. "Even if I believed you, I know this much: you tried to have me killed."

"You don't know that."

"I do." I shook my head and cocked the hammer.

His face drained with panic and tears now came to his red-veined eyes. "Look, anything I've done has been to protect my family. Song, you—for the last few days you have dedicated your life to coming after me, to taking away my wife and son. I mean you of all people—you know what it's like to pin a family together. And you know what can happen when you fail."

He waited, lip hanging, for me to cry and forgive him. "Bold card to play, Cook. I might have some sympathy, you know, but we're talking about murder. You can't just do whatever the fuck you want."

"Is there anything you wouldn't do to get your family back?"

I struggled with a knot in my throat, sudden, dry, and wooden. "Chaz, go grab him and let's take him to the car." I kept my gaze aimed at Cook's forehead, heated with bloodlust, while Chaz took him by the arms. Then, for an instant, Cook looked past my shoulder with a frightened, curious glint in his eye. By the time I thought to turn around, it was too late to react.

Someone jumped onto my shoulders and grabbed for my right arm with both hands. I uncocked the hammer and held on to it with all the strength I had left. But I was weak and exhausted, and I was on my knees with the weight on my back. As my assailant tore it from my hands, I saw Chaz and Cook wrestling, the physicality of the act surprising them both.

I stayed on the floor in a heap of skin and bones, the will to fight slipping out of my body like water from a toppled glass. My heart jammed against my chest, pumping, urgent and terrified. But the rest of me was more tired than scared, and my eyelids started to drop in anticipation of the big sleep. I jogged them back open so I could stare into the barrel of the gun.

Yujin stood over me in a black tank top and yoga pants. Her face was as worn and sleepless as Cook's, but her eyes bored down on me, alive with wild panic. I heard the steely click of the hammer for what seemed the thousandth time in my life.

"Where is she?" Her voice quivered with a tone as strained and thin as violin music in a horror film. It took me a few seconds to register that she had addressed me in Korean.

I responded in kind. "Your daughter is safe."

She shook her head, and I watched with disbelief as tears welled up in her blazing eyes. Then I understood, and I filled in the correct implied pronoun. "Where is he?"

I answered slowly, in my halting Korean, in a voice designed to be calm. "I don't know. We got into a crash downtown. He was unconscious when I left him, but I don't know how badly he was hurt."

Her hand was shaking now. "You bitch. What did you do to him?"

"He was trying to kill me. I was tied up. I was lucky we crashed." I felt no obligation to tell the whole truth. I continued carefully, trying my luck again. "Look, I didn't stick around to see how he was doing, but there was a lot of blood."

She moved the gun toward the pile of men. "Get away from him, Mr. Lindley."

Chaz looked up at the sound of his name, his mouth open, his eyes terrified. He and Cook disentangled themselves and he shuffled across the carpet on his knees.

Cook stood up where he was and looked down at me with fury and contempt. "Don't speak Korean," he said. "Yujin, what did she say?"

She turned to him, seething through clenched teeth. "John is hurt."

"What do you mean, John is hurt?"

"He has been in an accident. A bad one."

"Shit," he said, nearly spitting on the floor. "Shit."

"We need to help him," she said. Her hand had turned the gun back to point at me, but she was facing Cook, her eyes wide with authority. "We have to."

Cook slumped onto the piano bench. "Yujin." Out of his mouth, her name came out like "Eugene," long in the second syllable. "Let's think this through."

"What is there to think through?"

"If he was in an accident, the police probably have him by now. He's probably getting help."

"You do not know that."

"Come on, Yujin. He's probably at a hospital right now."

"Listen to me, Bill. We cannot just sit here waiting for news. We have to do something."

"What can we possibly do?"

"We have to go to him."

Cook looked at her with stern patience, like she was a child throwing a tantrum. "You know we can't do that."

I turned my eyes back to her face and I knew, right away, that she'd forgotten all about me, about Chaz. Her mouth fell open and her brow grew tight, stunned and furious. "I do not think I heard you, Bill."

"I know you heard me."

She let out a nervous laugh. "Your brother is somewhere dying because of you, so forgive me for hoping I misheard you."

"I'm sure he's being helped. We'd be giving ourselves up for nothing."

Her gun hand was now at her side, slack and vulnerable. I weighed the tension in the room, and I tried to force enough energy into my knees to allow me to spring for the weapon.

"Nothing?" she shouted. "It would not be nothing for me."

"I get it, but let's be rational here. We have ourselves to think about. He'll never give us up. The only way we can end up in jail tomorrow is if we go galloping after him and turn ourselves in."

I watched as the gun found its way up, its muzzle turned toward Cook. "We are going to help him."

"Put that thing down. We both know we can't go, and you're not going to shoot me over it."

Maybe Cook hadn't seen Yujin Chung as I'd seen her, just the day before. His voice betrayed less fear than it had when I had the same gun pointed at his head. He spoke with the same dismissive tone that he'd used when describing his brother as a troubled young man. As far as he was concerned, Yujin was in the palm of his hand. She was just a woman on his payroll, and she had lived thus far to please him at the expense of her own flesh and blood. He was smug.

"Can you take me to him?" There was another delay before I recognized that she was addressing me again.

"Hey, stop speaking Korean." Cook started toward her. "And Jesus, Yujin, give me that gun."

She repeated the question, faster this time. "Can you take me to him?"

There was only one answer I could give. "Yes," I said, and closed my eyes.

The gunshot was louder than I expected. It rang out, pulling the room and the world outside into the dark burst of sound, sharp and deep, tearing space. When I opened my eyes, Luke's dad was lying on the floor. Blood sprayed from a hole in his throat, an impossible amount with an impossible trajectory, onto his beautiful oriental rug, painting the keys of the grand piano. I looked away. This was an image that I'd never forget. It was nothing like the books, nothing like the movies. No clean shot leaving a single dark red stain to get the point of death across. I felt myself starting to cry.

Yujin stumbled and collapsed around folded knees, the gun falling to the floor with a heavy thud. She was white with shock, her eyes unable to move from Cook's corpse. It was a small window, I knew, and I collected my nerves and lunged for the gun. I didn't need to hurry. She sat very still for a long time.

"I had to do it," she said. She was speaking English again. "But I did not know it would be like that. I know what you think of me, but I have never killed anyone before."

I couldn't think of a thing to say. I was happy to have the gun back on my side.

"Where is John?" She was still looking at Cook.

"I don't know, but if he's alive he's getting help. I called in the accident before I came."

She started to sob and I got an uneasy feeling in my stomach that I recognized as guilt. I had been instrumental in the scene in front of me. I saw the love and panic in Yujin, and I saw the rift between my two enemies. I had a gun in my face, and, ignoring the fallout, I had done what I could to get it pointed elsewhere.

I stood up and kept the gun trained on Yujin as I backed away from her and Cook's body. From the corner of my eye I saw Chaz come to his feet. I'd forgotten he was there.

We were halfway to the front door when I heard her speak in a spectral whisper. "Tell Lori I am sorry," she said. "I only wanted to give her the kind of life I never had when I was young." Suddenly, she sounded like every first-generation Korean mother that I had ever known. "And you will not understand this, but I thought she could love him like a father. Now she has no one."

I took one last look at this woman, one unwilling glance at Luke's dead father beside her, and left the Cook mansion behind me.

Seventeen

For the first time in days, I was, in a sense, safe. The thought entered my head hot and pointed and taunting. I had witnessed a murder. All the bodies that had fallen around me, the deaths of those I loved most—none of that had prepared me for the actual sight of one person taking the life of another. And yet here I was, safe from the people who had tried to put me away just hours before. The murder, the shock of blood, had been my means of escape.

I wiped the gun down with my shirt and discarded it in a rose bush on the front lawn. It was now a confirmed murder weapon, and I never wanted to see it again.

Chaz didn't say a word until we were in the car, until the heavy, dark gate of the Cook mansion let us out.

He gave me his phone. His hairy hand was shaking. "Call them. Now."

I dialed 911 and reported a gunshot at Cook's address and left it at that. Chaz scowled at me, his eyes red and wet. "Will you tell me what the fuck just happened in there?"

I told him. "It's nothing I won't take to the police later."

"When?"

"I need to see Luke. I need to tell him that his father is dead."

"We just witnessed a murder. We got other things to do."

"Please, Chaz."

He continued to glower, but I thought I saw him start to soften. At this moment, at least, I was grateful that I was a woman. Marlowe could never count on the kindness of strangers, and he never bothered to try. But Marlowe had other methods, too.

"There's two hundred dollars in it for you if you'll just make this detour." He started to protest but I didn't let him. "Nothing illegal. It's just a delay. Please."

We drove downhill in silence. After a minute Chaz asked, "Where's Luke?"

"You've been there today. Marlowe Apartments. Rossmore and Beverly."

We made the trip to the Marlowe in half an hour. Chaz talked most of the way, and I answered his questions and listened to his scolding. Exhaustion still pulled at me, ate at me from inside, but I could no more fall asleep than I could turn back time. This was the last stretch. I had Chaz pull up to the back of the Marlowe and asked him to wait for me.

I made my way to the gate and buzzed Luke's apartment. I was half surprised when he let me in. He didn't even ask who I was.

The door opened when I was still a good ten feet away. Luke was in the same clothes, conscious, bounding to me, sobbing.

He caught me in a painful hug, arms low on my waist, squeezing. The wheezing came at first like whispers, then burst through, braying, dry, and percussive, like coughs in still air. They pulled at the last of my heartstrings until they snapped.

I lifted a hand to the back of his head, hovering next to mine. It was wet, with blood or sweat, it was hard to tell. I swallowed.

We separated and made our way to the open door. I closed it behind us and we sat on the couch.

"Song, I was so scared. I've never been so scared. Not in my entire life."

"Me neither." I couldn't look at him.

"What happened? How'd you get away? Tell me everything." He looked at me with genuine relief lightening his features. He hadn't heard about his dad, and I knew I couldn't tell him until I found out what I needed to know.

"He put me in handcuffs and we went for a drive. He was driving me downtown, I'm guessing he was taking me to where he killed Diego. It was my car, and it was as I'd left it, if you ignored the stack of Diego-related memorabilia in the backseat."

"What memorabilia?"

"Old letters and pictures, mostly." I realized with a quick pang that I might lose some of those last traces of Diego. I hoped I could recover them from the backseat.

"Where'd he find your car? And your stuff?"

"Lori's mom. I hadn't seen my car, my keys, my phone, nothing since I showed up at her doorstep and got myself drugged up." I laughed. It was quiet, but I could hear the scary timber of cracking sanity in the sound. "You know what I have on me now? Nothing but my clothes and around half the person I was before this weekend."

He looked down. "So how'd you get away?"

I told him, up to the part where I went to his father's house.

"I don't know whether your uncle is dead or alive, but he's in somebody else's hands now."

Luke's eyes went fuzzy and his lips separated, making a parched sound in the silence of the room.

"You still want me to believe you didn't know who was after me until today?"

His pupils flitted, unlocking and sliding away from mine.

I waited.

"Look, I didn't know for sure, Song. For a while, I didn't know my dad was involved in any of this. I didn't want to believe it. So maybe I was playing dumb for you, but I was playing dumb for me, too."

"Tell me something." I felt rage build like a storm cloud behind my eyes. "Why didn't I know about him? Why didn't I know he existed?"

He was quiet, and his mouth barely opened to a murmur. "I don't like that I'm from this family of crazy people. I know everyone has a crazy family, but mine—look, my mom is so gone in her own world that she's off God-knows-where for the twentieth time this year. My dad is the sane one, you know? Or, I mean," he laughed, squinting and sardonic, "I thought he was. But then he had a psycho brother and, I don't know, I never wanted to talk about him. I kept him at a distance. It wasn't hard, either. I wasn't lying when I told you he hates me."

I waited for the retort, the accusation that I kept my family problems locked away from him. It didn't come. "Okay. I get it. But make me understand something else. You didn't flinch when I said your uncle killed Diego."

His pallor grew paler. "When he came for you—"

"Luke . . . Luke." I closed my eyes and wished we were different people in a different place.

"I thought he was going to kill you, Junie." He reached for my head and took it in his hands. He kissed my eyelids and brows.

The only person who ever called me Junie was dead now, and I still had yet to bury him.

I stood up. "You have no right."

"What?"

"You're a bastard, Luke."

"Because I didn't tell you about John? Because of my dad? I'm not proud of these people, I'm sorry. I'm glad you came back instead of him."

"No, Luke. Because you were there."

His face turned a sickly oatmeal and his green eyes the flat dead color of old bills. "I don't—what?"

My eyes were hot and they leaked tears while I spoke. "He knew about Diego's baby, Luke. And he didn't just know about the baby, he wanted me to know that you told him. He was fucking smug about it. Because he knew more than I did. Because I figured out that Diego was tailing him before he died, but I didn't get to the part where you were in John's front seat."

I stayed standing. Luke held his hands together between his knees. He looked at his hands, then he looked around the room, but he kept his eyes below the level of mine. I didn't move, and the minutes swam by.

"Diego is dead and you were there when it happened. You could've stopped it. You've broken my heart, Luke. Tell me. You owe it to me."

He was looking at the floor and his shoulders swelled and bumped like ocean waves at a quiet hour. I saw the top of his head bob like he was praying and he lifted his face to meet my gaze with the pleading of a sinner searching for the wafer.

"I'm sorry."

"Tell it to me. Give it to me in one piece."

He lowered his head again and panned the room. "When you were in the bathroom at the Red Palace, I got a call from John. He said to meet him at my apartment in ten minutes if I wanted him to leave you alone. I thought it might be an empty threat, but I didn't know for sure until right then that he was the guy who'd been tormenting you. So I went.

"I should've known better, should've known he was— God!" The name in vain, phlegm-choked, aspirated. "When I got there, he was sitting in his car in the garage and he told me to get in. I did. When we came out to the street, I saw what he brought me out for. I saw Diego." His hands and legs shook as he spoke. "He was idling in his car just across the street and a few feet back from the garage. If he had any intention of staying hidden, he sure didn't act on it. According to John, Diego had been following him around for a couple hours. They ran into each other at Park La Brea. Diego must've been worried about you. He drove over and recognized John in the parking lot."

"Diego knew him?"

"They never met, but John would visit Stokel sometimes to meet with my dad. Diego could've seen him then and put things together."

"And did John recognize Diego?"

He trembled. "Of course he did. It's why he called me. I fucking know it."

"Did he say that?"

"No, he asked me if I recognized him. Asked if he was a friend of yours."

"And you told him what?"

He swallowed. "I—I wasn't thinking. He started asking me all about Diego, about his relationship to you, his relationship to

Greg Miller, all this stuff, question after question, real fast. And I was still putting the pieces together, trying to fit it so that my dad and my uncle weren't murderers, and he was getting excited and insistent, and I couldn't—I don't know, I didn't have time to think, time to be careful. I'm sorry."

"What did you tell him?"

"I don't know, that he was one of my best friends, that we went to school together and he worked for Stokel now. That he barely knew Greg Miller and that he had nothing to do with any of this."

"And about me and Diego?"

"I—" He sank into himself.

"He asked. Don't you dare tell me he didn't ask."

"I told him that you dated in college and for how long. And I told him—well, he asked me if—he asked me if Diego could still be in love with you."

I stepped back. I reached for words like I was reaching for books on a too-high shelf. When I found one, the rest came falling down after.

"You said yes." My eyes were hot again. "And that's why Diego's dead. Because he showed up at my apartment like an idiot, like the caring, worried idiot he always was, and John decided he was a problem. But he went to you because he didn't know how big of a problem he was, and you—you told him—you, Luke? And why? We both know it isn't even true. He would've done the same thing for you, and you—"

"He didn't ask me if Diego was in love with you, he asked me if he could be. And I said yes because I wasn't thinking, and because we don't know. I don't know, and be real, Song, you don't either."

I cleared my eyes with the heels of my hands and calmed

myself with three deep breaths. "I'm not going to argue about this now. I need to know what happened next."

"We drove, around and around, I don't know for how long. I kept asking him what we were doing, but he was evasive. But only in words, not in attitude. He was cheerful, and I don't know, I didn't think—I didn't think he was going to hurt him."

"And then at some point you made it to Skid Row."

"Right. But I thought—John lives downtown and I thought maybe we were just going home."

"Until he parked."

He nodded.

"And Diego parked."

He nodded.

"And Diego got out of the car. Like an idiot. Because he knew you were there, and he would've followed you into any dark alley you chose."

"He was coming towards the car, and at that point I saw that John was holding a gun. I panicked. I started begging. I told him about Jackie and the baby, I told him I'd never forgive him. When he ignored me, I got out and yelled to Diego to get back in his car." He closed his eyes so hard I saw the strain ride up into his forehead. "I didn't have a chance. Every time I blink I see him drop. It was so quick, so quiet. I didn't even see the bullet. Just blood and gravity. I don't remember much after that."

I shivered, shut my eyes, saw black. I sat down.

"And you still didn't want me to go to the police to protect myself. You thought you could save me like you tried to save Diego."

"I tried. My God, Song, it was no good but I tried. But it was different with you. My dad didn't know about Diego, he promised me up and down that he would never have allowed it. But I told him that wasn't good enough. I swore to him that if anything happened to you, he would no longer have a son. And he believed me. He said he would make sure you were left alone."

I drummed agitated fingers on my thighs.

"Well, Cook, I'm here in one piece, more or less."

He took a few seconds to respond, hoarse and quiet. "What does that mean?"

"There's no use in disowning your father now. You were ready to stay his son when you knew what he did to Diego." I meant to tell him what had happened, but instead I heard myself start to shout. "Diego had a wife and a kid. He was a good person, and we all needed him. Who the hell am I? What good am I doing for anyone? I have no people left, Luke. After tonight, I don't even have you."

"It's only luck that you're alive. I'm not going—"

"Listen to me, Luke." I grabbed his hands and peered into his face. This was someone I'd loved with all the force of family, and even as I severed our ties I felt his pain reflected in my chest. "Your dad is dead."

He let his eyes find mine and I watched his pupils shiver. "What?"

"I'm sorry." The tears came again, but they did nothing to blur the image, to soften the brilliant red of Cook's death.

We stayed still for a long time, until suddenly Luke shrank back. "You?" He almost choked on the word.

The accusation hit so hard it nearly knocked the wind out of me. I shook my head and let him go. "No."

"Then who?"

"It was Yujin," I said. "The police should be there by now. I'm sorry. I really am."

I waited for him to press for details, but he didn't. Instead, he sat, catatonic. Minutes later, he grabbed my hand again. "What do I do now, Song? Tell me, what do I do?"

He was crying and I had to pull my words from the coldest place in my heart. "I don't know, Luke, but I can't do a thing for you anymore."

"I'm sorry, Song. I'd do anything to undo this weekend, to bring Diego back. But I can't, and I need you right now. I need you to forgive me."

"I will not help you bury that man," I said. "Come with me to the police. Help me tell this story, with all its shitty details. Tell them about your dad. Tell them your part."

I saw him swallow. I couldn't take his nauseated eyes.

"I'm just kidding, Luke. I can't ask you to do that. Whatever he did, he's paid for in full. And as for you?" I hung my head. "I don't care what happens. I've seen enough of you for this lifetime. But I won't say a word to anyone. It's my last bit of goodwill to you, Luke. Because I know you didn't want Diego dead—you don't have to tell me that. But you were there, you let it happen, and you hid it. And like you said, it's only luck that's kept me alive. I know this, and you know, and if you think I'll ever forget, you're as crazy as anyone."

I could feel his eyes on me, begging, challenging me to take in his sorrow and walk away. I heard his lips part, but no words came out.

I let him have his best appeal. The whole of our friendship played through my mind, and I felt, deeply, the built tissue of affection, understanding, and trust. I gave remembrance to our most tender moments, and to the days of pain in which he had been my salve.

It wasn't enough.

"I need two hundred dollars." I tried to keep my voice low and matter-of-fact, but it came out full of cracks. "I'm demanding it."

He didn't move. He started to cry again.

I popped my knuckles. "Alright, I'll find it."

I walked into Luke's bedroom and riffled through his drawers. In his second desk drawer I found a stack of bills. There were eight hundreds at the bottom of the stack. I took two. When I came back out, Luke was clutching his head in his hands and wailing with abandon.

"Luke, stop it. You want me to hang around, pretend nothing's happened? Let's be real. There is nothing that can make us what we were. I love you like a brother, but I'm not your sister, and I don't think I ever want to see you again."

He didn't say anything else and after a minute of standing around and bearing witness to his misery, I left the Marlowe one last time.

Chaz was right where I left him, and when I climbed into the front seat, he touched me lightly on the shoulder.

"Jesus, are you okay?"

"I don't want to talk about it." My voice came out studded with hiccups, and for a few minutes I hugged my knees and sobbed. When I calmed down, I tried to hand him the bills. "Sorry about that." I was sniffling.

He rejected the money with a wave of his hand. "Keep it." He sighed loud and spoke soft. "I'll go to the police on my own. You can tell them your story tomorrow. Let's get you home—where am I going?"

My tired body filled with gratitude and I mouthed a series of thank-yous as I thought about the question. The world outside was full of morning and all I wanted was my bed and total darkness. As soon as I found a place to sleep, I'd be out for a long time.

"Start driving and I'll tell you in a minute."

It was Monday morning and the whole week lay before me, before Chaz, before Yujin, before Jackie, before Lori, before Luke—all the survivors, left to live every day, two dozen hours then two dozen more. No wonder no one liked Mondays. Mondays were beginnings.

The next days would be hell for Lori, and I didn't know how I could make them better, but I would try. In another phase of my life I had shown a talent for being a sister. When I lost Iris, I lost that badge. I was a failed sister, then no sister at all. I became nothing. A piece of driftwood, waiting for the wave that would finally take me under. But I'd been wrong. I'd had plenty to lose, and in the last few days I had lost it all.

I wanted to save Lori, to extract her from the grip of a monster, to take her away from the world that wrapped itself around her. In the end, I was a part of that world. Tomorrow, her mother would be in prison, and forever Lori's past would be littered with the bodies of dead men.

But I could save her still. Iris never gave me a second chance, but Lori was alive and young, and she would have a hard time facing the next act alone. If Lori wanted my help, I would be there.

"We're going to Santa Monica," I said. "Someone there needs me."